UNCHAINED BEAST

PIPER STONE

Copyright © 2022 by Stormy Night Publications and Piper Stone

All rights reserved. No part of this book may be reproduced or transmitted in any form or by any means, electronic or mechanical, including photocopying, recording, or by any information storage and retrieval system, without permission in writing from the publisher.

Published by Stormy Night Publications and Design, LLC.
www.StormyNightPublications.com

Stone, Piper
Unchained Beast

Cover Design by Korey Mae Johnson
Images by 123RF/feedough, Shutterstock/Carsten Reisinger, and Shutterstock/muratart

This book is intended for *adults only*. Spanking and other sexual activities represented in this book are fantasies only, intended for adults.

To my beloved Moose, who crossed the rainbow bridge far too many years ago.

Through your loving black lab eyes, I experienced the true meaning of selfless love for the first time in my life. Thank you for allowing me into your amazing, joy-filled world. You will never be far from your mommy and daddy's heart.

Piper

CHAPTER 1

abriel

Hunger, the kind that burns deep, scorching every nerve ending. A desire so strong that it cannot be denied.

Or else...

"We are very honored to have our special guest with us tonight, the reason for this gala, and isn't it a glorious event?" His voice boomed over the microphone, the thousand people in attendance cheering as the powerful man searched the crowd, the spotlight following his gaze.

As the bright beam washed across my table, I gave him a respectful nod as the closest guests congratulated me, several women squeezing my arm. I allowed them a few moments of attention as the chair of humanitarian causes clapped along with everyone else in the room.

However, I was eager to end the evening, tired of making small talk with influencers, politicians, and celebrities, something I usually enjoyed. I even considered it one of the perks of my billion-dollar business.

My vice president leaned over, lifting a single eyebrow. "Don't look so thrilled," Alex said, laughing.

"Oh, I assure you that this award is very special. Imagine the dollars that will be brought into our coffers." My response was met with a roll of his eyes.

"Everything is always about money."

"Absolutely, my dear friend. That's why you can afford the yacht you just purchased."

Alex seemed surprised that I knew. There wasn't a single thing that went on in *my* city I didn't know about. As the cheering died down, the chair finally lifted his arms to silence them. At that moment, I adjusted my bow tie. The money spent on the event could feed thousands.

As the chairman went on, expressing his gratitude for the people of Chicago, I closed my eyes. Almost instantly, I felt a swell of anguish in the pit of my stomach, the kind of intense hunger that I'd fought against becoming crippling. My palms were sweaty, my pulse increasing. With everything I had, I shoved aside the burning hunger erupting in my system as another vibrant vision swept into my mind. Her shimmering face. Her voluptuous body. My need only doubled, desire roaring through every cell and muscle.

. . .

"Who are you?" she asked before backing away, her lower lip quivering.

I inched closer. "I'm your worst nightmare. I'll also be your savior."

"I don't need a savior."

"Mmm... That's where you're wrong."

Her laugh was strained, her eyes never blinking as she stared at me. In the depth of her soul, she knew what I was, a beast who'd hunted and secured his prey. Yet her fear was subdued, her desire overwhelming. I sensed the changes in her body as her pussy lips swelled, her nipples becoming fully aroused. My mouth watered at the thought of tasting her, quenching my thirst on her sweet nectar.

My nostrils remained flared from her scent, the intoxicating fragrance creating filthy thoughts, boosting every need burdening my system. She was the one.

My mate.

My salvation.

And I would enjoy every moment of devouring her. As I continued advancing, her breath became scattered. Within seconds, she would succumb, offering more than just a taste. When she backed against a wall, I sensed her continued trepidation, her misunderstanding of what was required of her. Soon, she would learn.

And she would obey.

Yet she surprised me, the strong, virile human, darting for the door. I took a deep breath, allowing her to believe she'd gotten away into the darkness. Away from me. After issuing a primal growl, I bolted from the house, catching her easily. As I yanked her around to face me, she made the mistake of scratching her nails down the side of my face. The force she'd used had been enough to draw blood, but within seconds, the ridiculous injury had already healed. In the waning light of the afternoon sun, she watched in horror as the wounds closed. The moment her eyes opened wide in amazement, I threw her over my shoulder.

"What are you?" she mumbled, clearly shaken by what she'd just seen.

"Such a bad girl. You will learn not to disobey me. And the answer is, I'm your master."

After storming inside and slamming the door, I pushed her against the wall, raking my hand down the front of her dress, ripping it to shreds.

A look of rebellion crossed her face, and she slammed her hands against my chest, prepared to drive her fist into my gut. I snagged her hand in mid-action, cocking my head. My thoughts swirled around everything I wanted to do to her, my needs dragging me out of my ability to control them as my wolf crowded closer to the surface.

With a single snap of my wrist, I was able to remove her dress entirely, my chest heaving as I continued to drink in her delicious aroma. Every cell was on fire as I slipped a single finger into the waistband of her panties, easily pulling them away. When she stood completely naked in front of me, I had no ability to curtail my natural urges.

Those of a dangerous man.

And those of a carnal beast.

As she narrowed her eyes, allowing them to fall to my already throbbing cock, the temptress dared to defy me in another way, brushing the delicate tip of her tongue across her lips. Then she tilted her head, daring me to take her.

She had no idea what beckoning me would do. But she would soon learn.

I fisted her hair, jerking her onto her toes as I rubbed the rough pads of my fingers all the way down the length of her back. Her skin was so soft, like rose petals, the shimmer in her eyes exposing her body's betrayal. She longed to surrender, to let go of her inhibitions, but a thin layer of fear was keeping her from accepting her place.

Towering over her, I took several deep breaths before capturing her mouth, crushing her lips against mine. While she planted her palms against my chest, there was no resistance. As her touch continued to excite me into a frenzy, I enjoyed the moment of dominating her tongue. Everything about her was perfect, her lithe body molding against mine perfectly. Within seconds, she was mewing into the kiss, undulating against me.

My balls tightened as I squeezed her bottom. I ached to be inside of her, shoving my cock all the way into her womb. As the seconds passed, I was forced to accept I had no control left.

When I lifted her from the floor, she thrust her arms around my neck, tangling her long fingers into my hair. The second I broke the kiss, she whimpered, her breathing scattered.

"*I'm going to fuck you.*" *My words weren't said as a warning.*

They were expressed as a promise, not only for now but for years to come.

She wrapped her legs around me, clinging to me as her eyes shifted back and forth, her ability to focus stripped away.

There was no additional hesitation. I plunged my cock past her swollen folds, pleased at the way her pussy clamped around the thick invasion. Everything about the gorgeous blonde was tempting, including her defiant nature. There was a mixture of hatred, confusion, and excitement in her eyes. My mouth twisting, I could read every thought racing through her mind, her disbelief at what she was experiencing.

As I thrust hard and fast, every nerve seared from the touch of her alone, I slammed both hands against the wall, rising onto the balls of my feet.

Her cries filtered into the air as I fucked her savagely, pounding her against the surface until echoes rose above her whimpers.

Flesh of my flesh.

Blood of my blood.

The words tumbled in my mind, fueling the raging fire that remained desperate to be fed.

But the creature would never be satisfied.

As her breathing skipped, her heart beating in time with mine, I could tell she was close to coming. She lolled her head, gasping for the precious air she needed to survive, trying desperately to ignore her body's cravings.

It was no use. As her body began to shake, a powerful climax sweeping through her, I threw back my head and roared just before my release.

I had difficulty breathing as the vision faded, my skin remaining clammy. The vibrant images had been as real as the four I'd experienced over the last three weeks, perhaps even more so. The pain as well as the explosive desire remained, but my anger was increasing. What the fuck was going on? I'd never experienced anything like this before.

The rut. The need to mate. The desire to consume.

The thought was ridiculous but something I was finding it difficult to ignore.

"Whoa, buddy," Alex hissed, managing to snag my glass before I turned it over. "Are you okay?"

Hissing, I realized my cock was still twitching. "I'm fine."

"You're just about to be the star of the show. Do you want me to stop Jeff from introducing you?"

"Hell, no."

I could feel Alex's heated gaze remaining, his concern only increasing. While the vision was disconcerting as fuck, even more so was the fact I'd need to feed before the night ended.

"Now, may I present our Humanitarian of the Year award to a man who needs no other introduction. Mr. Gabriel Dupree."

I rose to my feet, taking my time to button my jacket before moving through the rounds of tables. All eyes were on me, especially the women, but I had no plans on indulging in my sadistic needs tonight. There was work to be done. I managed to curtail my savage nature before walking onto the stage, but I knew it was only a matter of time before I lost control.

Jeff Porter was a small man in comparison to my size. He seemed almost overwhelmed as he gazed up at me while handing over the crystal statue, backing away almost instantly. There wasn't a single person in the room who wasn't fearful of my regime.

However, my keen sense of smell allowed me to gather the delicious perfume of every woman, their scents boosted by just how wet they'd become. They had no idea what kind of man I was behind closed doors.

And they should hope to never find out.

As every guest rose to their feet, I could see the lineup of reporters ready to capture the moment. All three of the local television stations were represented, hungry for a sizzling story. I took a deep breath, waiting until the applause died down. Two minutes and fourteen seconds. I was losing my touch given the last time had been well over three.

Exhaling, I kept my smile, glancing from one side of the room to the other. "Thank you very much, Chairman Porter. I am deeply honored to be standing in front of you today. I am also thankful to the thousands who supported such a worthy cause. Without your assistance, this year's fundraising events would not have exceeded expectations by almost fifty percent. You should be congratulated." Another round of applause kept me silenced until I threw up my hands. "However, I would be remiss if I didn't offer my gratitude toward my vice president. Alex, you always go above and beyond, something I will never forget."

I lifted the award, holding it in his direction as the cameras were redirected toward our table.

Then I walked off the stage, forced to push my way through several people as they rushed toward me. After placing the award in front of Alex, he gave me a mischievous grin.

"You're good. I'll give you that," he said. "But you and I both know it's bullshit."

Smirking, I took a sip of my bourbon, knowing that in about ten seconds, every reporter in the room would advance like piranhas. As expected, I was surrounded, microphones stuck in my face.

"How do you plan on exceeding your fundraising activities next year?"

"What are your plans for Dupree Enterprises?"

"How do you feel about topping the city's most eligible bachelor list?"

At least the last question made me laugh. "How do I feel? Fantastic. Although sadly, I have no time for a personal life."

It would seem every woman in the room groaned.

As the questions continued, I noticed a reporter I didn't recognize inching closer, his eyes never leaving mine. When he managed to shift directly in front of me, I sensed easily that he was here for another purpose.

"Mr. Dupree. It's widely known that you are the first-born son of the most powerful mafia family in the entire United States. How can you honestly expect anyone to believe you actually care about hungry children?"

I found it interesting that such a small man would have such a powerful, booming voice, loud enough that he managed to drive his question over all the others.

His question caused confusion as well as additional curiosity.

As I turned to face him, the crowd surrounding me backed away, their expressions full of fear. To his credit, the unknown reporter didn't budge from where he stood, the wry smile on his face managing to piss me off. When

I'd closed the distance, I allowed an almost unrecognizable growl to slip from my throat.

He didn't seem fazed in the least.

I found the punk amusing as well as annoying. However, I wouldn't allow him to get under my skin. I'd worked far too hard on keeping my corporation entirely legitimate.

Even if there was a distinctly different and much more profitable side to my company.

"I don't believe I've had the pleasure of meeting you," I said, as if I'd located a long-lost friend.

"My name doesn't matter," he responded.

I tilted my head, allowing him to see the slight but often mesmerizing change in my eyes.

The reporter swallowed, a single bead of sweat appearing just below his hairline. At least he'd gotten the point not to fuck with me. I pushed my anger below the surface, waiting for his answer.

"Joe. Joe Brooks."

"Well, Mr. Brooks, now I'm happy to answer your pointed question. You are correct that I am Chandler Dupree's son, one of five. While I realize that my father has been involved with some… unscrupulous activities, the work I perform with several amazing charities should never be considered a reflection of any aspect of my father's life. And I will repeat. Never."

He opened his eyes wide, but I could tell the little asshole wasn't likely to let this go.

"This is a night of celebration," Alex interjected as he flanked my side. "If you would like to learn more about the significant number of hours Gabriel has worked with these various organizations or the millions of dollars we've donated, then I'll be happy to provide that for you."

I couldn't help but grin. I'd chosen the perfect man to stand by my side. He was honorable, highly respected, and there wasn't a bad bone in his body. He was also loyal and protective as hell. Alex knew about the other business opportunities I'd been involved with for years. He simply chose to look the other way.

He also knew that it wouldn't be in his best interest to cross me.

Ever.

"Very well, Mr. Dupree. However, I find it interesting that the FBI has opened an investigation on your business's activities." Joe threw it out to create a scandal.

He managed to enrage me. The thudding in my heart as well as the rumbling in my loins indicated I could lose control far too easily. I took a deep breath, holding it for several seconds, fascinated as several of the other reporters came to my defense.

"That's bullshit."

"Mr. Dupree is an honorable man."

"This is a celebration. You need to get out of here." Jeff finally made his way through the crowd, already looking for the security he'd hired.

Joe backed away, his eyes never leaving me. "Fine. I'll go. But now you know you can't hide behind your façade any longer."

If only he understood what kind of mask that I'd been forced to wear my entire life.

Even though Joe moved away without another incident, Jeff pushed the reporters away, mouthing 'I'm so sorry' before doing so.

"Fucking asshole. What the hell was he talking about?" Alex asked under his breath. He'd learned the rules of playing the events, making certain he never appeared flustered or on the edge.

One thing I knew, I had to get the fuck out of here before I lost all control.

Fortunately, the ringing of my phone interrupted me. "Yes?"

"I'm sorry to interrupt your evening, boss, but you need to get down here." My soldier's tone of voice concerned me.

"What's wrong?" I scanned the room for my Capo, easily able to see him over the others in the room. As soon as he caught my look, he moved in my direction.

"Let's just say I found a thief."

After telling me where he was located, another growl popped up from the bowels of my being. "I'll be right there."

"What's wrong?" Alex asked.

"Some business I need to take care of." When I gave him a look, he knew better than to ask what kind of business I was referring to.

"I'll take your award with me."

"I appreciate that." I kept my jacket buttoned as I moved toward Bronco. The man had been by my side for six years. While brutal in every aspect, he'd also learned how to blend into any situation.

"Problems?" Bronco asked.

"Nothing we can't handle. Let's go."

* * *

Traitors.

In my line of work, I'd experienced only a few, likely given my firm hold on every detail in both my legitimate as well as unsavory businesses. There wasn't a person working with me who didn't understand my intolerance for disloyalty of any kind. My punishments were swift and harsh, but only given when necessary.

Tonight was one of those nights.

The small house was unassuming, located in a decent neighborhood where hard laboring families lived. As I stepped out of the back of the Jeep, various odors assaulted my senses, some from over two blocks away. Garlic. Onions. Cigarette smoke. The odors would linger in my system for far too long.

I'd already pulled my weapon from the holster I'd left in the floor of the vehicle. Patrons of glamorous events didn't like the confrontational aspects of a man hiding a gun. Snickering, I didn't bother waiting for Bronco, heading straight for the front door. When I walked inside, I was underwhelmed by the surroundings. The asshole had made significant money from being in my employ over the last two years. It would seem the least he could do was purchase a few decent things.

As one of my soldiers eased into a doorway toward the back of the house, I could tell by the blood splattered on his face that he'd already worked the son of a bitch over. I heard Bronco closing the door after entering. He would ensure I didn't have any interference. When I walked into the kitchen, I was struck by the filth covering almost every surface. For some reason, that riled the fuck out of me.

"Did he give you any trouble?" I asked, glancing from Jackson to Miller, my main soldiers also loyal men.

Jackson laughed as he fisted and flexed his hand several times. "He thinks he's a tough guy."

"Interesting," I said under my breath.

I stared down at the man who'd dared defy not only my patience but my trust as well. Then I took another full minute to study his surroundings. Dirty dishes were piled in the sink, the surface of the oven covered in grease and food particles. My stomach churned as much as my anger continued to rise.

"Emilio," I said.

His breathing labored, Emilio managed to lift his head. As expected, I was able to notice resignation as well as utter terror in his eyes. He was fully aware his time of reckoning had arrived. "Gabriel."

It was interesting he'd resorted to calling me by my first name, which was strictly forbidden. Sighing, I inched closer, studying his countertops. "It would seem you've been a very bad boy."

"I'm sorry," he muttered, his voice strained given the puffiness of his face.

"Sorry. Well, I completely understand the desire to improve a situation; however, if appearances are accurate, you've done nothing but wallow in your fucking shit!" I'd raised my voice at the end, something I never did. I was extremely agitated, which went against my usual character.

I closed my eyes, trying to control my breathing. The reason for my rage was two-fold, the second being more concerning.

My desire to shift over the course of the last few weeks had been increasing. It had come to a point that I was no longer certain I'd be able to restrain my beast from surfacing at will. My hunger was to the point I found it difficult to focus. That had never occurred before.

"He has a brand new boat," Jackson offered.

"And a fancy new car in the garage," Miller stated.

Laughing, now I was fully able to understand. Emilio was planning on using that boat in an effort to sell the same stockpile of weapons he'd been stupid enough to steal from me. I moved in front of him, placing my foot on the rung of the chair he was tethered to. When I leaned over, he flinched. Well, good. He should be concerned about what I was going to do. "Do you have a family, Emilio?"

"Just a mom and my sister, sir."

"Sir. Oh, you seem to understand the error of your ways. Excellent." My head was pounding, the blood running through my veins creating a vibrant pulse on the side of my neck.

"Yes. I just lost my way," the man whined. "I swear to God it won't happen again."

"Yes, you did and you're right, it won't." I backhanded him, then moved away, contemplating what to do as I fisted my hand. A message had to be sent to maintain order. "First of all, we're confiscating your sexy new toys. Second, you're going to supply the names of every asshole you promised a sale."

I could hear his sigh of relief, which pissed me off even more.

Another lesson needed to be learned. While I'd normally handle it myself, the pain already coursing through my body indicated that wasn't going to happen. "I'm going to allow you to live, Emilio, but there are consequences you will endure. However, if you dare attempt to defy me in any manner again, there will be no leniency. None." My heart thudded against my chest, a snarl slipping up from my throat before I was able to curtail it.

Emilio stared at me, his expression reflecting gratitude.

Until he locked eyes with mine. I'd allowed my beast to surface, if only for a few seconds.

Then there was nothing but blatant horror crossing the asshole's face.

I backed away, doing what I could to keep from stumbling. The pain shifting into anguish, I lowered my head. "Provide him with a lesson he won't forget."

"You got it, boss," Jackson said. Only the most trusted individuals in my operation knew of my affliction.

That didn't include Alex, although I considered him a friend. The less he knew about my lineage the better.

I moved out of the kitchen, Bronco immediately realizing what was wrong with me.

"Where do you want to go?" he asked as he threw open the front door.

"Somewhere secluded." I could no longer recognize my voice. By the time I pitched myself into the backseat, the agony racing through every cell and muscle was almost unbearable. I hunkered over, barely cognizant that Bronco had already started the engine.

Why the fuck was this happening? I'd been able to control my urges my entire life. The voracious hunger in my system was more intense than ever before. I was losing my sanity as repulsive visions popped into my mind. As I dragged my tongue across my teeth, my gums were already receding, prepared to accept my canines.

I thought about my upcoming trip, the request for me to return home. I hadn't been to Baton Rouge in years, preferring the vibrant and tough atmosphere of Chicago. However, I'd already heard about some of the issues my father had been facing, certain factions attempting to muscle the family business out of several cities, including New Orleans. That wasn't going to happen. Maybe a show of force was needed.

Still, given the recent changes in my body as well as the accusations the reporter had made, I would need to return quickly. I sat back, taking several deep breaths, but within a few minutes, my control had almost slipped away.

"Hurry," I managed, my vision now cloudy.

"Just hang on, boss. We're almost there."

I struggled to breathe, my thoughts now centered around feeding. Whatever the fuck was going on was reprehensible. There was no accounting for time when I fell into a lust-filled haze, only my needs weren't something I'd ever wanted to participate in.

"We're pulling in," Bronco huffed. When he jerked the Jeep to a stop, I immediately began to rip off my clothes.

"Stay. Here." I knew my instructions would be followed. Bronco had been through this twice in the last two months alone.

He said nothing, ignoring me as I stumbled out the door. The raw scents of the forest filtered into my nostrils, easing some of the pain. As I scampered off in the dense woods, there was no way of holding back my wolf.

He was ready to hunt.

He was ready to feed.

And he refused to be denied any longer.

CHAPTER 2

 oraline

Frustration.

Exhaustion.

I wasn't certain which had the greater hold on me. Exhaling, I glanced around the clinic one last time before stumbling into my office and grabbing my purse. I'd spent somewhere close to sixteen hours that day alone making the final preparations in order to open my doors for business.

As if anyone had called to make an appointment.

Not that they could since my office phone wasn't working yet. Damn it. The assholes from the phone company had better be on time in the morning. Thirty-six hours and I was set to open the doors. So what if it was lean for a little while? I could survive. Maybe.

Thibodaux, Louisiana was certainly a far cry from New York City.

'Come home,' my mother had said. *'I have a great opportunity for you.'*

Huffing, I realized I wasn't certain where I'd put my keys. After searching for five minutes, I finally found them in the pile of trash on the floor. So much for my organizational skills. The 'great' opportunity was to own a veterinary clinic. However, I hadn't expected the existing business would be located in a rundown building in the freaking middle of nowhere.

Still, I'd wanted a quiet life, one with more meaning. Hell, I'd jumped at the chance without bothering to look at the location my mother had found. She'd even purchased the damn place for me, which had shocked me. How had my mother managed to squirrel away enough money to purchase a business for her only daughter?

Yeah, I found out quickly enough. At least I'd been able to hire a few contractors in a short amount of time so the bare electrical wires wouldn't start a fire.

When I opened the door, the humid air hit me in the face. Well, I guess it was better than the usual garlic stench that always seemed to cling to my clothes. Living in New York City had certainly been a fascinating experience.

I turned off the lights, making certain the outdoor fixture remained on. While I wasn't skittish since I'd been faced with enough dangerous assholes that I always carried a gun, the darkness surrounding the clinic was eerie at night. After locking the door, I realized I should stop and get some dog food. Poor Moose had maybe one meal left. Well, maybe he'd share my steak that I'd purchased two days before. I'd lost my appetite after looking at my bank account.

The car my mother had left me had seen better days, but at least it was adequate transportation. Thankfully, she'd sold me her house for a single dollar, her move to Florida or the Caribbean or somewhere else tropical unexpected. Then again, my mother had always been a wild wanderer, a trait I thankfully hadn't acquired.

The woman believed in black magic and monsters, and she'd assured me when I was growing up that the spirts of the earth had a special reason for my existence. In all the years I'd been alive, I hadn't asked her what that 'reason' was. Why I'd thought of it tonight was beyond me.

What I hated the most about the location of the clinic was the dark, tree-lined road I'd travel every day. I'd been the kid afraid of my own shadow. The ones the trees manifested in my headlights were huge and ugly, a reminder there were monsters lurking everywhere.

"Girl. You've been watching too many horror movies." I cranked the air conditioning then turned on the radio. Maybe a good rock and roll station would keep my mind occupied. When one of my favorite Bon Jovi songs came on, my mood improved. I'd open the celebratory bottle of wine my mother had left on the counter as soon as I walked in the door.

I deserved it after the last few days of good old-fashioned hard work.

After rounding a bend, my headlights picked up an object in the distance. Probably just a deer.

Or a serial killer.

Cringing, my inner voice was the glass half empty kind of gal. I laughed and slowed down, hoping the beautiful creature would just pass on by. Seconds later, the hair stood up on the back of my neck. Was that some dude standing in the middle of the road? I knew the road leading to the clinic also had other businesses just to the west, so it was entirely possible the guy had broken down on the side of the road. However, the lump in my throat was another flag provided by my instinct.

The man waved his arms as I approached, trying to flag me down. One thing was certain. He wasn't going to allow me to pass on by. As I slowed to just a crawl, I scanned both sides of the road, able to see a truck located just up ahead. From the way it was positioned, it was possible the guy had driven into a ditch. My senses on overload, I pulled to a stop, lowering my window only a couple of inches.

"Is something wrong?"

He raked his hands through his long hair before approaching. "Hey there, pretty lady. Thanks for stopping. Yeah, there's something wrong."

Almost immediately I had a sense of danger, but before I had a chance to roll the window closed, he'd managed to reach in, grabbing a fistful of my hair.

"Something's very wrong, you bitch."

Out of the corner of my eye, I noticed two more assholes trotting in the direction of the car. I could swear one of them held a rope.

"Let go of me," I screamed, fighting to get out of the man's grasp. He yanked my head, twisting me so I was unable to keep pressing on the button for the window.

"That's not going to happen. I suggest you unlock your door or things are going to get ugly," he snarled.

I slapped at his arms, able to scratch his skin, but that didn't faze him. Then I reached for my purse. Damn it. It was too far out of my reach. The other two men closed in, one moving to the passenger door while the other stayed in front. When he slammed on the hood, leaning over, his expression something that would haunt me for months to come, I let out another bloodcurdling scream.

As if anyone was going to come to my rescue.

"This little lady is a real treasure," the first guy huffed.

I managed to bring my leg up from the floorboard, fighting with everything I had to slide it across the console. Panting, I continued fighting him with one hand, reaching out with the other after I was able to snag the strap. *Please. Please. Please!* I was able to drag it a few inches, but the asshole figured out what I was doing.

The hard slap of something steel against the window made me yelp.

"We can do this the easy way or the hard way. It's entirely up to you. You got three seconds to unlock that door or a bullet is going to come through your window. After that, you won't like what happens to you."

All the stories about developing superhuman strength in this kind of situation were bullshit. I was terrified, still fighting to get my gun from the heavy purse I carried.

"She is a little bitch," one of the others stated, laughing like some freaking lunatic.

"We'll take care of that. Won't we, darlin'?"

Everything seemed to shift into slow motion, tears forming in my eyes.

"I can see you like it the hard way. Then that's exactly what we're going to give you. One. Two."

The thudding of my heart in my ears was suddenly replaced with an unrecognizable noise. Then I was able to hear a dark and husky growl of some animal.

Either the bastards couldn't hear the animal's approach, or they didn't give a damn.

Unable to see anything, I could tell I was losing the fight.

Then I heard a horrible bellow from the man holding me, the growl increasing in volume. When he let go of my hair, I immediately scrambled for my purse, my hands shaking as I retrieved my weapon. I froze as I heard all three men screaming. Then the one who'd been on the passenger side was tossed back like a rag doll.

While everything was a horrific blur, there was no doubt given the amount of blood splattered across my windshield that the men were being torn apart.

I hunkered over, gasping for air, doing everything I could to remain calm. Oh, God. Oh, dear God.

Pop! Pop!

The next sound was a terrible yelp, the cry coming from the animal. I expected at least one of the men would come after me again but there was no movement of any kind outside.

I peered out my driver's door, every part of me shaking like a leaf. After blinking several times in order to focus, I managed to see one of the men lying face down close to the tree line. Very slowly I turned off the radio, the open window rolling in the stench of blood. I held my hand over my face, unbuckling my seatbelt. When I leaned over the steering wheel, I was horrified to see one of the attackers was lying smack in the middle of the road.

There was no way to get around him given the narrowness of the road. I'd be forced to move him or drive over his... body. Those were the only two choices. "Damn it. Damn it." I closed my eyes until I heard a single woeful whimper. Not from the men but from the creature that had undoubtedly saved me from being kidnapped or worse. With my gun still in my hand, I unlocked the door, carefully easing outside. The second I stepped away from the side, I had to toss my other hand over my mouth.

While I'd anticipated the men would be mauled, I was shocked at the horrible sight in front of me. Instantly nauseous, I turned around. I'd seen terrible injuries animals had been forced to endure, human monsters doing unspeakable things, but this was entirely different.

After taking several deep breaths to keep from tossing what little food I'd eaten that day, I backed against the car, sliding around until I reached the trunk. The creature was a dog, a beautiful black male dog. Oh, my God. He'd fought to save my life. I raced over, hunkering down, my fingers immediately brushing through blood. Fuck. "You've been shot, baby. Jesus. What the hell am I going to do?"

Courage. Get the dog to your clinic.

Yes. Yes, that's what I had to do. I stroked the side of his face, startled when he opened his eyes. "It's okay, baby. I know you're hurt, and you don't know me, but just like you saved my life, I'm going to save yours, but you'll need to trust me. Do you think you can do that?" Whether or not he understood anything I couldn't be certain of. For all I knew, he could be rabid, which had allowed him the incredible strength he'd obviously had.

However, I refused to leave him on the side of the road. I realized I had a blanket in the trunk. Maybe that would help. "Stay right here." I scrambled to the back of the car, shoving the weapon into the small of my back then fighting my shaking hands in order to get inside, constantly looking from one side to the other. I half expected one or all of the bastards to stand, even though what was left of my rational mind knew better.

Breathe. Just breathe.

That did little to help but I managed to yank the blanket into my hand, fighting another wave of terror as I returned to the dog's side. "Okay. I'm going to gather you into my arms." That would take a damn miracle. The dog had to weigh eighty pounds, maybe more.

By the grace of something holy, I managed to get him into my arms just enough I was able to place him into the backseat. Tomorrow, I was exchanging the car for a truck. Whew. After settling in, I slowly backed away, cognizant a bump occurred under at least one of my tires. I bit back a moan, trying to keep myself as calm as possible. An injured animal could turn vicious at any moment.

I pressed down the accelerator, wasting no time getting back to the clinic. "I'm not leaving you. Just getting something to help me." By the time I attempted to unlock the door, my hands were steady. The fear had left, my anger surpassing every other emotion. Who the hell were those men? "Okay, let's get you on the table." Thank God I'd thought of the rolling platform. The dog definitely seemed a hell of a lot heavier than before.

After getting him inside, I locked the door, gasping for air.

Then I realized he was barely breathing.

"Fuck. Fuck!" I wasted no additional time, placing my weapon on one of the cabinets then scrubbing my hands.

There were two bullets lodged in his chest, deep enough I was forced to give the dog a sedative. I wasn't set up to do emergency surgeries yet, which meant there was no way I could put him under anesthesia. Oh, this was bad, but there was nothing else I could do.

As I started to clean his wounds, the dog jerked his head up, staring at me intently.

He had the bluest eyes I'd ever seen before in my life. That's the moment I realized the patient wasn't a dog.

He was a wolf.

I held my breath, fighting a trickle of fear. Wolves were some of the most intelligent creatures on earth. They could sense terror from a mile away, homing in on their prey. As I stared into his eyes, I realized my breathing was shallow, but my reaction wasn't out of fear. It was out of fascination.

The beast cocked his head, lowering his gaze and letting off a single growl, one that should have pushed me away, but the sound drew me in. My entire body tingled, my heart racing as a wave of adrenaline flowed into my system. I suddenly felt like I was drawn into his world, my gut telling me he could read my thoughts.

Hunger. The beast was hungry, but not to rip me apart limb from limb. He wanted me. To take me.

To use me.

To… fuck me.

Coraline…

I jerked back but only for an instant, certain I'd heard the creature speak my name. Damn it. I needed a long night's sleep. Now I thought an animal could talk to me.

Blinking, I forced myself to look away, surprised goosebumps had covered my arms. *Think like a doctor. He's injured. He needs your help.* After taking several shallow breaths, I offered a smile.

"Hi, there. I hope you can still trust me because this is going to hurt. But I promise I can make it better. Okay?" My God. I was talking to him like he could really understand. His gaze was unnerving, making my skin crawl. I gathered everything I needed, proceeding to set up an IV with pain medication. I had to be damn careful.

For several reasons.

The creature never took his eyes off me as I started the surgery. He didn't yelp or even move. He just… studied me. I only hoped he wasn't considering me for his next meal.

After twenty minutes, I managed to pull the second bullet. One more inch and his spine would have been severed. "You're a lucky pup. I think you're going to make a full recovery." Now what the hell was I supposed to do with him? As I stood back, his blood still covering my gloves, I studied him. He was without a doubt one of the most beautiful creatures I'd ever laid my eyes on.

So regal.

So enthralling.

So predatory.

There was an electricity about him, an aura that drew me in and I had no idea why. Other than the fact he'd saved my life. When he finally closed his eyes, resting his head, I made a calculated decision, opening one of the large cages then disconnecting his IV. As I slid my arms under his massive body, I was thankful he was breathing easier.

While moving him was a struggle, I managed to get him into the cage without disturbing him, reattaching the IV line and adding a blanket before closing the door. When I eased away, ripping off my gloves, only then did the adrenaline rush start to pour out of my system.

I knew I should call the police. Of course I should. That's what any sane person would do. The jerks who'd attacked me certainly weren't going anywhere. After a few seconds of hesitation, I grabbed my purse, retrieving my phone, prepared to make the call. This was the first time I'd noticed there was absolutely no reception in the building. No freaking reception.

Why, oh, why had I moved to bumfuck again, a place I'd sworn I'd never return to. Because something had drawn me here other than just my mother's offer. I'd almost felt compelled to return home. Maybe the attack was actually karma kicking me in the butt for being stupid.

I moved into my office, dragging out my chair as well as a bottle of water. So much for the glass of wine. Moose was home all alone. At least there was a doggy door at my mother's house, a product of her futile attempt at keeping a pet. Ugh. When I sat down, every last ounce of steam was gone, ripped away. As tears started to slide down both sides of my face, all I could do was laugh.

There were no friends left that I'd grown up with, no immediate family, and I had no idea where my mother was. Perfect. "You're an idiot, Coraline." I gazed down at the cage then rubbed my eyes before closing them. My mind often worked in mysterious ways. As aches settled into my system, words tumbled from my mouth.

"There's no place like home. There's no place… like… home."

* * *

"What?" I jerked my head up, gasping as I tried to focus. When I realized it was light outside, I almost panicked, fighting the tenseness in my body to get to my feet.

Then I remembered the horrors from the night before.

"Oh, no!" I'd fallen asleep, not checking on the wolf a single time. I snapped my head in the direction of the cage. Then I froze.

There was no sign of the creature.

Without moving, I scanned the room, expecting to see items toppled over, the front door scratched. Then I realized I'd locked it. Unless the wolf was a magician, he wouldn't have been able to get out of here. Wait. The window in the other room. I rose to my feet, grabbing my gun before inching toward the back room. There was no glass on the floor or any other sign the wolf had entered the space.

This didn't make any sense. Fuck. Did I dream the entire thing? I moved from room to room, discovering the exact same conditions. When I hunkered down, peering into the open cage door, I realized the IV had been disconnected, not ripped out. That wasn't possible. Out of frustration, I walked toward the front door, finding it unlocked.

I backed against it, staring up at the ceiling. "Let me get this straight. A severely injured wolf inside a closed cage managed not only to get out of his cage, but out of the building without destroying anything or killing me. Uh-huh."

But as I walked into the main room, turning in a full circle, I was forced to accept the wolf had disappeared. As

I leaned against the counter, all I could think about were monsters.

"Monsters are real, ghosts are real too. They live inside us, and sometimes they win."

Stephen King

CHAPTER 3

abriel

Palace.

That's the way my parents had described their new home. With over twenty-five thousand square feet of polished Venetian marble, massive stone fireplaces, and Macassar Ebony wooden floors, I could see why they used the favored reference. As I wandered into the kitchen, a smile crossed my face. My mother had always said she wanted a kitchen large enough that she would be able to cook for at least two hundred guests.

Not that my mother had spent much time in any kitchen since I could remember. When I moved toward one of the four islands, my footsteps echoed. I preferred my high-rise condo to something so... fancy. I noticed a tray with an iced beverage of some sort, several glasses surrounding it. While I'd been greeted within seconds by a friendly face, the lovely girl knowing exactly who I was, I'd yet to see anyone else wandering the many corridors.

I poured a glass, surprised when I brought it to my lips that it was freshly squeezed lemonade. I couldn't remember the last time I'd enjoyed something so refreshing. "Hmmm…" I took another sip before moving toward the bank of all glass doors. The day was steamy and humid, yet the outdoor space was inviting, including the pool that went from one end of the house to the other.

"Impressive, Pops. You certainly made good on your promise to be the big man in town." I don't know why I'd muttered the words out loud. There was no one around to hear me. After touring the expansive space, I took up residence in one of the lounge chairs, yanking my sunglasses from my pocket.

Why not soak up a few rays while I was here. As I waited, I thought about the events of the last few days. At least I knew Alex would handle one side of the company, Bronco assuring me he'd keep close eye on the other portion, letting me know immediately if anything had gone awry. A major shipment would occur at the end of the week, which made the timing of this trip bothersome. While I'd investigated what Joe Brooks had spouted off, including talking to one of the higher-ranking officials within the FBI, a man who owed me his life, there was no validity to the reporter's comments. Why had he attempted to rile me?

Men like that never did anything without a reason.

The only reason I could think of was notoriety.

I took a deep breath, my thoughts drifting to the beautiful woman from the night before. I'd been drawn to Thibodaux, a location I'd only been to once in my life. I'd gathered her scent and had been unable to break away from finding her. That troubled me more than the need I'd had the night before that, my feeding frenzy lasting for hours.

I rubbed my chest, the ache of being shot and the subsequent surgery remaining as a dull reminder of what had happened. While I'd been able to fight off the sedative she'd used, shifting healing the wounds almost entirely, the treachery of what the men had done remained as a bad taste in my mouth. They'd targeted her specifically, likely figuring no one would care.

My thoughts turned in another direction as need swelled within me. The connection I'd felt with her had been far too strong to be coincidental. There was no doubt in my mind the lovely veterinarian was the woman from my visions. I rubbed my eyes, trying to rid myself of the furrowing hunger. I'd saved her life, for fuck's sake. My instinct had drawn me to her.

Hissing, I took another gulp, swirling the ice in my glass. Damn if my cock wasn't aching. I'd reacted when her life had been placed in danger, ripping the three apart without any rational thought entering my mind. Our kind were careful, practiced. We never lost control.

But that's all I'd been doing lately.

As I closed my eyes, I could still see her pained expression, so concerned about what had happened to me. She had no understanding of just how much danger she had been in. I'd been able to read the thoughts of the men. They'd been planning on abducting her, but why? She was a veterinarian. And why the hell had I been there in the first place?

I'd been lucky I was able to get open the cage door before returning to human form. The entire last few months had been troubling. There had to be a reason for my bizarre behavior.

When I heard footsteps, I stayed right where I was. The lounger was actually very comfortable.

"Gabriel."

I lifted my sunglasses, surprised how well rested my father appeared. "It would seem the grandiose house has provided you with a new lease on life." As I rose to a standing position, his smile grew large.

Then he threw his arms around me, slapping me on the back. "It's good to have you home."

"Except this isn't my home, Pops, but I admit, it's pretty nice."

He laughed as he backed away. In his hand was an alcoholic beverage. It didn't seem to matter what time of the day it was, he refused to give up on his private indulgences. "Your mother loves it."

"I should hope so."

"Yes, it allows her some private time." He threw me a mischievous look then glanced at his watch.

"Are you expecting someone else?"

He took his time answering me. "This is a family meeting."

"Okay. Why wasn't I informed?"

"Because it's my meeting."

Now I could tell something was troubling him. "What's going on, Pops?"

"We'll wait until your brothers are here. Why don't you tell me how Dupree Enterprises is going?"

The man could easily exasperate me. "I think you already know since you receive quarterly dividends."

"Mmm... Yes, but that's from the technological side. I understand you won another award."

"Nothing gets by you. Does it, Pops?"

He lifted a single eyebrow. "No, and that's something you should keep in mind."

At least the man was in a good mood. "Have you had anyone tell you the FBI is investigating the family?"

The fact he didn't answer right away wasn't surprising. How many times had our family been under investigation by some organization or another? While we'd done everything over the last ten years to all but eliminate our criminal activities from the public eye, there were always people willing to talk for a price.

Or for a promise of freedom.

"Son, you have some of the keenest senses I've ever known. You have this ability to know when the family is facing danger. Do you have any fears that our world is about to be compromised?" The way he was looking at me was fascinating, as if this was a test of some kind.

I took a deep breath, able to see at least one of my brothers walking into the kitchen. "You're aware of my increased appetite."

He nodded, still searching my eyes. "It's something the entire Dupree family has been experiencing, some unable to control their reaction to the change."

"Meaning what?" As he walked closer, I gathered an understanding of what he was saying. "They've injured humans."

"Yes, enough so the entire Bayou is rumbling with concerns and accusations that monsters have appeared out of the darkness, running off with newborn babies. At least that hasn't come to pass, but several innocent lives have been affected," he answered, his eyes showing an emotion I wasn't certain of.

"But you fear the situation is going to get worse."

He suddenly looked extremely tired, as if holding onto the information had been taking a toll.

"What aren't you telling me?" I demanded just as Marcel swaggered onto the veranda.

If my father noticed his arrival, he didn't react. His hard, cold stare was unnerving. "You will soon understand."

"What about Dax?"

He inhaled, finally looking away, but not before I saw the sadness in his eyes. One of my younger brothers had been in prison for years for a brutal crime. His actions had been completely out of character, surprising all of us at the time. Now I had the distinct feeling it was in direct correlation to whatever revelation he was prepared to expose.

Marcel had a grin on his face as he approached, his usual dark demeanor tossed away for the afternoon. I was curious how long that would last.

"My big brother, as I live and breathe. How long has it been?" he asked before taking a deep breath. "Nice place, Dad. You did well."

"It's only been a year, brother." My answer was curt, but I was in no mood for a family gathering, no matter the reason.

"I'm glad you made it, son. I know you had difficulties," Pops said in passing.

Shrugging, Marcel kept his gaze locked on me. "It's okay. I handled the situation. Just an incident of theft, but the perpetrator has been taken care of."

I found it interesting that both of us had been forced to deal with the same kind of betrayal. Before I had a chance to ask, Sebastian walked onto the veranda. He seemed more perturbed than normal.

"I've love to say I'm glad the family is getting back together, but I have a huge shipment coming in tomorrow night," he stated, obviously annoyed.

"You'll be able to return by then, son. Incidentally, Christoff might be late. His plane was delayed."

"Why don't you go ahead and break the bad news, Pops. We all have businesses to return to." The demanding tone in my voice remained.

While my father was a brutal man and always had been, he'd never raised his voice to any of us. He never had to. I was surprised at the rage in his eyes as he took two long strides in my direction. "We will wait for your brother just like I said, Gabriel. I don't want to hear any crap from your mouths. You are all wealthy beyond your dreams because of the sacrifices I made, your grandfather made, and all the ancestors before him. Do you understand?"

All three of us glanced at each other. "Absolutely." I knew better than to push him. Whatever duress he was under was indeed taking a significant toll.

I gave him a nod of respect before walking away, Sebastian following me.

"What the hell is going on?" he asked quietly.

"Are you experiencing uncontrollable urges?"

He stopped where he was, lifting his head before shaking it. "That's what this is about."

"Evidently and I'll take that as a yes."

Sebastian appeared uncomfortable. "My need to shift is getting bad enough I almost lost it with one of my soldiers. I wanted nothing more than to rip him apart."

"My shifts are more frequent and longer. That can't happen. They need to be controlled."

"Then we need answers."

I turned and watched our father as he bantered with Marcel, my other brother smart enough to know the man shouldn't be pushed. At least Pops appeared more relaxed than seconds before. I also found it curious our mother hadn't greeted us. She never missed the opportunity.

We stood together quietly, but I knew Sebastian was just as much on edge as I was. We were by far the closest both in age and as well as our ability to connect. When we were kids, we'd rarely talked, our ability to connect mentally even in our human form uncanny.

My brother was afraid, an emotion he almost never felt. He was a strong leader, as ruthless as our father yet fair in all aspects of business.

Fortunately, we didn't have to wait long. As Christoff walked through the door, both Sebastian and I couldn't help but laugh. He appeared very much a man residing in LA. From his glowing tan to his expensive yet casual attire, he looked every bit the media mogul he'd become over the last few years. He was also the playboy, enjoying whatever flavor of the month more often than I'd been able to think about.

While I'd enjoyed women over the years, no one had captured my attention for longer than a few weeks. Perhaps I was destined to remain a bachelor all my life. We walked closer as Christoff surveyed the new house.

"Wow. And I thought my digs were lavish," he said then stared at our glasses. "Please tell me there's something stronger than a chick's drink."

"Let's go into my office," Pops said without wasting any additional time finding out how everyone was doing.

When he turned away, Sebastian growled under his breath. "This is going to be good," he half whispered.

I was the last one to trail behind the others, taking my time as our father headed down a series of corridors. When we finally walked into his oversized office, he waited then closed the door behind us.

"I can't take the chance of any of the staff overhearing our conversation," he said after we all gave him a curious look. He pointed toward the bar, still nursing on his drink. "Make whatever you'd like. I suspect you'll need something stronger."

Now my hackles were raised. What in the hell was going on?

As we all prepared drinks, he moved toward one of his windows, staring out and remaining unblinking. He'd masked his thoughts, which also surprised me. But there was no denying his concerns. He could tell the moment all four of us had given him our full attention. Although he threw a glance over his shoulder, he remained in the same position.

"Do you remember what I told each of you when you were old enough to question why you were different?" he asked in such a somber tone that I strained to hear him.

"To me, you said that a curse had been placed on the family and we were lucky to be able to live as humans while experiencing the joys of a hunt. That's pretty much all you told me." Christoff's answer held a hint of animosity. As the youngest of the siblings, he'd often felt as if he was thrown scraps of everything involved with the family, including being forced all the way to the other side of the country. He'd worked diligently to make Pops proud.

Our father chuckled then lowered his head. "Which I still believe; however, there is much more to the story."

I'd likely been the only one to learn the full history from the early nineteen hundreds, our past generation even more brutal than we were today. However, I wanted to hear everything directly from our father's mouth before I made any kind of response.

"Why don't you cut to the chase, Pops. I doubt there's a single one of us who hasn't had difficulty containing our urges. True?" Sebastian asked as he looked around at all of us.

I nodded first, the others following.

Our father was a distinguished man. He loathed drama, although he enjoyed taking his time eliminating his enemies, forcing them to endure hours of torment when necessary. I realized after a full thirty seconds that he wasn't certain how to tell us the bad news.

"You've heard me talk about Jade Brousseau over the years," he said in a solemn voice.

"The mystical voodoo priestess who issued the curse on our family," Marcel answered, laughing softly after doing so.

Pops shot him a hateful look. "She was an extremely brutal leader. She believed in the dark side of using voodoo to allow the world her family had created to thrive. Her ancestors had developed a powerful community, thriving off the land. They were some of the first settlers in the Bayou in the eighteen hundreds, prospering off the land for an entire century. Things were much different during that time, violence an everyday part of life."

For some reason, an uneasy feeling shifted through my mind.

Sebastian turned his head in my direction. My brother was pragmatic. There'd been times over the years that he'd refused to believe a part of him was Lycan. He'd struggled with the knowledge, refusing to turn even when his beast needed to feed. Fortunately, up until this point, we'd been able to keep our carnal desires at a minimum. Everything had changed during the course of a few months.

"We've heard this, Pops. I think you need to move past the history lesson," I stated with as much respect as I was able to manage.

He took another sip of his drink, and I couldn't help but notice his hand was shaking. "Did I tell you that she was burned at the stake like some common witch?"

Christoff muttered his disgust under his breath.

"Enough!" my father snarled. "You will listen to what I have to say. Hundreds were strung up to makeshift crosses, their bodies burned, the charred remains left for others to see what would happen if they dared to cross the Dupree dynasty. They were innocent people! They didn't deserve to die. They didn't…"

As our father's voice died off, there was no doubt he was riddled with guilt from reliving the events passed on through the generations.

"Let me guess. She didn't die, hence the curse," I said with no emotion in my voice. All of us needed to hear this out.

Pops nodded, barely glancing in my direction. "Jade was clever in placing the curse, knowing that our family would continue to thrive even though we'd been turned into beasts. Therefore, the cunning woman decided to seal our fate."

The room was absolutely silent until Christoff burst into laughter. "She's dead. What the fuck does it matter now?"

"The Cajuns believe she remains alive, living in a dark cave still close to the land she loved with all her heart. Regardless, her ancestors live on, the children sent away when the group got wind of an impending attack," Pops countered, a snarl erupting from his throat. "One thing is certain. She damned us, all of us. Every single descendant and there are hundreds of us, maybe thousands."

"A fascinating and tragic story, Pops. However, what the hell does it mean exactly?" Marcel asked, his expression one of rage as well as frustration.

For some reason, my father took a few seconds locking eyes with mine. A cold wave settled into my system. "It means," he started, "that her intent was for us to destroy all those around us, the men and women who aided us in annihilating their community. She was very conniving in her actions, realizing that exacting her revenge early would be far too easy. She wanted to inflict the same torturous pain that had been doled out to her people."

"Why are you telling us this now?" I asked, giving each brother a stern look.

He returned to the window, gazing up at the sky. "This year marks an anomaly, an occurrence that even the scientists couldn't predict."

"Jesus, Dad, get to the chase. This is getting old," Sebastian huffed.

"Stop talking!" our father demanded. I'd never seen him so angry, his beast close to the surface.

The room was silent once again.

"There will be two blue moons this year. They are powerful to our kind, drawing us closer to the intense, primal desires that all Lycans experience. We've been lucky for decades, over a hundred years to be exact. We've prospered. We've excelled at everything. And we became filthy rich because of the horrible deed performed by our ancestors. Now, we must pay the price for murdering their people, destroying everything they'd worked so hard to achieve." He lowered his head, taking several rattled breaths. "You are the direct descendants of those responsible, the pure bloodline of our family. And because of that, you will be punished severely. What happens over the upcoming months will be an indication of how much brutality our family must go through."

I'd learned as much about the Brousseau family as possible over the years. Pops had taught me early on that knowledge of your enemy was necessary, although from what I knew about Jade's descendants, they'd scattered to the four corners of the earth after the annihilation in the early nineteen hundreds.

Sebastian narrowed his eyes as he looked at me, biting back a laugh. He'd never believed in the legend, making fun of our father behind his back. Today was no different.

"According to this legend?" I asked.

Pops nodded. "The effects have already started, and they will only increase in need and duration. There is almost nothing we can do."

Marcel exhaled audibly, daring to be the first one to try to clarify what the hell our father was talking about. "Our increasing hunger is an addition to this curse. Is that what you're telling us?"

"Yes," Pops said far too quietly, which wasn't like him under any circumstances.

Even Sebastian seemed lost in his own thoughts, uncertain of what to say.

"What do the two blue moons have to do with what's happening to us?" I asked after a full minute had passed.

When he turned his head to look at me, I could swear there were tears in his eyes. "All five of you must mate this year. If you don't, then every single descendant will be forced to live out the rest of their lives as the beast Jade cursed us to become."

I knew my father well enough to know that there was more to this wretched curse that had been placed on us. "What else?"

"Your hunger will continue to increase to the point that soon you won't be able to control it, as will every other member of our extended family. No longer will creatures of the night satisfy your needs. You will require more."

"Humans," Marcel managed.

"Yes," our father hissed. "You must find your fated mate or what is unleashed will be catastrophic. There will be almost no way of stopping the bloodshed."

I felt cold, emotionless. I also wasn't shocked by what he'd told us. Perhaps I'd known all along that our ancestors had damned the entire family.

"A mate," Sebastian snarled. "Ridiculous."

"I suggest you listen instead of talking," I snapped.

Sebastian rolled his eyes before looking away.

"If this is really the truth then how the hell are we supposed to find that… person?" Christoff struggled to say, my brother always allowing his emotions to get in the way of his ability to think clearly. I could sense his beast had risen to the surface.

"You will know the very moment you meet her, or least that's what I was told, but it is likely you will need to search for her. It won't be easy. Jade never intended for our lives to be easy." Our father's words seemed to trail off, a single tear sliding down his cheek.

I couldn't remember if or when I'd ever seen our father this emotional. He'd prided himself on being able to handle any situation.

"Let me get this straight," Sebastian scoffed, his eyes filled with venom. "Someone *told* you that this was going to happen? You don't have actual proof that any of this is true?"

"Who is this someone?" Marcel demanded.

Our father glared from one to the other, his chest heaving and his face reddening. "This was passed down by our people. My father told me, his father before him. We are Lycans! That is all the proof you need."

A moment of quiet, blistering tension remained between us, anger running high.

"So what you're telling us is that there is no proof of this curse, only a legend passed down through generations, which means the story has likely been embellished over the years. Is that correct?" Marcel continued.

All our father did was nod.

Snarling, I threw my brothers a harsh glare. While I realized the situation was farfetched, the fact we were Lycans gave credibility to the story. Pops had never been prone to drama, refusing to buy bullshit from anyone providing an excuse. While I didn't want to believe a word he'd said, I'd experienced the visions, felt the desperate need, and lost all control when I'd believed my intended mate's life was in danger.

"And the Brousseau family? I assume they have also been made aware of this… legend." I asked, shaking my head. He'd kept this from us all these years. Maybe he'd hoped that two blue moons wouldn't happen in our lifetime. Whatever the case, I was furious that he'd maintained the secret all these years.

"Of course they have. They were indoctrinated into hating our family from the minute they were born. Jade's descendants will stop at nothing to keep your mating from happening. And they will do everything in their power to hunt all five of you down."

Our father's words were haunting, even if there was only partial truth in what he was saying.

All three of my brothers laughed.

"Let's assume this garbage you're spewing off is true, then what about Dax? He's in fucking prison. How in the hell are we supposed to get him out?" Sebastian's demanding question was one that needed to be asked.

"You'll need to do whatever it takes to get him released, and I do mean anything feasible. Your brother is already experiencing significant difficulties hiding his true identity. I fear he will break sooner than the rest of you. If that occurs, all our livelihoods will be in jeopardy. We can't allow that to happen."

I closed my eyes briefly, allowing our father's words to sink in. As my thoughts drifted to the night before, I realized that the woman I'd saved was my mate. There was no question in my mind. The electricity we'd shared had been undeniable. The fact I'd slaughtered three men in coming to her rescue just the beginning. I no longer was certain what I was capable of or if I could control my wolf.

"Un-freaking believable," Sebastian huffed.

"But you've felt additional hunger. Right? I know I have," Christoff countered.

"We all have, son," Pops said quietly. "There hasn't been a day in the last month I haven't thought about hunting. Only your mother has been able to keep me from doing so. That won't last and soon all five of you will start to lose control more frequently."

"This is bullshit!" Marcel snapped, tossing back the rest of his drink then slamming his glass on the bar. "If you really think some dead woman's curse is going to affect us after fucking two hundred years, then you are deranged, Pops. I'm not going to allow my life to be altered by some legend." As he stormed toward the door, my father reacted instantly, taking long strides after him.

Pops slammed his hand on his desk. "Do you honestly believe that what we've become is anything but a curse? We hunger for flesh and blood, and no matter how sophisticated or educated we've become over these decades, the simple fact is that we are creatures that have been allowed to remain in human form. What we did to an entire group of people is unforgiveable. Hundreds if not thousands of Jade's followers were murdered all because they refused to hand over their land. We are responsible for the near extermination of their kind. However, a few survived, enough to build their community once again. While they remain in the shadows, many of them also refusing to believe in the old ways, moving to other states and countries, they will not be able to deny their ancestry. They will return in force, doing their own version of hunting. And they will do everything in their power to destroy us."

While his words hung in the air, all four of us remained incapable of accepting what we'd been told.

Marcel lowered his head, his shoulders heaving.

Then he walked out.

Sebastian and Christoff looked at each other, both taking only a few seconds before following in Marcel's footsteps.

There was so much anger, total denial.

When I was left with my father, I walked toward the bar, refilling my drink. Then I took the bottle with me, pouring another hefty amount in his glass before easing it down onto the surface of his desk.

We both remained quiet for several minutes, although I sensed his increased despair. He'd fought to keep from telling us the truth, which had likely eaten at him for years.

"Why didn't you tell us years ago?" I finally asked.

He swirled his drink, taking a huge gulp before answering. "I wanted all of you to live normal lives." Even though he laughed, I could tell he was close to breaking down emotionally. "As normal as possible. Our kind is an anomaly."

"There are more Lycans?"

"I don't honestly know, but I can't believe the curse wasn't used before."

"Interesting." What else was there to say? My instinct told me that man was hiding something.

"You need to protect yourselves at all times," he said.

"We certainly know how to do that."

"I hope so, although you don't know what the Brousseau family is capable of. They will use less than honorable methods to achieve their goal." he said quietly.

I lifted my glass, resisting bursting into laughter. As if our family hadn't used unscrupulous, brutal methods of getting what we wanted for decades. "Then we'll be ready."

"I hope so," he said almost too casually. "I want to retire, son. That means you're going to be the new Don of our regime very soon."

"This is the first I've heard of your plans."

He shook his head. "It's time. Maybe it's past time. Your mother and I purchased this house to be able to enjoy our lives, not to have me working all the time. She's been nagging me relentlessly."

"And your hunger? Is it really that bad?"

"Yes, but as I said, I've found ways to… keep it in check." He laughed after issuing the words. "As I mentioned, other family members are experiencing it as well, fortunately most not in the severity that we are."

"Because we are direct descendants of the people who exterminated the Brousseaus."

"A pure bloodline." The fact he'd repeated the words seemed odd. I'd heard him before.

My father was worried that he didn't have long to live as a full human. The thought filled me with anger.

"What do you expect out of me in return?" I asked after a full minute had passed.

"First, you need to get Dax out of prison. Then I want you to allow him to take over Chicago."

I wanted to laugh in his face. "Dax isn't capable of handling Dupree Enterprises. He's a freaking loose cannon. He was a murderer long before this… blue moon crap started."

"That may be the case, but you're needed here. This curse is…" He swallowed hard, unable to look me in the eyes.

I couldn't believe he was asking me to leave everything I'd worked so hard to achieve. "Why?"

He took his time answering. "Because in addition to the curse, there is another family threatening our organization. They have nothing to do with the curse. They are hungry to take over everything we've worked so hard to achieve."

"You're worried they will use this ridiculous curse against us."

"Yes. They are ruthless, using their own powerful influences to expand their territory."

"The Fontenots?" I knew the answer, the same crime syndicate who'd caused disruption in our supply chain several times, managing to destroy several of our ships in the process. Up to this point, Pops had been able to keep them from formally crowding into our territory. The last thing we needed was another crime syndicate feeding off our difficulties.

"You are correct. We can't allow that to happen anymore than losing our humanity. I will need your support. From the reactions of your brothers, I doubt they'll be of much use."

My father's fear was palpable. "When are the two moons expected?"

His features softened hearing my voice. When he turned toward me, I could swear he'd aged by at least ten years in the last half hour. "It's January. There will be one in March and the other in October. As I understand, all five of you will soon be unable to ignore your cravings. You have limited time, but it's vital that you find your mate immediately. You are the king in waiting, the man who will assume the role of Don. To the Brousseau family, you are their greatest threat."

"What does Mother think about all this?" While Josephine wasn't a Lycan, she'd never seemed troubled by the fact her husband and children had been endowed with the affliction.

"She is… disturbed by what will happen, but you know your mother. She is confident we will endure." At least thinking about her gave my father a smile. Their love story was straight out of a romance novel.

The information weighed heavily on me, the responsibility almost too much to bear. "I murdered three men last night."

He chuckled after a few seconds, lifting his glass. "A product of our regime."

"Not for business, Pops. I saved a woman's life. In doing so, I couldn't control my anger. I was…" I held up my hand, remembering the way my claws pierced their skin, the joy I'd felt in punishing them for attacking the beautiful girl.

Exhaling, he remained silent for a few seconds. "In Chicago?"

"In Thibodaux. After my flight landed, I was drawn there, unable to keep from driving to a deserted road in the middle of nowhere."

"And the woman?"

"She's alive, but she was forced to tend to my injuries. I sensed she innately knew I was drawn to her."

As he narrowed his eyes, I could tell he was having difficulty breathing, but there was excitement in his eyes. Hope. "Does she know what you really are?"

"I remained a wolf until she fell asleep. Then I managed to escape. However…" I licked the rim of the glass, trying to fathom what the hell I was supposed to do.

"Was there a connection?"

"Yes. I've never felt the way I did last night. I wanted nothing more than to devour her, fucking her like a wild animal. I've been having visions for weeks. They all revolved around her. I'm certain of it."

He placed his hand on my shoulder, digging his fingers in. "Then that's exactly what you need to do, mate with her before it's too late. If my suspicions are true, then her life is in danger. I suspect the men you killed were Jade's direct descendants. If that is the case, they knew before you did that this woman belonged to you. I think we're running out of time. If either you or your mate is killed, there is no way of stopping the effects of the curse. You must protect both yourself and this woman at all costs."

"If these descendants are planning an attack, then we will treat them like any other enemy we've faced. We will exterminate them." I pulled away, studying his eyes.

Another smile crossed his face. "You are ready to take the helm, son. I've already put out some feelers to people I trust. We will know soon enough if we have a real issue with Jade's ancestors. You deal with the woman. Let me find out what I can."

"That might necessitate taking this woman to Chicago until I can get a handle on my business. I can't just walk away. I've worked far too hard to lose control in that area as well."

"I understand."

"What haven't you told us, Pops? I know there's more."

When he couldn't look me in the eyes, another wave of anger soared.

"There's nothing to tell that matters any longer. All hope is placed on your shoulders. As firstborn son, you must mate first or nothing else will matter."

"My brothers are right. This is bullshit."

"I've lived with the guilt of not telling you for years. Time has run out. If you want to protect her, you must mate with her. You don't have any other choice if you want our kind to live."

Our kind.

I'd spent my entire life pretending that I hadn't been born a half breed, forced to surrender to the wolf living inside of me. Even as I wanted nothing more than to deny what my father had told us, my instincts as well as my hunger were screaming otherwise.

The lovely veterinarian with the gorgeous eyes and kind spirit belonged to me.

Soon, I would make her mine.

CHAPTER 4

 oraline

I paced the floor, wringing my hands as my heart continued erratic heartbeats. I'd raced away from the clinic, purposely driving the other way when I'd gotten to the main road. Fortunately, my GPS had allowed me to find an alternative way of getting back to my house. I hadn't been able to stand the thought of driving past the horrible scene.

Visions.

I'd had constant visions of the night before, the horror I'd experienced. I could swear the three brutes knew who I was. They'd tracked me on purpose. No, that wasn't possible. Was it? Knots remained in my stomach, my heart racing.

And I couldn't get the wolf's face out of my mind. The craziest thing is that I'd felt close to him, almost as if I knew him, which was absolutely ludicrous. "I'm losing it, Moose."

Woof!

"Thanks for the vote of confidence."

I want you. I need you.

Oh, my God. I was losing my freaking mind. The words had floated through my mind more than once.

"Where are they, Moose? The entire damn police department should have been here by now." I snarled, shifting my gaze toward my Labrador. He was a big, beautiful hundred-pound boy who'd been with me for two years. He was loving and protective, his bark alone saving me more than once in New York. Sadly, I wasn't certain he could protect me from the nightmares I knew would never end.

I'd called the local sheriff's office, babbling on about what had happened. I wasn't entirely certain I'd made any sense. I hadn't been able to process what had occurred the night before. A wolf saved my life, then disappeared despite the impossibility of doing so. Three men who were going to abduct me out of the blue. Nope. Maybe I'd imagined the entire thing.

Moose whined then moved closer, cocking his head as he always did when trying to figure out what I was saying.

"I know. I should have found a way to call the police last night. I was foolish. I was…" How was I supposed to describe my behavior? I'd saved a wolf instead of fleeing. What had I been thinking? Groaning, I wrung my hands, still able to envision the way the creature had stared at me.

Hunkering down, my hand remained shaky as shit as I stroked his head. Then I heard the sound of an engine roaring up the driveway. Exhaling, I rose to my feet, glancing past a slat in the blinds. At least seeing the sheriff's car clearly marked gave me some peace. "Stay here, boy. I'll be right back."

When I moved outside, I folded my arms, remaining on the front porch. The man who exited the vehicle glanced around my property before yanking his hat from the car, tossing it onto his head. Then he walked forward, keeping his sunglasses in place.

"Ms. LeBlanc?"

"That's me. What did you find, Sheriff?"

He took his time walking closer, giving me more than just a onceover. I didn't need to hear his answer to know he thought I was some kind of crazy woman.

"Well, I didn't find a thing on that road. Maybe whatever you thought you saw were animals."

His answer almost made me laugh. Was he kidding me? I wanted to shout about the fact I'd witnessed three men ripped apart, but I didn't think that would go over well.

"Nothing? No vehicle or any indication there was an incident?"

After a few seconds, he removed his sunglasses, staring at me in a way that told me he was amused more than anything. "It was a dark night."

Oh, my God. He thought I'd hallucinated. "Sheriff, I assure you that my headlights are working just fine. They not only allowed me to see the three men and gather a view of their truck, but they also enabled me to see one big, black wolf." Why had I bothered to tell him? It was more than obvious he couldn't give a shit. I was disgusted, giving him a nasty glare.

"You live here alone, Ms. LeBlanc?"

"What does that have to do with anything?"

"Well, it's kind of a long way from town. Your clinic is as well. The road leading to the building you purchased is dark at night. I'm kind of surprised you bought the place."

Jesus Christ. Not only did he not believe me, but he was criticizing my choices. I yanked in my anger, stepping off the porch. "Well, I did. Just so you know. I don't scare easily, if that's what you're getting at. Something happened last night. Three men attacked me." I'd left the part out where a wolf had come to my rescue, although I wasn't certain why.

"It's not that I don't believe you, miss, but I didn't find any evidence other than some blood."

"Then analyze it. Find DNA."

He laughed in a haughty manner, which pissed me off even more. "Do you know how many wild animals live in those woods? Do you realize how many unsuspecting people hit a deer or a fox during any given month? Even if I was willing to collect blood samples, it would be useless. Tainted."

"Three men attacked me last night, Sheriff. They were driving a Ford pickup truck. That much I'm certain of."

"Did you get a license plate?"

"No, it was dark, and I was concentrating on not being kidnapped!" I sucked in my breath after raising my voice, my gut telling me the man couldn't care less.

"Can you give me a description of the men at least?"

I thought about his question, trying to shift my mind to what had happened. Unfortunately, I'd been too terrified to remember much of anything. "All three were tall and very large. I'm sorry I can't provide any additional details. It was dark and I was distraught."

"Distraught. Yes, I can imagine. Well, I'll continue the investigation, but I suggest you keep your doors locked at night. You never know when the beasts of the Bayou might come calling. A word of advice, Ms. LeBlanc. Don't venture into the woods. I won't be able to save you if you do." With that, he turned around and slid into his car, immediately starting the engine.

What the fuck had just happened? Was he warning or threatening me?

And beasts of the Bayou?

I watched as he drove away, realizing there wasn't an inch of my skin that didn't have goosebumps.

* * *

Starving.

I'd never felt so hungry in my life. What few groceries I had in the house were abysmal. There wasn't enough to make a decent pasta sauce, let alone a box of linguine or fettuccini. I also had no desire to cook, the exhaustion finally starting to take a toll. At least I had a working phone in the clinic. Tomorrow would be a long day.

Even if I didn't have a single appointment.

I'd decided to venture out of my comfort zone, refusing to remain terrified. However, my weapon was fully loaded, more ammunition in the glove compartment. If some asshole wanted to attack me again, I would be prepared.

As I drove into town, it seemed the entire city had remained frozen in time. Even as a kid, I'd realized that while quaint, it would never suit my aspirations. Then I'd moved back. What had I been thinking?

At least one of my mother's favorite old sites had remained, a combination bar and restaurant that she used to rave about after I'd left for college. I'd have to take her advice that the place had some of the best Cajun food in the south. As I drove into the parking lot, I shook my head. The place was rocking more than I would have imagined. I was lucky to find a spot close to the front.

After easing onto the pavement, I stared down at my worn jeans, grimacing. I hadn't taken the time to change, although I had no intentions of doing anything but picking up the order that I'd already called in.

Still, I remained self-conscious as I walked inside. I'd never felt so lonely in my life. At least the music was incredible, whatever country band holding court on the stage one of the best I'd ever heard.

"Can I help you?" the girl at the hostess stand asked.

"I called in an order for LeBlanc."

"Let me check."

I was shocked at the number of customers already inside. The building hadn't seemed that large to me. I moved closer to the doorway leading to the bar, drinking in the atmosphere. How long had it been since I'd danced or been on a date? I couldn't even remember. A very long time. Finding someone to share my life with hadn't seemed important, at least not as much as building my career.

I was almost thirty-two years old and what did I have to show for it? I'd returned to the small town I'd grown up in on a whim. I had almost no money in my account, a business that would take years to grow, and a beaten-up car that really didn't belong to me.

Good going, power girl.

"Ms. LeBlanc?"

I heard the girl's voice from behind me and immediately reached into my back pocket for the money I'd brought with me.

"I'm sorry, but there's going to be a slight delay in getting you your order," she said in a far too chipper manner.

"Why?"

"Well, there was a small fire in the kitchen. Small." She offered the kind of smile that given my level of exhaustion, I wanted to wipe off her face. "But drinks are on the house. I asked my manager and he said it would be fine."

Groovy. A drink might be the last thing I needed. Oh, what the hell? At least I could enjoy some music, which would be a nice change of pace. I realized I must have been glaring at her by the way her eyes had widened.

"The bar is through those doors. I'll come find you when it's ready. The bartender already knows to expect you."

"Okay, fine. Thank you." Growling at the poor girl wasn't going to do me any good. I tentatively walked into the room, grateful I wouldn't have to go through the crowd to get to the bar. Suddenly, a drink sounded like exactly what I needed.

Within seconds, the bartender sashayed his way in my direction. Too bad he was at least ten years younger. "Whatever you want is on the house."

Another person that was far too gregarious. "Just a glass of red wine."

"Cabernet? You look like a cabernet kind of gal."

Was everyone in the town happy? Except for the three assholes and the sheriff anyway. "Sounds wonderful."

I crowded as close to the edge of the bar as possible, trying my best to relax. The bartender wasted no time, sliding a glass in my direction without spilling a drop on the cocktail napkin.

The moment I took a sip, I felt a presence behind me, crowding close enough my skin crawled.

I'd always had keen senses, the ability to know when someone was watching me. However, this was entirely different. My entire body was electrified, my breath stolen. I wasn't the kind of girl to believe in fate or any of that crap. However, as the prickles rose on my arm, butterflies churning in my stomach, I was fearful of turning around and there was no logical reason why.

But I did.

I was floored by my reaction, although even in the dim lighting, I was forced to admit he was one hell of a looker. Tall, dark, and handsome. Wasn't that the depiction of Prince Charming? He was at least six foot five, but instead of being dressed in jeans and some flannel shirt, he wore a suit. And not just any suit, one that was tailored to fit him perfectly. He seemed so out of place in what could be described as a honky-tonk bar. And there was no doubt he was staring at me. Blinking, I tried to keep my cool, turning my attention toward the band.

Damn the man for walking closer.

I held my breath, uncertain of what to expect. Then he shifted a few feet away, crowding closer to the bar. I bit back a laugh, chastising my ridiculous behavior. I didn't bother glancing in his direction, just kept reminding myself that after the night before, I wanted nothing more than to get home and lock the doors, hiding away until morning light slipped in past the blinds.

The electricity remained, surging through every muscle. I nursed the wine, fearful I'd become lightheaded. The best thing for me to do was ignore him.

"Interesting place."

I closed my eyes the moment he made the statement. The richness of his tone, so deep and husky, was enough to arouse every part of me. "I wouldn't know."

"You're not from around here?"

Exhaling, I tried to remind myself again that I wasn't here for anything but a hot meal. "Nope. Just stopping by."

The quiet that settled between us wasn't nearly as unnerving as the way my body continued to react. My mouth was dry, filthy thoughts racing in the back of my mind. When he eased away from the bar, I was relieved.

Then he moved directly in front of me, the shadowed light unable to hide the intense look in his eyes. He lowered his head, taking a deep whiff, holding it for several seconds. The man was obviously sure that tonight was his night to get laid. I wasn't that stupid or that easy.

"If you don't mind, I'm trying to enjoy my wine." His scent was intoxicating, forcing my nipples to harden. I remained floored, dragging my tongue across my lips without realizing what I was doing at first. He continued to stare at me, his eyes piercing mine. Just his demeanor alone kept my heart hammering in my chest, fire lighting up every molecule. However, his arrogance was almost enough to pull me out of the spell.

Almost.

"I apologize for my directness. I'm Gabriel Dupree."

He made the statement as if his name should mean something to me. "Mr. Dupree, while I very much appreciate the attention, I don't know you. In fact, I don't know anyone in this town. I've had a difficult few days and I simply wanted to get something to eat." Why in the hell did I find myself so attracted to him? The intensity in his gaze was overwhelming, and for some odd reason, it felt like I already knew him. That was impossible, but the attraction was undeniable.

A look of amusement crossed his face. Then he did something completely unexpected, lifting his hand slowly and brushing the tip of his index finger along my jawline. I was no longer certain I was breathing. This was insane. I couldn't be this attracted to a man I didn't know.

"I think we should dance. In fact, I know we should."

"I don't know you," I stated, doing my best to give him the brushoff.

"That's the beauty of meeting someone for the first time."

He didn't make a request, but it wasn't entirely a command either. Yet the somewhere in between managed to turn me on to the point that my panties became damp. I debated his... request, darting a look toward the dance floor. He certainly wasn't like the men from the night before. Why not enjoy a single dance? What did I have to lose?

"All right. But only one. I need to get back to my practice."

As he took my glass from my hand, another wave of current blasted through me from our touch alone. He was very dominant in the way he placed both glasses on the bar. Then he wrapped his hand around my arm, pulling me deeper into the crowd. Even his hold was possessive, as if he wouldn't have taken no for an answer.

The aura around him was just as powerful as his actions, almost everyone within a few feet easing away, gawking as we passed. I felt small in his presence, his grip remaining firm. The moment we stepped onto the dance floor, he took me into his arms, pulling me tightly against his chest. For a few seconds, I was overwhelmed with desire, my vision hazy. My instinct told me to pull away, but the draw to him was incredible, the way he held me protective.

Within seconds, I was comfortable in his arms, sweeping mine around his neck.

"Do you mind if I ask your name?" His gravelly voice filtered through me with a wave of electricity attached.

"Coraline."

"What a beautiful name," he half whispered, although his deep bass sounded more like a primal growl, enough so shivers danced down the length of my spine.

As he held me close, I relaxed in his arms. We didn't talk as one song turned into a second. By the time the third started, I was lost in the moment. There was nothing wrong with dancing, even with a stranger.

"Coraline."

The guttural sound of his voice blasted another wave of tingles down my legs. I was wet, embarrassed that my panties were damp, fearful he was able to gather a scent of my condition. This wasn't like me. I gazed into his eyes, hating the fact my breathing was shallow. When he lightly brushed his fingers across my cheek, my mouth became completely dry. As he lowered his head, I could swear he was going to kiss me. Even worse, I wanted him to.

Every sound he made was dark, a fierce reminder that he was all male.

"This isn't your kind of place," I managed, blinking several times.

"I'm curious as to why you've come to that conclusion?"

"Because of the way you're dressed, but even more than that, you don't seem like the type who enjoys beer and peanuts or barroom brawls."

Laughing, his eyes lit up even in the darkened space. "Your assumption would be correct."

"Then why are you here?" Every answer he gave me was guarded, his eyes never leaving mine.

"I was drawn here, unable to resist."

Red flag. Damn it. I was actually enjoying the moment, the possessive yet gentle touches. Too bad it would appear he was just another typical predator.

I pushed my hand against him. "Look, while I appreciate the full court press, I'm not that kind of girl."

"Then what kind are you?"

Even though I thought about his question, I had no decent answer. "I don't give in that easily to any man under any circumstances. In truth, I prefer being alone." It was certainly much easier than dealing with the usual baggage a man brought to the table. I'd experienced enough losers to prefer spending time with Moose. That had to be a country song.

"What a pity. Someone as beautiful as you should never be alone, especially in the Bayou."

"Why do you say that?"

"Because the swamps and surrounding areas are dangerous places."

The way he said the words made me shudder. "Well, lucky me that I don't intend on doing any swamp diving coming up. And I can take care of myself. Trust me. My daddy taught me how to shoot a gun and I carry a weapon with me at all times." My thoughts drifted to the night before. I wasn't entirely certain if I'd been able to reach my gun that I could have managed to shoot the asshole.

"Guns don't always prevent someone from being harmed or worse, Coraline. There are many evils in this world."

The way he said my name was seductive, almost making me swoon, but I'd been around the block for long enough not to allow myself to fall for anyone's bullshit.

Even a man as extremely good-looking like Gabriel.

Although his words rang true, the experience from the night before remaining haunting. My mother had continuously told me stories of horrible crimes, although always in other locations. I pulled away from him, my instinct screaming that he was the dangerous one. While I wasn't afraid of him, my hackles were raised, and I wasn't certain why. I needed time to think. No, the best thing for me to do was to leave before I allowed my guard to fall.

"I need to leave. I'm sorry. I'm exhausted."

I was surprised when Gabriel didn't try to stop me, but there was something about the way he was staring at me, the intensity making it almost impossible to breathe. I'd never had bouts of claustrophobia before, but the sensations rocketing through me were like claws clamping around my throat.

"Be careful, Coraline." He stood where he was, shoving his hands into his pockets. I stared at him for a few seconds, finding myself mesmerized by the man. Why? When the stage lighting suddenly changed, he was caught in one of the beams, the powerful shimmer highlighting his powerful physique.

And his incredible sapphire blue eyes.

There was no way. None. It was a sheer coincidence. I'd obviously lost a small portion of my mind during the attack.

Stunned, I backed away, almost stumbling over a chair that had been pulled too close to the dance floor. "I'm sorry," I said, unable to take my eyes off him.

Gabriel remained where he was standing, the distance as I continued to back away unable to keep his eyes from piercing mine.

I turned abruptly, no longer hungry. All I wanted to do was to get home, hide behind closed and locked doors. The flood of visions from the night before hindered my ability to push through the crowd. By the time I managed to make to the entrance to the lobby, I was out of breath.

"Hey, pretty lady. It's early. Why don't you and me have a dance?"

There was something sinister about the way the stranger asked the question, or maybe my mind was still in shock from the events of the night before. Either way, I had to get the hell out of the place. "Sorry. I have other plans."

He didn't allow me to get even a few inches away before snagging my arm. "I don't think you heard what I said. It wasn't a request. You will dance with me."

Snarling, I yanked my arm away, using an influx of new customers to stay out of his reach. My keys were in my hand by the time I made it out the door. I threw my head over my shoulder, trying to keep my wits. The bastard was nowhere to be seen. Was it possible the jerk was connected to the guys from the night before? I moved quickly into the barely lit parking lot, chastising myself for being so stupid as to leave my house after dark.

Maybe there really were monsters lurking in the shadows.

The hard yank was shocking, the brutal push against the side of the building knocking the breath out of me.

The bastard slapped his hand against my mouth, pulling me around the corner of the building, the area even darker than the other. "You don't seem to understand, little girl. I'm not taking no for an answer."

Terror rushed through me, but I refused to allow some asshole to drag me off. When I gave him a hard jab with my elbow, he hissed and lost his hold for a few seconds. It was enough time for me to dart away from him, yelling at the top of my lungs.

I expected either a tackle to the ground or something even worse. When a hard thud filtered into my ears, I dared to stop, still backing away as I turned around. While a small crowd had gathered, trying to figure out what the hell was going on, I was still able to see the reason for the sound.

Gabriel had the jerk against the building, his hand tightly wrapped around his throat. I folded my arms, my breath still labored as I walked closer. What I heard should have made my skin crawl. Instead, the dark words made me smile.

"I'm not the kind of man to provide warnings, but it's your lucky day. I'm in a generous mood. There won't be another one. You will never touch that beautiful woman or any other in that manner or I assure you that my next visit will provide a painful lesson in behavior."

The asshole clearly couldn't breathe, wheezing as he continuously slapped his hands against Gabriel's chest, although it was clear to see the much shorter man was no match.

"Do you understand?" Gabriel hissed.

At least the asshole nodded.

When Gabriel let him down, I could swear I heard a deep, rumbling growl. Whether I did or not, what my newfound hero had done had obviously scared the crap out of the jerk. He tumbled into the parking lot, his hand still wrapped around his throat. Gabriel turned around slowly, doing nothing but glancing back and forth at the crowd of customers.

The man's powerful aura was enough that every one of them backed away. Then he took a deep breath, slowly turning his head in my direction. As he walked closer, he never blinked, nor did his expression soften.

But his jacket was unbuttoned, allowing me to see a weapon.

"As I said, Coraline, this town and those in the same parish are dangerous. I'm taking you home."

"Not so fast. While I appreciate what you just did, I don't know you. I have my car here, my gun in my purse. I'll drive straight home, lock the door, and refuse to allow anyone inside. My killer dog will protect me as well."

He inhaled, holding his breath for at least thirty seconds before scanning the parking lot. "It's apparent you don't know who I am."

"No, I don't. I'm not certain why that matters."

I'll be damned if he didn't crowd my space. Even worse, I didn't mind. What the hell was wrong with me?

"As I said, my name is Gabriel Dupree. My father is Chandler Dupree of Baton Rouge, the owner of the Dupree Corporation."

When I tilted my head, a look of amusement crossed his face. "I'm sorry, but if that's meant to impress or to keep my thoughts from drifting to the serial killer mode, it didn't."

He chuckled, lifting a single eyebrow. It was obvious he was used to people cowering at his feet. "Let's just say I'm a dangerous man, the kind who doles out severe punishment without second guessing my decision. I assure you that you are much safer with me than anyone else you'll come in contact with."

Now his arrogance pissed me off. "Okay, thank you again, but I can handle myself. Really." The surprises kept coming for the night. He allowed me to head to my car, although he trailed behind me even though he kept his distance.

When I was safely in the car, the doors locked, I yanked my gun from my purse. I had a terrible feeling I'd need to use it sooner versus later.

My gut also told me I hadn't seen the last of assholes like the one from the bar.

Or of the dangerous, seductive man.

CHAPTER 5

 *oraline*

Darkness.

It hovered around me, the whistling of wind through the trees creating wave after wave of jitters. I couldn't shake the ominous feelings flowing in my mind. I scanned the trees, the light from the porch barely doing anything to illuminate more than a few yards. Christ. I hated feeling so alone.

"Come on, baby. Do your business," I said absently as I remained just off the front porch of my mother's house. I should get used to calling it my house, but I hadn't allowed myself more than an hour to unpack anything. While I loved the area, the beautiful cottage serene and full of good memories, the night seemed more oppressive than usual. I remained skittish, half expecting some asshole to jump out of the bushes. At least Moose would warn me, his keen senses unlike any other dog I'd known.

Almost as sensitive as a… wolf.

Moose barked once, making me jump. "Are you okay? Where are you?" I took several steps away, cursing under my breath. I hadn't counted on needing a flashlight. The pup never strayed far away. "Moose. Come to Mommy or she's going to be very angry." I turned in a full circle, holding my breath.

The crackle of twigs forced me to yank my weapon into my hand. When Moose came bounding out of the darkness, my knees almost buckled.

Woof!

Exhaling, I wagged my finger seeing the stick in his mouth. "You scared me, buddy. Let's get inside." I ushered him onto the porch, laughing when he didn't want to give up his 'toy.' Before retreating inside, I scanned the area for the third time. A sickening feeling washed over me that I was being watched.

With the door secured, I took a deep breath before moving into the kitchen, refreshing his water bowl then dumping three scoops of kibble into his food bowl. I'd grabbed a bag of his food, although he'd go through it in three days given the small size. I hadn't seen a Costco anywhere, the local grocery stores another reminder the town remained almost exactly the same as when I'd left.

"Enjoy, big man." Tomorrow I'd go to the grocery store again before it got dark, stocking up instead of tossing a few items in my basket. Laughing, I realized I was still as nervous as a kitty cat, taking long strides toward the kitchen window and snapping the blinds shut. At least I had enough wine to soothe my nerves.

For now.

What about the next night and the one after that? I refused to live in fear. The two incidents weren't connected. They were both just random... acts of violence. Right? I took a sip of wine and eyed my computer, more curious than ever about just who Gabriel thought he was. As soon as I pulled up his name, the first listings on Google were for Dupree Enterprises. I scrolled through the corporate website, realizing that the guy must be worth billions. The second entry was just as enticing, pictures of a glamorous charity event only a few nights before.

As I stared at the group of pictures, I realized my breasts were aching, my nipples remaining just as hard as they'd been when I was dancing with him.

He'd called himself a dangerous man. That meant there was another side of him.

I didn't have to search long to realize exactly who and what he was.

Some would call him a savvy businessman while others would call him a vile, reprehensible criminal.

His father was head of the Dupree crime syndicate and Gabriel was next in line for the throne.

I shut the lid on my laptop, moving away from the counter. Okay, now I was concerned. I doubted a man like Gabriel had just stopped by the little town on his way to see his father. The area was a far cry from the posh surroundings of his office in Chicago. While I wasn't prone to believing in either coincidences or in some crazy aspect of karma, the events that had occurred in the last three months skittered into my mind.

My mother had called out of the blue, suggesting I come home, then calling again insisting on it without providing a decent reason.

My mother signing over her house in pretense of retiring to Florida.

My mother finding the perfect—well, almost perfect—location for my clinic, purchasing it then telling me after the fact.

An attack out of nowhere on a dark, deserted road.

Then the wolf.

Then… the mysterious man who was tied to all things treacherous.

"Get a grip, girl." I was just overwrought. I hadn't realized that Moose had already finished his food, leaving the kitchen for his favorite spot on the couch. After glancing at my computer, I trailed behind him, unable to shake the questions that had formed in my mind.

"*Gggrrr...*"

The hair on the back of my neck stood up on end. I immediately retrieved my weapon from the kitchen. "What did you hear, buddy?"

Moose huffed then jumped off the couch, immediately going into a barking frenzy. Even though the front blinds were closed, the lamp on the end table still turned on, I was able to see headlights, could feel the rumble of an engine.

"This might get rough, baby." After checking to make certain the safety was off, I moved to where I'd dropped my purse, grabbing my cell phone and shoving it into my pocket. If I called the sheriff for a bogus reason, he'd sign off on the insanity idea.

Moose continued barking, lunging at the door. Then he backed away, his tail between his legs, which was something he'd never done before. I inched closer, placing my hand on his head, keeping my arm outstretched, the gun firmly planted in my hand.

The knock on the door sounded more like gunshots in my mind. I remained quiet, trying to consider the best option.

"Coraline. I know you're inside. Open the door."

Gabriel's words weren't a request. They were a command. Just like in the restaurant. I should say no, forcing him away. I should threaten him with calling the police, although he'd saved me from another unsavory jerk. Or maybe the asshole had intended on doing what the others had planned. Yes, I should do one or both of those things.

Yet I opened the door.

Moose immediately growled, the sound deep and entirely different than I'd heard him use before.

Gabriel's massive frame loomed in the doorway, his gaze remaining on my face for a few seconds before lowering it to the weapon I had in my hand.

"I suggest you leave," I said defiantly.

"That's not going to happen. Hand me your weapon." He held out his hand, those damn gorgeous eyes of his piercing mine.

Piercing my very soul.

I want you. I need you.

The haunting words rushed into my mind. Hell, no, I wasn't going to fall for a round of exhaustion.

"Then I'll be forced to shoot you if necessary."

Exhaling, Gabriel shook his head. Then he yanked the weapon from my hand, shoving it into his pocket. After that, he stormed inside, slamming and locking the door.

"You bastard!" I snarled, although instead of terror prickling every cell, there was excitement. I knew exactly what he wanted. Me. All of me.

"I've been called many things, Coraline." Maybe it was the way he looked at me in such a carnal manner or maybe it was my refusal to accept my body wanted him, but I reacted without hesitation.

I bolted toward the door. "Come on, Moose!" My God. I didn't hear the scramble of my dog's claws on the hardwood floor or a single growl. He'd remained inside. What the hell?

"Enough, Coraline. You will obey me." Gabriel was right behind me, wrapping his arms around my waist and dragging me inside.

I smashed my fists against him, able to get away from his hold. He stood still, shaking his head, disapproval in his eyes.

I was breathless, uncertain if the man was going to kill me even though my instinct told me he was here to provide protection. The burning question was why?

When Moose didn't make another sound, instead moving by Gabriel's side, I couldn't take my eyes off the man. Gabriel reached down, brushing the backs of his knuckles across Moose's nose. My pup seemed to be in heaven, his eyes half closed. I couldn't believe how much he trusted the stranger.

Still, I backed away, my mind having difficulty processing everything that had recently occurred. "I know who you are." I spat out the words with as much hatred as possible.

"I'm certain you do. You're an intelligent woman, Coraline, which means you know what I'm capable of."

"You're going to kill me."

Laughing, he kicked the door shut again. "If I wanted to kill you, I assure you that we wouldn't be standing here talking."

"Fine. Then you need to tell me exactly why you're here."

"Why?" he asked as he removed his jacket ever so slowly, placing it over the arm of my chair. As he started to unfasten his sleeves, I realized I was holding my breath.

The dim lighting from before hadn't done him justice. He wasn't just handsome. He was gorgeous, tall and muscular with incredible obsidian hair and full red lips. He exuded the kind of savagery that was only depicted in romance novels. But he was a living, breathing man standing in my living room.

And my God, my body had already betrayed me, desire unlike anything I'd ever known shifting through me like a wildfire.

As he moved closer, a wry smile crossed his face, the look of hunger in his eyes unmistakable. "Because we are connected, you and I."

"Connected. How?"

I took two additional long strides away, but I was losing real estate, almost at the back wall. I could barely swallow, my heart was thumping so hard.

He took three long strides, coming within a few inches. With one inhale, the scent of his exotic cologne filled not only my nostrils but also every cell. I was lightheaded, trying to maintain some sense of focus.

There was something so primal about him as well as his actions. However, I felt no fear.

"You will learn that soon enough," he muttered, his husky tone washing over me.

When he cupped my jaw, I pressed my hand against him. Whatever was happening between us, I couldn't seem to avoid.

Nor did I want to.

His grip firm, he pulled me onto my toes, forcing my back to arch. There was no hesitation this time. He simply lowered his head, capturing my mouth. I found myself clinging to him, fisting his shirt as he lightly brushed his thumb back and forth across my skin. The heat built between us, tingling every portion of my body. Within seconds, I fell into the kiss.

While he was gentle at first, pushing his tongue past my pursed lips, I sensed his needs increasing, his actions becoming rougher. He dominated my tongue, dancing his back and forth as his breathing increased, his chest heaving. I could feel a rumble erupting from deep within him, the guttural sounds he made like an animal.

Like a wolf.

The taste of him was spicy, evoking a series of filthy thoughts in my mind. I'd never felt this way around a man, my desire surging while my rational mind still wanted nothing more than to push away. I shouldn't want this man. I didn't need any complications in my life and this was one complex individual, the mystery surrounding him creating another haze in my mind.

He slid his arm around me, cupping my bottom and lifting me off my feet. I could sense his hunger becoming more explosive, was able to sense he wasn't going to be tender in any way. When he broke the kiss, he shoved me against the wall, his fingers shifting to my neck. A dark chuckle erupted from his throat as he dragged his tongue down the side of my face, nipping my chin.

"I'm going to enjoy fucking you, Coraline."

I was even more lightheaded than before, holding onto his arms as he licked down the side of my neck.

No. No! I couldn't do this. This was completely out of character for me. When he eased away, a lurid smile remained on his face as he yanked his shirt over his head with one hand.

Another moment of clarity filtered past the haze of lust. I jerked to the right, heading around the other side of the couch, able to slide my hand into his jacket and grab my weapon. His reflexes were immediate, but not nearly as much as mine. I pointed the gun at his chest, holding it with both hands.

"You get one more chance to get the hell out of here, Gabriel. I don't care if you are the prince of some mafia family. I couldn't care less if you're a criminal. I have a quiet life I intend to live. Without you!"

Instead of lunging at me, he remained exactly where he was, scanning the room as if I'd invited him inside as a guest. "They will return for you."

Snorting, I was forced to wipe beads of perspiration from my face. "I don't think so. Some animal ripped them apart."

Gabriel snapped his head in my direction, a sly smile forming on his face. "There are more of them, Coraline."

"Okay, why and who the hell are these people? I'm nobody. I just arrived back in town to run a clinic. They can't know me."

"You were born here."

"Yes, so?" Why was he telling me this?

"You are a member of the community as was your family."

I cocked my head, trying to keep my hands from shaking. "Yes, for at least three generations. I think. What the hell does that have anything to do with this moment?"

He took a step closer. "Because you're important to them."

I lifted my gun then pointed it once again, shaking my head. "I wouldn't do that if I were you."

"I'm going to take the gun from your hand. Then I'm going to punish you."

Now I couldn't stop from laughing. "Are you out of your mind? I don't know who you think you are, but you're not going to touch me."

"You hunger just like I do. You need, just like I do. Soon, you will become insatiable. Just like… I… will."

Why did his words bother me so much?

"Just go. Just get out and I won't call the police," I said, barely able to recognize my words.

"That's not going to happen." Now the bastard lunged toward me.

And I fired a single shot.

All time stopped. Ceased to exist, frozen like my mind as well as my heart. I'd just killed a man. After blinking, I realized he wasn't dead. In fact, the force of the bullet hadn't pummeled him backwards by a single inch. He stood with his massive chest heaving, glaring at the wound on his shoulder.

Fuck. Fuck!

After a few seconds, he moved his arm.

"Please, Gabriel. Just…" Of course I wasn't going to let him bleed out or something. If the bullet was lodged inside, I would need to get it out and tend to the wound. Wait a minute. He was a freaking criminal, a murderer.

Maybe I'd been shoved into a moment of shock. Or maybe my mind had shut down. Either way, I wasn't aware of what he was doing until it was too late.

He easily wrangled the gun from my hand, tossing it all the way into another room. Then he wrapped his hand around my wrist, yanking me toward the couch. To my surprise and horror, he sat down. What the hell?

"Remove your jeans and panties."

His command was so unexpected, I couldn't respond for a full five seconds. "What did you say?"

"You heard me. If I need to remove them for you, they will be shredded. It's your choice."

"I… Whoa, asshole. I just shot you. What the hell do you think you're doing?"

"As I told you, I *will* punish you." His gravelly voice was now unworldly, wrapping around me like a thick, warm blanket.

The man was serious. Blood was trickling down his arm and he was going to punish me? I must have had a psychotic break. There was no other explanation.

Because I hesitated, he growled, deep and throaty. Like a monster.

No, like a wolf.

Fuck me. Jesus.

"Three seconds, Coraline."

The man was serious. My mouth remained dry but for some crazy reason, I obeyed him, unfastening my jeans then struggling to rip off my tennis shoes. A powerful feeling of hot embarrassment formed the minute I shoved the dense fabric down my hips. Then I couldn't look at him, my body swaying. Hunger. Yes, I'd felt hunger, but what woman didn't? I'd also felt a pull to him that was unexplainable. Fine. What the hell was he trying to tell me?

When I looked down, I realized I'd complied with his command, now shaking like a leaf as heat rose from my chest to my cheeks. Panting, I'd never felt so awkward in my life.

Or so stupid.

He didn't speak, only pulled me over his lap. Fuck me. The asshole was going to spank me like some stupid child. The big, bad mafia dude was resorting to this? I lifted my head, hissing at my beautiful dog. He wasn't paying a damn bit of attention, comfortable on his bed with his eyes closed. Did that mean Gabriel wasn't actually a bad man after all?

Ha. Not a chance.

I squirmed until he pressed his hand on the small of my back. Instantly, I felt more comfortable, at peace with what was about to happen. I also had another round of intense visions, even stronger than the night before in the clinic. Why was I drawn to this man with such explosive power that I couldn't breathe normally?

There were no definitive answers, at least none that a sane person would use.

When he brought his hand down, I jerked up out of shock more than pain. Reality settled in, the hard-working rational woman kicking in again. "Bastard!"

"Yes."

Every word he issued was seductive in nature. He wasn't threatening me. He was simply enjoying being in control. God, I wanted to hate him, to feel justified about shooting him, but I remained mortified.

He smacked me several times, the pain finally starting to roll up from my toes. Panting, the moment I wiggled again, two things happened. I felt his throbbing cock and he grabbed my arm, holding me in place. Both were… There were no words.

The spanking began in earnest, his hand moving from one side to the other in rapid succession.

"Ouch! That hurts. You asshole."

"If you don't stop fighting me, I will pull off my belt. Are we clear?"

If he wanted confirmation, he was going to be disappointed.

While I did everything that I could to hide my anger as well as the almost all-consuming anguish, I couldn't seem to stop fighting him. When he thrust his leg over mine, I was forced to take a deep breath. This was really happening. A man I didn't know was spanking me. It remained laughable that Moose wasn't bothered in the least, his slumber obviously a good one, his body twitching as he chased rabbits in his sleep. While he'd always been accepting of people around me given his happy nature, the fact he had no concerns about the man holding me hostage was incomprehensible.

After another round of brutal cracks of his hand, hatred for my body's reaction only intensified. My pussy was wet, likely trickling down my thighs and staining his expensive trousers. While a part of me didn't give a shit, another continued to feel shame that a single part of me had accepted this on any level. Who the hell did he think he was? My savior?

Only seconds later, the pain was significant enough I issued several whimpers, unable to hide how much the fierce man was getting to me. Grimacing, when he rubbed his fingers across my heated and bruised bottom, I bit back a moan, undulating my body against his hardness involuntarily.

His breathing remained ragged, the sound filtering into my ears as he continued stroking me like a pet he'd just purchased. He rubbed the tips of his fingers down one leg then the other, creating such a wave of desire that I was fearful I'd orgasm from the simple touch alone.

But I didn't.

I refused.

No man would get the satisfaction of knowing their domination pleasured me. I closed my eyes, praying this horrible moment would be over soon. I remained stupefied that the arm he was using was the one I'd shot. Clearly the man had no sense of the kind of agony he should be facing.

When he trailed a single finger down the crack of my ass, lingering over my pussy lips, I held my breath. A part of me wanted to beg him to drive his fingers inside, another terrified that if I did, there would be no turning back. The moment he slid the tip of his finger around my already swollen clit, I almost lost my resolve, begging for even more.

This couldn't be happening. I shouldn't be attracted to him for any reason, but I couldn't deny the pulsing electricity. I was thrown into another dimension, no longer able to feel my fingers or toes.

He slapped his hand down four more time then squeezed one side of my bottom. I didn't have to be a mind reader to know what he wanted, what he craved.

There was something so intimate about the way he eased me off his lap, taking his time to perform the act as if I would break in the process. My survival instincts kicked in and before I knew what I was doing, I slapped him hard across the face.

Then I noticed his wound.

It had almost entirely healed.

That wasn't possible.

I realized I was digging my fingers into his arms as I stared at his shoulder. "How is that possible? You're almost healed."

The savage man didn't bother to answer me. As he rose to his feet, towering over me, I lost all my ability to breathe. He didn't waste any time, using both hands to rip my shirt apart, yanking the sleeves off my shoulders and pitching the unwanted material aside. His intense glare kept me mesmerized, the lust I'd felt earlier only increasing.

Even the way he slipped his arms behind me, unfastening my bra then removing it entirely didn't push me into a tailspin. I allowed him to. I almost encouraged him to. Unblinking, I locked eyes with his before moving my hands to unfasten his belt then unzipping his trousers. I couldn't stand to look at him as I rolled the material over his chiseled hips, pushing until gravity allowed the hindrance to fall to the floor.

The man wasn't wearing underwear, as if going commando allowed him to fuck any woman he craved whenever he made the determination to do so. Somehow, my instinct told me that he wasn't that kind of man. How ridiculous. I didn't know him. I wasn't certain I wanted to. This was nothing more than a blip in time.

His cock was already standing at full attention, veins throbbing on both sides, the tip the color of crushed purple velvet. I was ashamed my mouth watered at the sight, longing to have his thick shaft in my mouth.

Unable to resist, I trailed my hand down the length of his chest, marveling in his muscular structure. He was built like no other man I'd been with, as if he'd spend years in a gym perfecting his body. Somehow, I knew that not to be true. Given the scars crisscrossing his torso, I had a feeling every muscle had been earned by something else entirely. I shuddered to think what that would be. The man was a killer. I knew that by instinct alone, but he was also a savior, a man with a conscience.

That had to make him an anomaly in his dark and dangerous world.

When he kicked his pants away, I took a step back, trying to control my nerves. Nothing made rational sense any longer. Not the circumstances. Not the desire for the stranger standing in front of me.

But I couldn't seem to resist him, the draw becoming more powerful with every passing moment. Lights flashed in front of my eyes as he advanced. There would be no denying him.

Not that I wanted to.

I'd spent my entire life being a good girl, playing by all the rules. Tonight, I wanted nothing more than to live on the edge, to forget about all my responsibilities and inhibitions. Now was my chance.

His approach was slow, the look on his face unrecognizable. However, I knew what was about to happen, the savagery he would display. While I'd thought his actions predictable, he approached cautiously, cocking his head when he was finally only inches away. His breathing became irregular, his nostrils flaring. Then he slid his hand around to the back of my neck, squeezing seductively as he pulled me against him.

Breathless, I had no idea what to expect. When he tilted my head, forcing me to look into his eyes, I knew there was no way I could look away. He had me locked in a world of his own, a man ready to consume a woman for entirely different reasons than I'd experienced before.

As if the need was unbearable.

As if I belonged to him.

While nothing made any sense, the moment he crushed his mouth against mine, there was little else I could do. All thoughts of fighting him were put on hold, my body taking over and demanding satisfaction. Before I knew what I was doing, I threw my arms around his neck, arching my back until I was able to feel the pulse of his cock pressing against my stomach.

The kiss was no longer gentle like the one from the bar. His actions were forceful and demanding, pushing me to the limits of acceptance.

But I did.

I entangled my fingers in his hair as I wrapped one leg around him, my nipples so hard they ached. Every part of my body was on fire as he dragged his fingers down my spine, cupping my bruised bottom and lifting me into his arms. As he explored the wet heat of my mouth, I kept my eyes closed, every nerve standing on end. The taste of him only added to the excitement surging through my body, my pussy clamping then releasing several times.

There was no possible way this was real.

Seconds later, he broke the kiss, pushing my head back with his until he was able to breathe across my cheek. I closed my eyes, issuing several scattered moans as I squeezed his muscular forearms. Nothing had ever felt this incredible in my life, vibrations shooting down my legs until I could no longer feel them.

His breathing wasn't just labored, it was laced with the same dark and husky growls I'd heard before. They enticed me. Hell, they excited me, pushing me into a fantasy world if only for a precious and very limited amount of time.

He wound one hand around my hair, yanking until I was placed in a deep arc. Chuckling softly, he rolled his lips across my chin then down from my neck to my breast. When he pulled my nipple into his mouth, I couldn't hold back a moan. Still lightheaded, I did everything I could to keep my grip on his arms, but it was almost impossible. Every sound he made only added to the desire that continued to build between us. His actions were almost feral, as if he wouldn't be able to survive without fucking me.

"So beautiful," he whispered before rubbing his lips across to my other breast, engulfing my hardened bud.

I shifted my hips back and forth, gasping for air. There was no doubt in my mind I would have fallen to my knees if he wasn't holding me in place. He bit down on my tender tissue, the pain blinding yet his action almost threw me into a climax.

Only a few seconds later, I was in his arms. He took two long strides toward the couch, sitting down, his eyes never leaving mine. There was no pretense, no other foreplay. He simply positioned the tip of his cock against my pussy lips then yanked me down with enough force the wind was knocked out of me.

"Oh. Oh. Oh…"

There was no adequate way to describe the utter dazzling sensations rocketing through me. His cock was so large my muscles were forced to stretch in order to accommodate his girth, yet there was no hint of discomfort, only blinding and beautiful rapture rushing through me.

"Ride me, Coraline. Ride me hard."

The sound of his voice as well as his intense command spurred me on, dragging me out of my comfort zone. I did exactly as he asked, bucking against him as I tossed my hair back and forth. Within seconds, I was no longer the girl I'd once been, turning into someone I didn't recognize.

His cock continued to expand, filling me completely, throbbing against my pussy walls. Every guttural sound he made only fueled the fire raging between us. Stars in vivid colors floated in front of my eyes, preventing me from focusing on anything. Not that I wanted to. Everything became savage in nature as he gripped my hips, yanking me almost all the way off his shaft then pulling me down.

The jarring motions as he repeated the move several times were spectacular. This wasn't about romance. This was about hard fucking, brutal in nature and delicious in execution.

I clawed at his chest, still finding it difficult to breathe as I bucked against him. He was ferocious. Even his eyes had changed colors, his golden irises shimmering in the light. I couldn't help but remain mesmerized, drawn to him like a lamb to slaughter. The thought should have been revolting but I found it adding to the desire since it was the truth.

While the man obviously meant me no harm, this wasn't about starting a love affair. There was no true definition for why my attraction was this strong.

Without notice, he pitched me onto the sofa, throwing one of my legs over his shoulder as he thrust hard and fast, the force he used tossing me up and down by several inches. He continued leaning over me, planting one hand on the edge of the couch, the other along the back edge. A smile crossed his handsome face as he angled his hips, the sounds of our bodies slamming together further fueling his animalistic behavior.

I pressed my hand against his chest, digging my nails in, realizing within seconds that an orgasm was close. Everything about the interlude was sinful, but I knew neither one of us could stop our actions.

The climax still managed to catch me off guard, shooting into my aching pussy. Gasping, I arched my back, throwing one hand over my head and clenching my fingers around the decorative pillow.

"Yes. Yes. Yes!" There was no holding back, no possibility of stopping the powerful blast of raw ecstasy. Shaking almost violently, I shut my eyes tight as my pussy muscles clenched and released dozens of times. One climax burst into a second, this one even more intense than the one before. I'd never felt this kind of pleasure, never knew it existed.

When I finally stopped shaking, I slid my hand away, dangling my fingers over my mouth. He slowed, but there was no doubt he continued to stare at me. Seconds later, he gathered me into his arms, pulling me onto my knees. Why I thought he was going to be softer in his actions was beyond me.

As he'd done before, he tossed me over the back of the sofa, yanking my legs apart, once against plunging his cock inside my tight channel.

His silence was almost unnerving as he continued fucking me, his actions so brutal that the springs in the couch squeaked. I had no idea how long he continued driving like a wild beast. Within several seconds, I lolled my head, doing everything I could to control my breathing.

But I knew the minute he was unable to control his needs by the harshness of his growls, the shaking of his body. I closed my eyes, biting back a scream as I clenched my muscles on purpose.

I'd heard men roar before, but the primal bellow he released was entirely different. Deeper. More resonant.

More like a true animal.

As he erupted deep inside of me, he wrapped one hand around my throat, holding me in place. When he lowered his head, blowing another swath of hot air across my skin, that was the moment fear entered my system.

This wasn't the last I'd see of him.

Whatever plans he had in store for me, I sensed his thoughts, knew what he was intending.

He was going to force me to belong to him, whether I agreed or not.

When he finally pulled away, I shifted around to see him.

To my shock and horror, his wound had completely healed.

CHAPTER 6

abriel

Anger.

I was a brutal man; however, I'd never been prone to dealing with bouts of anger. In truth, I'd never had to up to this point. Given my position in society as well as in the underworld, no one dared cross me. When they did, punishment was swift and without a second thought. I'd been fortunate, able to recognize my enemies, prepared for almost any action they'd been stupid enough to make. This was an entirely different situation. The name of the enemy might be known, but that didn't mean I was able to believe the ridiculousness of the legend in its entirety. Acting without additional proof would lead to violence the small town wouldn't recover from.

That would jeopardize not only my life and reputation, but that of my entire family as well. My patience level was going to be tested.

However, there was an ominous stench in the air, the odor reminiscent of swamp water, but much worse. Only my kind could detect something so putrid, typical humans incapable of doing so.

While I wanted to discount everything my father had said, I'd known since I was a child that there were secrets surrounding the reason that we were Lycans. While the myth of our existence was strong, some believing in the folklore enough they feared the darkness and even the full moon, most people simply went about their everyday lives. They'd shoved aside mystical creatures when turning into adults, laughing at those who continued to hold onto their beliefs.

Right now, I was full of rage, enough so my wolf remained just below the surface. Fortunately, this was a situation I could control, at least for the time being. That too would change as the blue moon drew near. Even the moon from the night before seemed oddly different in color, the orb's fullness a reminder that time was short.

I'd been forced to leave Coraline alone, although I'd checked the perimeter both before I'd taken her and after I'd left. My behavior had been disconcerting, but my needs as well as my father's words had been a force I couldn't avoid. Her scent remained covering me, staining my skin, which did nothing more than fuel my hunger. While the last thing I wanted was to use her as bait, I needed to find out just how widespread the danger truly was.

Unfortunately, our mating wasn't finalized. Forcing the issue would only have pushed her away. Her resolve was strong, enough so I was well aware her defiance could get her into additional trouble. I'd spent the morning combing over the site of the attack. Finding no evidence other than a few strings of blood meant the Brousseaus had organized the event. They'd anticipated the possibilities that the plan would fail, which disturbed me almost as much as what had transpired.

That also meant the danger was much more significant that I'd originally thought. Hell, I wasn't certain what had gone through my mind after meeting with my father. One thing was certain. He was petrified we'd be altered forever.

Like hell that was going to happen.

"What's going on down there, boss?" Bronco asked.

For me to command him to send Jackson and Miller to the freaking Bayou was unexpected. It also likely raised red flags. He was the one person I'd trusted enough to learn that I never had any intentions of returning to Baton Rouge. "Just get them here, Bronco. And make certain we don't have any issues until I return."

"Which is when? I mean if you don't mind me asking."

"Hell if I know. Maybe a few days, maybe a week. Keep a close eye on Emilio. I don't trust the bastard. He's likely to return to his old ways."

Bronco chuckled. "I can handle him."

"Yeah, I know, but call me if you hear anything on the street. I don't want anyone to know of my absence. You got that?"

"You bet, boss. I'll have Jackson and Miller get to the airport within the hour."

"Good." As I hung up the phone, I glanced around the room of the small motel. The small city was charming, but there was something about a good number of the people that made my skin crawl. As if they knew who I was, able to identify my ancestry just by looking. I'd also spent some time on my laptop, trying to find out as much information about the lovely Coraline. While the name LeBlanc was Cajun in nature, that meant little in Louisiana, the surname prevalent.

I found almost nothing in my search regarding her, which didn't raise a red flag. The Cajun people kept to themselves, either moving away when they had the chance or entrenching themselves in the slow-moving environment that they'd been brought up in. Even with my connections, I found nothing of any importance on the family or the surname itself. From what I could tell, LeBlanc had nothing to do with the Brousseau family.

Then again, I wasn't shoving aside any possibilities.

I'd left Coraline with the explicit instructions to call me if anything suspicious occurred. I half laughed just thinking about it. She was enough of a rebel that I had a feeling she didn't like to follow anyone's orders. What we'd experienced had been explosive, but I knew that she'd regret what had happened.

That wouldn't bode well for my ability to protect her, especially since the house where she lived was even further in the sticks than her veterinary clinic.

I was perturbed when I heard a knock on the door, immediately reaching for my loaded weapon, which remained on the bed. I slipped it under my waistband in the small of my back before answering the door.

"I'm surprised to see you. I would have thought you'd be long gone by now."

Sebastian gave me a nasty look before scanning the room and walking inside. "Soon enough. Nice place you got here. Took me a little while to find you."

"Yeah, well, there are no five-star establishments in Thibodaux." As I closed the door behind him, I sensed his tenseness. Sebastian's merciless control of Miami had put the fear of God into the majority of criminals, including some members of the Puerto Rican Cartel. Nothing bothered him. On this late morning, he was disturbed as hell. "And as far as being found, I don't find it necessary. The less people who know where I am, the better. I'd surprised you're not on a plane to Miami."

He shifted back and forth, his hands on his hips. "Trust me, I'm headed to the airport after our meeting."

"Trouble in paradise?"

"Something like that. Does that mean you buy this bullshit about the curse?"

I moved toward the cheap wooden dresser, sitting on the edge and removing my gun. He eyed it carefully, shaking his head. "I think there's some credibility to what Pops told us."

"Credibility," he huffed, his gaze following my actions. "Did trouble follow you or did you have a run-in with the Brousseaus already? You're tense as fuck." He laughed until he noticed my face. "You did."

"That happened before we had a meeting with Pops."

"What the hell?"

"I was drawn to this city for some reason. In fact, after getting off the plane, I lost track of time, ending up in a forest just off a two-lane road on the outskirts of town."

He shrank back, narrowing his eyes. "That's not like you."

"Exactly. What transpired over the next two hours is just as troubling."

"Meaning what?"

I looked toward the window, the ugly view of the parking lot lights a reminder of where I was. "I ripped three men apart in order to save a woman."

I could hear the glitch in his voice. "I take it what you did had nothing to do with business."

"No, it certainly did not. I didn't know the girl, but I was drawn to her. I realized instinctively that she was in danger. I followed my instinct, the bastards almost succeeding in abducting her."

"So your premonition was true." He exhaled, the sound exaggerated. "Your mate?"

Nodding, I realized I had zero guilt about what I'd done. "It would appear so."

"This shit is just getting more difficult to believe. What did you do with her?"

"Nothing. I was injured, enough damage I was knocked unconscious for a short period of time. The woman believed she needed to save my life. She pushed aside the carnage and pulled me into her vehicle."

"You're shitting me."

"No, she's that kind of woman. A veterinarian who just returned to the area. For some crazy ass reason."

Sebastian took a deep whiff. "I can see you've already explored a carnal relationship."

"To a point."

"If you believe what our father says, just mate with her. Maybe that will stop the bullshit."

My brother's cavalier actions always made me laugh. "Are you such a barbarian that you take any woman you hunger for without questioning if she wants it?"

He gave me a sly smile. "Something like that. Wouldn't she feel the same?"

"If you're asking if I knew about the second part of this curse, I didn't. However, I knew all along there was more to the story." I wasn't yet ready to tell him I suspected there was a third blow that would likely destroy our family. "Coraline and I have intense chemistry, but there's nothing more."

"And you're hesitating?"

I gave him a hard look.

Whistling, he lifted his eyebrows. "You're trying to figure out who might be in charge of this other family. Right?"

"I am. However, I won't risk her life by doing so." I walked toward the window, peering outside at nothing but cracked pavement and a leaning light pole, snickering under my breath. Maybe the best thing to do was to take her with me back to Chicago. "I found only limited information on the Brousseau family, including anything concrete regarding what happened a century ago."

Sebastian eyed me carefully. "You're thinking they're underground on purpose."

"I am, which is another reason I need to protect Coraline."

"You like this girl." He chuckled, a sly smile crossing his face.

"You know me better than that, Sebastian. I don't give a shit about anyone. Remember?"

He flanked my side, leaning against the glass. "According to someone from your past."

"And she was right."

"And I don't buy it for a second. I'm the playboy. You're the homebody."

It was my turn to laugh. "I've changed since I last saw you."

"I kind of hope not, brother," he said after a few seconds. "I don't know what to think. If only there was some evidence to back this up other than just stories told over the years."

"Yeah, but I doubt we'll find that. The Cajun people were tighter with regard to their beliefs then than they are now. What I suspect is that the Brousseau family has grown stronger in numbers over the years."

"So has the Dupree family," he said then snorted. "What the hell am I saying? Am I buying into this garbage?"

"Pops is retiring, which means I'll be taking his place. Whatever happens, Sebastian, as the Underboss, I'm going to need to rely on you. Do you understand?" When I turned my head, staring him in the eyes, he exhaled.

"I take it that's your first order as new Don. Fall into line with this curse. Find my mate."

"What I'm telling you is that you're next in line. If there is any validity to this legend, then you need to be prepared."

"Finding this person where?"

"That, I don't know."

"A freaking needle in a haystack."

I thought about his comment. "The one thing I've learned over the years is that karma has a way of putting two people together."

"Since when did you become the philosopher?"

"Since I realized that this curse has haunted our father his entire life. There is a reason for it. The hunger is real and it's only getting worse."

He took a few seconds before answering. "Agreed. Keep me informed as to what is going on."

"I plan on doing some sniffing around town, although I think my arrival has already been detected."

"Interesting." He placed his hand on my shoulder then walked toward the door. "What about Dax?"

"I'm not certain. I'll put out a few feelers, but I'm not going to promise that even with my connections can I get him out of maximum security." The fact Dax had been sent to the only remaining super-max prison in Colorado continued to piss me off. He'd been railroaded; not one of the high-ranking members of law enforcement and judges we'd paid very well to stay out of our business had been able to prevent it from happening. The task wasn't just daunting. It was impossible.

Especially since he was guilty of the crime.

"If anyone can, you will. However, I'll be happy to help anyway I can." He hesitated, staring me in the eyes. "I have to tell you, Gabriel. I don't like this shit. All these years, I've thought that being a Lycan was just another gift like precognition or bending spoons. But now?" His laugh was bitter.

"I don't like what has been forced on us either. Whatever happens, you need to do everything in your power to curtail your hunger."

Sebastian rolled his eyes. "That may become impossible. What little feeding I've succumbed to hasn't been satisfying, my anger increasing. I've done everything to avoid it. It's changed my behavior."

"Find a way, brother. We could destroy everything our family has built if we succumb. Any of us."

"What about the extended family?"

"I can't be concerned about them at this point." None of us had experienced a close relationship with any of our immediate families, including our only uncle and four cousins. They'd stayed away from Louisiana, ignoring their affliction as well as the fact their family members were brutal criminals.

"Agreed," Sebastian said under his breath.

While I could tell my words troubled him, he gave me a single nod. It was only a matter of time before all five of us lost control.

Then God help everyone in our path.

"Why did you come here, Sebastian? Just to find out if I bought the story?"

"I came here to warn you. I've had issues with a smuggler, the bastard managing to sabotage two shipments," Sebastian said in passing.

"A single asshole?" That was surprising given the number of soldiers my brother employed.

"Hard to believe but yes. There's no doubt he's had some help, but I haven't been able to flush out the traitor yet. I caught wind he was headed in this direction just before Pops called. I gathered his disgusting scent the moment I stepped off the plane. It would appear that this shit of a little town is where he's holed up, which I admit I find curious as hell. I don't have time to hunt him down given a large shipment arriving from Brazil tomorrow, but there's a chance he's working for someone else."

"Meaning what?" Given I'd never believed in coincidences, curious wasn't the word. If father's predictions were correct, the asshole might be a member of the Brousseau family engaging in another method of revenge. It was something that couldn't be ignored.

"Meaning I have a strong sense that his attacks on my shipments were planned, others to follow but not necessarily in my domain."

I took a deep breath. "His name?"

"Goes by the Iceman. I've never seen him, but an informant told me the man's face has a jagged scar on one side. He's managed to kill four of my men with an icepick. I'm told he's frequented one of the bars I own, perhaps to gather information."

"Interesting. While I'm here, I'll certainly keep my eyes open."

"Just be careful."

Chuckling, I lifted my eyebrows. "I'm surprised you'd say that to me, dear brother. You know how I am."

"That's what I'm afraid of," he said, grinning.

I watched him walk out the door, realizing every decision I made would affect the entire family, most of which I'd never met. I didn't like the odds or the tasks that I'd have to face. One thing was certain. I would not allow my mate to be harmed in any way.

If anyone tried, I would allow my beast to surface.

Unfortunately, there might not be any going back.

Soon, night would fall. The time for creatures to creep from their shadowed existence, feasting on their prey. The hunger I was experiencing continued to surge in waves, prickling my skin. I'd spent the better part of three hours observing people in the town. Everywhere I'd gone, people had distanced themselves from me, avoiding eye contact. I'd been wrong that the Brousseau family kept to themselves. There were dozens of them in town, many running the various establishments I'd gone to. From what I'd been able to ascertain, those under thirty had no apparent knowledge of the curse placed on my family.

Or they'd been taught to hide their animosity well.

However, the hatred remained strong. More than one of them had been pulled away from answering my questions or even serving me in a coffee shop. I'd come away with nothing more than a better understanding that in Thibodaux, the name Dupree was shunned.

Abhorred.

I'd been able to find almost nothing on the Iceman, but given the town's obvious dislike of strangers, I had a feeling I'd discover little.

As I pulled into the small parking lot of the veterinary clinic, a dull ache occurred in my gut from the wounds inflicted by the men who'd attacked her. However, what continued to remain even more sensitive was the area just under my shoulder where Coraline had shot me. Unlike the two bullets that had been positioned in the center of my chest, the one she'd fired off had gone straight through, allowing me to heal within minutes.

Much to her horror and surprise.

The bond we'd already formed allowed me to sense her emotions as well as to be able to read a portion of her thoughts. She remained confused about everything that had happened, including her inability to thwart the rush of electricity that had awakened her carnal needs. I also sensed more determination, refusal to allow the bastards who'd attacked her to sway her from the reason she'd returned to her hometown.

Even if she wasn't certain of it herself.

Two cars were parked in the lot, her beaten-up older vehicle positioned off to the side. That meant she had a client inside. At least there were no signs of obvious danger. I waited as my soldiers exited their rental vehicle, both studying the small building in front of us with curious looks on their faces.

"Bronco told us almost nothing about this assignment, boss," Jackson said after moving by my side. "Not that I'm complaining about getting out of the city for a few days."

"There's nothing to tell other than you are to protect the woman inside, no matter the cost." My answer was succinct. There was no need for them to learn about the curse, or that it was entirely possible their lives were in more danger here than on the streets of Chicago.

"Who is she, boss?" Miller asked as he removed his sunglasses.

"Someone important. That's all you need to know. Maintain surveillance twenty-four/seven."

Jackson moved away several feet, studying the woods surrounding the building. "Just who are we protecting her from? Another rival family?"

"Of sorts. They are just as dangerous, their methods Neanderthalic, although lethal." There were two animals inside, one of which I suspected was the Labrador that Coraline adored. At least the oversized pup seemed to recognize exactly what I was. Chuckling, I shifted my weapon under my jacket to ensure it wouldn't be seen. "I'm going to pay her a visit. Then I have business to attend to, which could take me into the early evening."

"We'll keep her safe," Miller answered.

"Make certain you do." As I headed toward the front porch, I was struck once again by how far removed the business was from the rest of the town. From my perspective, the purchase wasn't the best if the girl wanted to make money. There had to be another reason she was here.

There was no receptionist at the front desk to greet patients, no sign of life at all. However, the area was decorated in beautiful colors, the floor gleaming and soft music playing. Moose lifted his head from the fluffy bed positioned in the corner, his thumping tail keeping time to the music.

There was something incredible about his big brown eyes. "Hiya, boy." I hunkered down, taking a few seconds to scratch behind his ears. He was trusting of me, which wasn't necessarily in Coraline's best interest. "Just rest, buddy. I'm here to see your mommy." He closed his eyes, falling into a deep sleep almost immediately. I'd noticed my ability to control a certain number of smaller creatures was increasing as rapidly as my hunger. Perhaps I was obtaining another powerful weapon. Sighing, I rose to my feet. The building itself wasn't secure, even with the two locks on the front door. The windows were old, some of the wood rotten. Anyone who intended on coming inside could do so without issue. Her house was much the same way. With the thick woods surrounding both properties, it would be difficult for my men to detect danger until it was upon them.

Only one of the doors leading to another area in the building was closed. I moved from one to the other. There were two examination rooms and what appeared to be a storeroom as well as a hallway leading to another part of the building beside.

I headed down the corridor, noticing another open door. When I walked inside, I was surprised to see state of the art computer equipment positioned on an ancient metal desk, the room so small Coraline was forced to squeeze beside the desk in order to sit in her chair. She had several pictures on the surface, all of which were ones taken of

Moose. The photographs provided interesting information.

She had no boyfriend, no large group of friends she wanted to remember. That surprised the hell out of me.

The sound of movement behind me forced a usual reaction. I immediately reached for my weapon as I turned toward the noise.

"Just a second, Mrs. Martin." Coraline bounded inside, her initial look of shock turning to a glimmer of fear as her gaze fell to my hand holding my weapon. At least five seconds passed as we stared at each other. "What the hell are you doing here?"

"Is that any way to greet the man you were writhing under only a few hours ago?" I realized my words were crass, but I was curious as to her reaction.

Her mouth twisted as anger replaced any hint of trepidation. "This is my office. My private space. We don't know each other and at this point, I don't want to get any closer. Period. I have a patient. I suggest you leave."

"I'm afraid I can't do that, Coraline." I eased from around her desk, buttoning my jacket.

Huffing, she shifted past me, the close proximity of our bodies allowing another wave of current to encapsulate both of us. She did her best to ignore the electricity, grumbling under her breath and remaining standing as she typed furiously on her keyboard. Within seconds, the printer came to life, a single piece of paper rolling from the tray.

"Why the hell is that, *Gabriel?*" Her insolence was even more aggressive than the night before.

"Because you're in danger."

She stared at me with an incredulous look on her face. Then she shook her head. "As I said, I have a patient. Do not interfere." She pointed her finger at me before walking away quickly.

I sat on the edge of the desk, smiling from the way the lilt in her voice had changed. She was very good with her patients and their owners. Just thinking about her brought another wave of desire so intense that my cock ached with need. I purposely thought about the Iceman, concerned that a single entity had been able to breach my brother's security. If there was a plan instigated by someone who considered our entire family their enemy, things could get dicey as I attempted to discover the truth around the legend.

Only minutes later she returned, her hands on her hips and the same rebellious look on her face. "Explain why I'm in danger. I already told you that the three men who attacked me were killed. They don't have another chance to get to me." She narrowed her eyes, her breath skipping. The woman was doing everything she could to try to figure out why she thought about the wolf that had saved her life just after she thought about our encounter.

"Because they weren't the only ones who mean you harm."

"What are you getting at? I'm a target of what? And why? That makes no sense, unless these people are attached to you and your criminal activity."

The moment I moved away from the desk, she took a giant stride, shifting out of her office. "The danger surrounding you has nothing yet everything to do with your connection with me."

"We don't have a connection. We just fucked. That won't happen again. I thought I made that clear to you."

I took a deep breath, almost instantly intoxicated by her perfume. When I exhaled, she partially closed her eyes, taking scattered breaths. She didn't take another step as I closed the distance. "We did more than just fuck, Coraline. And we're going to do it again."

Hissing, she acted as if she wanted to slap me, raising her arm then closing her hand. "You're an arrogant bastard and no, you're wrong. Just leave. Okay? I have work to do."

"You have no additional patients for the day, none on the schedule for tomorrow. You're in the middle of nowhere in a clinic that has seen better days. I find that more than just curious for a woman of your intelligence. Why would you return to a small town after spending time in New York?"

She wrinkled her nose as she rolled her eyes. "That's my business. Not yours. And why the hell are you interested in the first place?"

I could feel my beast pushing against the surface. "Did you tell anyone about your attack?"

"What do you think? I'm not an idiot, no matter how odd the circumstances." She looked away, heat rising on her face. "I called the sheriff the next morning."

"Why not right after it occurred?" I could tell she was already jumping to conclusions about the wolf, her mind still foggy about details regarding the incident, but she would begin to ask questions. I had to know if she'd told anyone.

Exhaling, she rubbed her eyes before returning her gaze, exasperated as hell. "I don't owe you an explanation, Gabriel, no matter what you think."

I folded my arms, waiting as she tried to calm down.

"Fine. A wolf was the reason my life was spared, okay? I thought the creature was a dog at first. Only when I got him back here did I realize what I was dealing with. The wolf was severely injured, so I followed my oath as a veterinarian and saved his life. There is no freaking cell phone coverage in this damn place. That's why I didn't call until in the morning. And don't you dare say I should have allowed that creature to die!"

"Did you tell the sheriff about this wolf?"

"Yes. No. I'm not sure. I was rattled. Okay? I think I did."

Her conviction gave me a smile. "And what was the sheriff's reaction?"

She continued to seem galled that I was grilling her, but her tone of voice had already softened. "He couldn't care less. He said he drove by the location where I supposedly had a little trouble and found nothing. No bodies. No body parts. What little blood there was he refused to test. So, case closed."

If I had to make a calculated guess, I would say the sheriff's ancestry was tied to the Brousseau family. I would find that out soon enough. As I stood over her, I could tell my presence both excited as well as annoyed her. Within seconds, her desire was winning.

"You are so beautiful," I half whispered.

"Gabriel. I just… As I asked you before. Why are you so interested in what happens to me? I'm a stranger. Nobody. I'm just a girl trying to make something out of her life."

As I cupped the side of her face, a single growl erupted, low and husky. She wasn't terrified of the man standing in front of her, even though she'd guessed correctly that I was a killer. Instead, she wanted nothing more than to push my boundaries.

As well as hers.

I hesitated, brushing my thumb back and forth across her heated skin until she closed her eyes, her breathing irregular. Her scent filled me, exciting every molecule. My God, I craved this woman.

"I care because you belong to me." I crushed my mouth over hers, anticipating her pushback. When she slammed her fists against my chest, that only fueled the embers, turning them into a raging fire. I thrust my tongue inside her mouth, savoring the taste of cinnamon. Everything about her enticed not only the creature living inside of me but the man who'd been able to taste any woman he'd set his sights on.

I slid my hand around her waist, dragging her against my chest. The feel of having her in my arms added to the desire to protect her just as strongly as to my longing to force her to succumb. She had no idea the kind of emotions or needs erupting deep inside of me. Just digging my fingers into the softness of her skin evoked more emotions that I'd felt in years, my hunger swelling to the point I required relief.

Within seconds, her body melted against mine, her pulse continuing to climb as her yearning became the only thing she could concentrate on. Her soft mews quickly turned into ragged purrs as she clung to me.

While the passionate kiss excited me, every muscle in my body tense, I craved more. I would have more. After dominating her tongue, tasting the heat of her mouth, I shifted my hand to the back of her neck, holding her in place as I broke the kiss. My vision was clouded as my wolf managed to claw its way to the surface, enough that every action became even more savage.

I shoved her against her desk, sliding my hands under the hem of her skirt, forcing the dense material around her waist.

"What are you doing?" she managed, every sound breathless.

"Fucking you." The second I bunched her panties in my hand, she flinched, tossing her head back and forth. But there was no denying the heated moment or the need that threatened to consume us. She wanted me as much as I craved her.

I ripped the thin lace away with a single snap of my wrist, pushing her legs wide open before unfastening my trousers.

Panting, she wrapped her fingers around my shirt, yanking until she was able to slide her hand underneath, fingering my stomach.

I threw my head back and roared, my entire body shaking from the explosive adrenaline rush. There was something even more powerful about fucking her now than the night before, the vibrations dancing through my body creating sensations that erupted like firecrackers. She kept her hand against my heated skin until I'd freed my cock. Then she leaned back, planting both her hands on the surface of the desk as she wrapped her legs around my thighs.

My heart thudding against my chest, I yanked her naked bottom to the edge of the desk, wasting no time before plunging the entire length of my cock into her swollen folds.

"Oh. Oh!" She closed her eyes, moving into a deep arch as she gasped over and over again.

I dug my fingers into her thighs, pumping into her like a wild animal. A series of bright lights flashed in front of my eyes, the strings of colors fucking with my mind as I did everything I could to keep from shifting. As her pussy muscles wrapped around my shaft, drawing me in even deeper, I fisted her hair and lowered my head until I was able to lock eyes with hers.

Her sly smile was provocative as hell, only fueling my actions. I pumped hard and fast, my actions becoming more brutal. She smashed one hand on her desk as she clung to my arm with the other, dragging her tongue across her lips. We were nothing but wild animals, unable to keep our hunger at bay.

Every sound she made added to my need to ravage her for hours, but that would have to wait. This was nothing more than intensifying our need for each other, staining her with my scent to keep other predators away. Any member of the Brousseau family would know she belonged to me. That would protect her only to a point.

They would come after her again, only this time in force. I couldn't allow that to happen. If they dared to try, they would face my wrath.

"Yes. Yes..." Her moans increased as she tossed her head from side to side. Within seconds, I could tell she was close to a massive orgasm.

I drove harder and faster, beads of sweat forming along my hairline. I couldn't seem to get enough of her. There was no light or sound, only what was happening between us. I was able to hear her heartbeat, the thumping sound echoing in my ears. When her pussy muscles clenched and released several times, I rolled onto the balls of my feet, powering into her brutally.

"Oh, God. I... I..." She threw her head back, a scream erupting from her throat. Her entire body was shaking as the climax ripped through her system. She was so damn beautiful, her skin shimmering as the pleasure drove her into ecstasy.

I refused to stop, every thrust savage, my balls swelling to the point I wasn't going to be able to hold back much longer.

As I tangled my fingers in her hair, keeping her in a deep arch, she kept her eyes open, never blinking. I could swear the woman had managed to claw her way through the man, finding the wolf hidden inside.

After she was thrown into another tidal wave, one orgasm after the other, I pulled all the way out, brutally turning then tossing her over the edge of the desk.

"What are you doing?" she managed, still taking gasping breaths.

"Fucking you in the ass. Every hole belongs to me. That's something for you to keep in mind." I was too much in need to be gentle, although I was able to control my savagery for a few seconds as I pushed against her dark hole, every muscle tensing in anticipation.

"Oh. Oh!" She smashed her hands on the desk, bucking against me.

"Breathe for me, Coraline."

She tossed her head, shaking all over, a series of moans slipping past her lips as I pushed several inches inside. "So huge. God!"

I leaned over, pressing my chest against her then thrusting the remainder inside. Her bedraggled scream was my reward, creating a wave of vibrations. Her muscles clamped around my shaft, pulsing as they stretched to accommodate my size. As I pumped in and out, her moans increased in volume, her body writhing underneath me. Within seconds, I was pounding into her like a crazed man, beads of sweat trickling down both sides of my face.

While I wanted nothing more than to do this for hours, the explosive nature of our coupling wouldn't allow it.

"Yes. Yes. Yes…" she whimpered, further fueling the fire.

Suddenly, I lost the ability to control my body's reaction, shaking violently just seconds before I filled her with my seed.

Soon she would become my mate. Soon there would be no turning back.

God help us both, but a new dynasty was about to take control.

One that would rule not as men, but as beasts of the darkness.

And there would be nothing the Brousseau family could do to stop us.

CHAPTER 7

 abriel

Silence.

Coraline had pulled away from me, her face reddening as she'd adjusted her skirt, moving out of the room quickly. I found her staring out the window near the reception desk, her back heaving as she continued to process what had occurred between us.

She seemed to sense my presence, her body stiffening. I noticed Moose had moved by her side, pressing his muzzle against her leg as she absently stroked his head. "How did you know I didn't have any other appointments?"

I kept my distance, taking my time to answer. "I learn things, Coraline. I make it my business to do so. That keeps me aware of everything happening around me. That's also helped to keep me alive."

"I don't want to be a part of your world. Do you understand? I want to build this business. At least I had one customer today. I call that a win. So what if I had to stay later than I'd expected? At least I was able to help that poor beagle." She was exasperated, second guessing her move.

"Why did you come here?"

"Why? Let's see. I came here for..." She laughed, pressing the palm of her hand against the expansive and wide-open glass. Another aspect of the building I couldn't tolerate. "I have no real idea why I returned. Isn't that crazy? My mother thought it would be a good idea. She encouraged me to do so. No, it was more than just encouragement. It was... odd, as if she wouldn't take no for an answer. Hell, she even bought this place for me, which I likely wouldn't have selected. But I'm here and I plan on making a damn good life. Do you hear me?" She threw her head over her shoulder, biting down on her lower lip.

I found it curious her mother had insisted she return. That was far too coincidental in my mind. I glanced out the window, my loins aching for another reason.

The sun had already set. My need to hunt was becoming almost impossible to ignore. However, I would hold it together long enough to hunt for the Iceman, if only for tonight. My instinct told me the asshole was close, although there was no reason to be certain. At this point, she needed to understand I wasn't taking no for an answer.

I would protect her.

"You are going to listen to me and follow my orders, Coraline. I have two men outside who are going to ensure you are protected. You will not attempt to get away from them. I assure you that won't happen." My words didn't seem to register at first. Then she turned around, folding her arms as she glared at me.

"Your men? Are you kidding me? As I told you before. I. Don't. Know. You. This is my life. How dare you think you're going to assign two… what are they, killers? I can take care of myself."

"So you've said, but you underestimate what could happen to you. I can't take the chance."

"Why? You expect me to trust you when you've told me almost nothing. Besides, why the hell do you even care?" When I didn't answer right away, she laughed. "Fine. If you want two goons to follow around me like lapdogs, I hope they don't get bored easily. I'm going to the grocery store to purchase some food and lots of wine. Then I'm going home to lick my wounds of not having another patient on the books. After consuming an entire bottle of vino, I might watch a movie. What the heck, a horror movie. That might be more fascinating than what my life has become. Maybe tomorrow, you can finally tell me what the hell you think you're doing. Now, get out." She pointed toward the door, giving me a nasty look.

I scanned the room as I took several deep breaths, unable to sense any immediate danger. "Do not go anywhere else. Do you understand me?"

"You really do believe you can give me orders now. I don't think so. Go. Just go. Come back only if you're willing to tell me what the hell is going on."

I inched closer until she put her palm into the air, shaking her head. "Do as I say, Coraline. You *are* going to need to trust me."

"Sure. Whatever you say."

Her defiance was noteworthy, more so than several opponents I'd faced over the years, but she would be forced to obey my rules soon enough. I took long strides toward the door. "Don't fight me on this."

"Uh-huh."

As I walked out into the darkness, I felt an overwhelming need to feed. That would be forced to wait.

"She'll be leaving soon," I said to Jackson before heading to my rental car.

"We won't let her out of our sight."

As the wind rustled through the trees, I felt another strong urge to shift and snarled.

* * *

I'd learned in my observations of people over the years that behaviors never changed. If the Iceman was used to either securing information or simply indulging in one of his proclivities by frequenting a bar, then there was only one logical place for him in town.

The parking lot was even more crowded than the night before, forcing me to park on the street. After taking a deep whiff of the area, I buttoned my jacket before heading inside. The crowd was even more rambunctious, heavy consumption of alcohol the reason even at this early hour. I gathered the scent of sex as well as stale cigars, both assaulting my senses. As I made my way to the bar, I continually scanned the area. Fortunately, the amount of alcohol that had been consumed was enough to shove aside any instincts of who or what I was.

After ordering a scotch, I allowed my keen eyesight to search the room. A swell of anger surfaced when I noticed the person at the opposite end of the bar. With one whiff, I sensed he was carrying a weapon. When he shifted his position, I didn't need the dim lighting of the bar to highlight the scar covering one side of his face. I resisted a growl, my hackles raised.

I continued nursing my drink, waiting to see what he would do. The asshole powered down three shots of some liquor before polishing off his beer. Then he slid money across the bar and headed toward the entrance. When he passed by only a few feet away, there was no indication he'd realized that a predator was within striking distance.

I finished my drink before following him outside. He'd already jumped into a truck, revving his engine as it idled. Either he still didn't detect my presence or was luring me into a dangerous situation. Whatever the case, we would have a frank discussion.

There was no difficulty in following him, although I kept my distance, my anger increasing with every mile driven. I knew I had to be careful. Any mistake would destroy my ability to protect Coraline. He drove out of the city limits and into another rural area. While far removed from where the lovely veterinarian lived, my hackles remained on high alert. When he pulled onto a gravel driveway, I eased the car in front, watching until his taillights disappeared before parking.

After grabbing a second clip of ammunition, I made the half mile trek to his cabin on foot. With only one car in the driveway, I anticipated he was alone. I scanned the area one last time before pounding on the wooden surface. Then I took a step away.

Until he opened the door.

I threw a hard punch to his jaw, the force enough he was pummeled backwards, the gun he'd had in his hand tossed to the side upon impact. I wasted no time moving over him, kicking the weapon away then pointing my Glock directly at his face.

"What the fuck? Who the hell are you?" he bellowed as he rubbed his jaw, attempting to get to his feet.

I slammed my foot against his chest, pinning him down. "Not so fast. You're going to answer some questions. If you're a good boy, I'll let you live. If not, you'll soon learn what crossing someone in my position means."

He snarled yet held up his hands. "Whatever. What kind of questions?"

"Who are you working for?"

Huffing, he narrowed his eyes. "I don't work for anyone. Just myself. I think you have your wires crossed, buddy."

The look in his eyes indicated he was fucking with me. I took a deep whiff, loathing the man's stench. However, he wasn't of Brousseau blood. I shifted my foot to the tender area between his torso and upper thigh, digging my heel in. While he grimaced from the pain, I could sense he was contemplating reaching for his weapon. I almost wanted him to try.

Then I'd tear him apart.

When I moved my foot away, he wasted no time grabbing my leg, twisting until I thrown off balance. He didn't expect my quick reaction, able to grab him around the neck and hoisting him off his feet. I issued a primal hiss before tossing him against the wall.

Stunned, he slowly slipped to the floor, pressing his hand against his chest as he gasped for air. The look in his eyes was murderous, just like his intentions.

"I'm going to ask you one last time. Who are you working for? There won't be a third."

He struggled but managed to rise to his feet, darting a single glance in the direction of his weapon. I alleviated his temptation, retrieving and pocketing his weapon. He grinned after my actions. Yes, the fucker knew exactly who I was.

"Gabriel Dupree. I hear you're taking over from your old man soon. What a shame you won't get that chance."

While no one could have known that information, unless my father had mentioned his intentions prior to telling me, I couldn't allow that to interfere. "If you know who I am, then you're aware of why I'm here."

"I really don't give a shit. You obviously know why I'm here. I think we have a draw."

He dared laugh in my face, his hazel eyes lighting up as if he held some kind of secret. That only antagonized the hell out of me, forcing me to rethink what I would do to him. I lifted my weapon, holding it with both hands. "You have five seconds to share with me who you are working for."

The Iceman continued his hard, cold stare, the smirk on his face increasing. "You have no idea who you're fucking with."

"Now, I don't give a shit. I asked you a question. Three seconds."

"Go fuck yourself. By the way, there's no way you're going to be able to protect that woman. Her death will avenge mine."

The line of no return had been crossed.

There was only the need to fire a single bullet. While the smile remained, his body slowly slid to the floor, a trail of blood the only affirmation I needed he was dead. Hissing, I scanned the perimeter of his cabin. The sight of two suitcases positioned only a few feet away indicated he'd yet to spend a night in the location.

It was obvious he was a hired gun, likely given limited information about the marks he was paid to eliminate. Wasting time on looking for anything helpful wasn't in my best interest. I shoved the weapon in my jacket, giving the asshole another quick gaze before walking out the front door.

There would be more like him attacking within a short period of time. While the methods would change, the goal would remain the same. Disrupt our establishment then destroy the Dupree family.

My rage continued to grow, enough so that before reaching my vehicle, I was pitched to the ground. There was no way to shake off the transition. I threw my head back and bellowed, fighting to return to my feet, the transition already starting as I struggled to remove my clothes. The pain had never been this intense. My blood was already on fire, my muscles in anguish as they started to stretch.

Gasping, when I'd tossed my clothes aside, I fell back to the ground, clawing the earth beneath my fingers. My vision cloudy, I tossed my head from side to side, echoes of my bones breaking floating into the air around me. I was sucked into a fog, the pressure on my chest suffocating. As my wolf breached the surface, my spine curled, my ribs popping one after the other.

A series of growls spewed from my throat, each one more animalistic than the one before. Within seconds, my entire body was shaking as the transformation moved to the final stage, claws erupting from my fingers. I threw back my head, blinking as I studied the sky, the hunger reaching an impossible state.

My beast broke free, the electricity surging through my body invigorating, every odor coming from the darkness of the woods enticing me.

But there was only one thing that would satisfy my hunger.

I looked over my shoulder, clearly able to see the single light from the cabin.

Then I took off racing toward the structure.

Tonight, the feast would fulfill me, but soon, more would be needed. After issuing a low-slung growl, I advanced.

***

Panting, I remained on the ground, still aching from the recent shift. At least I was able to focus, no longer consumed by the burning hunger or with the rage that had almost devoured me. After taking several deep breaths, still fueled by the intense odors of the forest, I rose to my feet. The sound of my phone brought me all the way back to reality. I swung my head toward my clothes, fighting my aching muscles until I managed to grab my jacket, yanking it into my hand. "Jackson." I immediately sensed something was wrong.

"We were attacked, two bastards coming out of nowhere the second she reached her house." Panting, I was surprised at his exasperation. Jackson always remained cool no matter the situation.

"And the woman?"

"She's fine. Terrified."

"What about the bastards?" I growled.

"Handled, although it wasn't clean. What do you want us to do?"

My gut told me there was no additional time to waste. "Get her to the airport."

"What about the dog?"

I thought about the situation and sighed. "He goes with her. If she gives you any trouble, which she will, do whatever is necessary to get her to safety. Notify the pilot we're leaving sooner than expected."

"We'll do that, boss. You should know, those assholes were heavily armed, their vehicle indicating they were planning on kidnapping her."

"Dump the bodies inside then take the vehicle to the forest," I instructed.

"Already on it, boss."

As I stared at the sky, I was finally able to calm my breathing.

The war was just beginning.

After dressing, I took one last look at the cabin. The carnage I'd left would be found, the kill a strong warning to anyone attempting to get in our way. We would use what we'd been cursed with to survive the two blue moons. I wasted no time leaving the area, driving in excess of the speed limit. The Iceman had been ordered to Thibodaux to carry out my demise. The question remained as to by whom.

As I headed toward the motel to retrieve my things, I dialed my father's number. It was time for him to fill in some blanks.

"What's happened?" he answered.

Exhaling, I continuously scanned the rearview and both side mirrors. "You sensed an issue."

"As I always have with my boys. The woman?"

"Another attack. I'm leaving at least until I can get a handle on what's going on. An assassin was sent, the same bastard Sebastian has been having issues with over his shipments. There will be more of them in the near future. We need to find the identity of the person controlling the assassination attempts."

He sighed, the sound haunting. "Yes, we do. The four of you must stick together in order to beat this."

"What haven't you told us?"

"There's nothing left to tell you, son. What you heard was passed down to me."

"That's bullshit, Pops. I saw the look on your face. For a man who never shows his emotions, it was clear to see how disturbed you've been. What. Else." I was just as furious as before, more so given the lack of information my father had supplied. I knew when he lied, and it had nothing to do with our Lycan abilities.

"When are you leaving?"

His attempt to deflect only fueled my anger. "Within two hours. Why?" I fisted the steering wheel, hissing under my breath given his hesitation.

"You will be receiving a package at your Chicago address."

"A package. You need to tell me what we're all facing."

"I think you will finally understand, son, as well as accept our fate," Pops said with sadness in his voice. "Understand that there is only one copy, the information passed down from generation to generation. Now that you will become the alpha, it's important that you know in order to pass the legend down to your children. Even if you beat the blue moons, there will be another curse then another until our family is destroyed."

I didn't like the way he was talking, as if in taking a step back, he was disengaging himself from the curse as well. My hackles remained raised. Whatever he hadn't wanted to share was the reason for his despair. That much was certain. My gut told me whatever it was would alter the course of our existence in an entirely different way. "You've risked every member of our family by not telling us whatever you're holding back."

"It's been necessary. Everything I told you and your brothers is correct. There is no disputing the upcoming two blue moons or the fact your intended mate has already been under attack not once but twice. What does that tell you about the situation we're all dealing with?"

My father's hackles had also been raised, the low rumbling growl he issued indicating he was reaching the end of his patience. A sudden understanding shifted into my mind. "You've been threatened."

"Nothing I can't handle, son. You forget how tenacious and brutal my soldiers are. I've made a few phone calls. It's possible I might be able to get Dax transferred to a prison closer to Louisiana while he awaits a retrial. However, it's going to take some time."

"You mean time we don't have."

"Keep me informed, son. As you well understand, we have a lot at stake."

I wasn't surprised when he ended the call. He was the kind of man who never liked to be challenged.

As soon as I rolled into the parking lot, I sensed I'd had at least one visitor. I parked the car away in the shadows, adding a fresh clip of ammunition before exiting the vehicle. After taking a deep whiff, I snarled under my breath. At least one of them had Brousseau blood flowing through their body. The aging three-story motel had doors leading to an exterior balcony. I'd purposely asked for a room in the back, the location allowing me to see the parking lot. It was also the darkest side of the building.

I moved up the stairs, my Glock positioned in both hands. By the time I rounded the corner, I was able to see the door to my room remained cracked, a slender shimmer of light streaming into the darkness. I approached cautiously, unable to detect any sounds, the waning scents of the two individuals indicating they'd been gone for at least fifteen minutes. When I kicked open the door, an instant snarl rushed from my lips.

The bastards had come and gone, tossing the entire room. I walked inside, keeping my weapon in position until I checked the bathroom. Exhaling, I shoved my weapon into my jacket, surveying the area. Whether or not they were looking for something in particular was impossible to tell. What I was able to ascertain was their heightened anger, the bedding and mattress, the single chair all slashed with a jagged knife. My clothes were tossed in various corners of the room, one of the lamps smashed against the floor.

A laugh bubbled to the surface as I noticed the string of blood splattered across the dresser mirror. Still fresh, it indicated they hadn't been gone for very long. If the bastards thought they were going to scare me, they certainly didn't have an idea of who they'd gone up against. However, it was just another clear indication that leaving town was the best decision.

For now.

I gathered a few of the more pertinent items, shoving them into my suitcase then locking down the room. As I walked to my car, I resisted releasing a howl into the night sky. Maybe my departure would drag them onto my turf. The fuckers would pay.

The drive took much longer than I'd planned, the accident backing up traffic for twenty minutes. By the time I reached the airstrip, I was seething.

The Baton Rouge airport had a single runway for smaller commercial flights. While I knew Jackson would handle making certain the pilot was ready, prepared to leave as soon after I arrived as possible, there was always a chance we'd be forced to wait on the runway until our number was called. Now I knew for certain I'd been watched since my arrival, likely because the sheriff had been notified about a wolf killing three members of his parish.

I moved quickly toward the plane, taking a few seconds to scan the lot before moving inside.

"You alright, boss?" Miller asked as he closed the door after my arrival.

"Get this plane off the ground as soon as possible," I instructed, immediately noticing Coraline was slumped in a seat, her head listing to the side and her hands tied with thick rope. "Why the fuck is she tied?" I moved toward her, Moose blocking my ability to get to her.

The dog shifted his head, a growl erupting from the depths of his being. While his response wasn't directed toward me, I could sense he remained in protective mode given the way Coraline had been treated.

"You were right. She put up one hell of a fight," Jackson said. "I would have untied her, but the damn dog wouldn't let us get within two feet."

I glared at him, issuing a growl of my own. "Why is she unconscious?"

"She has a damn hard right hook. And she kicked me between the legs," Miller answered. "We had to use chloroform to get her to calm down and get her into the car."

Chloroform. I could kill the man right here. "Bring me some water and get this goddamn plane off the fucking ground! Where is Moose's water bowl?"

"Um, we didn't bring it," Miller admitted, his eyes opening wide.

"And his food?" I barked.

"No," Jackson answered. "We figured it was best to get her out of her house as quickly as possible, boss. Isn't that what you wanted?"

I closed my eyes, furious as hell. "Grab me two bottles of water and a goddamned bowl." Only after my soldiers had moved away did I bend over, petting Moose on the head. "It's going to be all right. I'll take care of your mommy; however, I need to see how she is. Is that alright with you?"

He stared at me with large eyes, remaining tense for a few seconds. Then he wagged his tail, pressing his face and muzzle against my leg.

"Good boy." I sat beside her, brushing my fingers across her cheek. At least she was breathing normally. Depending on how much she breathed in, she could be out for hours. Hissing, I shook my head as I thought about everything that had occurred. The shit was getting out of hand. As I struggled with the knot securing her hands, I realized I had no idea what the hell I was going to do with her in Chicago. Keeping her in my condo wasn't the best option, although the building was secure. I'd be forced to make difficult choices, but they would be necessary. I hadn't seen the last of the organized assassins yet.

When her hands were freed, I rubbed her skin, furious everything had come to this. I would enjoy hunting down those responsible.

I could tell Jackson was arguing with the pilot. That meant we'd be sitting on the damn runway for an extended period of time. We were sitting ducks, the sheriff able to shut down the plane and arrest me as a suspect to any number of crimes. I couldn't put it past the local law enforcement to prevent us from leaving the city.

Miller arrived with the water and a silver bowl, still acting sheepish as fuck.

"I'm real sorry, boss. I've never had an animal before. I didn't think about getting him anything." He bent down, wincing as Moose moved closer, issuing the same deep-throated growl.

"Shush, Moose. He won't raise a hand to you or your mother. If he does, he won't have long to live."

Miller glanced into my eyes, giving me a nod of respect then twisting the cap off one of the bottles. Then he poured the liquid into the bowl, backing away almost immediately.

"Looks like we're fourth in line for takeoff. Busy night at the airport." Jackson glanced at Coraline, his gaze lasting far too long for my liking.

I knew the pilot was unable to do anything, but it continued to piss me off. "Keep watch on out the windows. If you see any headlights, you instruct the pilot he *will* take off, no matter the risk. Am I clear?"

"I..." Miller stuttered.

All I had to do was shoot him another harsh look.

"Yes, boss. I'll explain it to the pilot."

"You do that."

Hissing, I closed my eyes for a few seconds, remembering the first time Pops had told me about the curse. I'd been seven or eight, peppering him with dozens of questions about wolves when I'd yet to shift. I almost laughed as the memory came as the forefront of my mind. I remember thinking it was the coolest thing in the world, until my father laid down the law, telling me in no uncertain terms that if I dared to shift, punishment would be involved.

I'd only gone against his wishes once. His method of punishment had been enough to help me learn control.

Now I was losing it.

It had also allowed me to stay alive, thriving instead of losing control as other descendants. At least there'd been no national news media on monsters who'd left a stream of blood. Fuck.

I shifted forward, staring out the window then shutting the blind. As I studied her serene face, I wanted to feel guilty for removing her from her life, but that wasn't going to happen. Every inch of her now belonged to me.

She would soon learn to obey my every command or face harsh discipline. Maybe that would help keep her alive.

I growled as an ugly realization settled in.

Like father, like son.

CHAPTER 8

oraline

"Obey me, Coraline."

His words were dark and ugly, his tone unrecognizable. He towered over me in my bare feet, his chest heaving from the anger he'd already expressed.

"No. I will never obey you," I retorted, backing away even though I knew there was no place to go. I was locked in my room for twenty-three hours a day, forced to comply to his wishes, no matter how brutal or sadistic in nature. I hated him, but I still couldn't fight the attraction between us.

He narrowed his eyes, letting off a deep and husky growl, the kind that both thrilled and angered me. On the dark and stormy night, it electrified my system more than the flashes of lightning. My nipples ached, the hard points pressing against the delicate silk of my gown only adding to my arousal. I gathered a whiff of my wet pussy, juice already trickling down both inner thighs. Every time he walked into the room, my body's reaction was the same.

I was disgusted with my burning need, but unable to do anything about it.

"Then you will be punished every day until you do." He continued advancing, his chest heaving and his cock pushing hard against his trousers.

My mouth watered at the sight of the huge bulge, my excitement only building. While I loathed the spankings, they also increased my desire, keeping me wet and hot, something I would never be able to understand. When he was only a few inches away, I darted to the left, racing toward the door.

He grabbed me within seconds, yanking me back. While still holding me with one hand, he raked his fingers down the front of my gown, ripping it into shreds. I watched in fascination, certain in the candlelit room that claws had appeared on the tips of his fingers. Unable to breathe, I shuddered to my core as he tore away the remnants of what little I'd been allowed to wear, tossing it aside as if I was meant to remain naked around him.

Then he advanced like the predator he was, cupping and squeezing both breasts before flicking his index fingers back and forth across my nipples.

"You are going to learn that disobedience isn't in your best interest, Coraline. I will help you realize that very soon." His *upper lip curling, he pinched my nipples, twisting and pulling on both until I cried out in pain.*

Yet I closed my eyes as a series of vibrations tickled every muscle, driving me to the edge of the kind of intense cravings that I'd never be able to escape. Panting, I realized I was arching my back, no longer able to feel my legs. I felt his hot mouth engulfing one, replacing the anguish with utter pleasure.

Every sound he made was guttural, the deep bass resonating in my ears. As always, goosebumps appeared on my skin. I was so alive, more so than I'd ever felt in my life. I wrapped my hands around his wrists, holding myself in place as he brushed his lips to my other hardened bud, taking his time nipping and sucking, pushing me closer and closer to ecstasy.

"Mmm... Yes, oh, yes."

When he dragged his lips up to my throat, I stiffened. He bit down with enough force I moved onto my tiptoes. I could swear his teeth were sharp canines, ready to eat me alive. Seconds later, he pulled away, breathing a trail of hot air across my face.

"Look at me, Coraline," he commanded.

A smile crossed my face as I kept my eyes closed.

"I said. Look. At. Me."

His tone had changed completely, almost unrecognizable. Moaning, I opened my eyes slowly, gazing into his.

Gone were the gorgeous sapphire blue eyes I'd fallen into months before. They were now crimson, their vibrant hue shimmering in the darkness.

Gabriel fisted my hair, pulling me upright. When he captured my mouth, I pushed my hands against him, able to feel his hammering heart next to my palm. He held me that way for several minutes, exploring my mouth as his tongue swept from one side to the other. Only when he broke the embrace did I issue a single whimper.

"Lie down on the bed."

I knew this command I couldn't deny. As I backed away, I wanted to continue looking into his eyes, but he'd lowered his gaze, taking his time to unfasten his belt. Swallowing, I wasn't certain if the candlelight had been playing tricks on my mind or if the lightning had caused a crazy but gorgeous sheen. Either way, I knew he wasn't completely human.

He couldn't be.

I settled onto the bed, shoving a pillow under me, crushing my fingers around the soft bedding. My breathing remained ragged, my mind a huge blur. Was it possible? I bit back another whimper as he approached. When he slapped the folded belt in the air, the whooshing sound made me jump.

Then I closed my eyes once again, holding my breath in preparation of the exploding anguish.

As he brought down the thick strap several times in rapid succession, my mind continued to play tricks on me. But there was no immediate pain, only a heightened level of heat rushing into my system.

Gabriel delivered at least six more, one coming immediately after the other. I gasped, shoving my face into the comforter, doing everything I could to remain in position.

"My beautiful Coraline."

As the sound of his husky voice settled into my eardrums, a vision popped into my mind, one so incredible that it took my breath away.

It was at that moment I was forced to realize that the man I adored as well as hated, the same man who'd abducted me against my will wasn't human at all.

He was... Lycan.

"Oh!" I hissed, trying to swim up from the fog. My breathing remained difficult, my vision blurry. I tried to make sense of what had just gone through my mind. Had it been real? A wolf. In my mind, an image remained of the gorgeous black wolf I'd treated, his fur softer than I knew it should be. And his eyes, just as blue as... Gabriel's.

The man had awakened something in me, the kind of dark, delicious, and dirty need that was never satisfied. My mind remained a blur as I continued to envision the very moment that he'd taken me. Was it possible that I meant something to him other than the brutal, carnal acts we'd committed? The images remained vivid, as if they'd just happened. But was I remembering a dream?

Or just the reality of a nightmare?

No. No! Oh, God. I jerked up, blinking several times as ugly memories rushed into my mind. I'd been taken from my house. Terror ripped through me, almost stopping my heart from beating. As my vision finally cleared, I slowly turned my head, noticing a blind on a small window. What? I was in a plane? There was no way. When I lifted the blind, I shrank back, doing everything I could to keep from whimpering.

I'd been kidnapped and taken out of Louisiana.

Moose! Oh, God, no! He'd tried to protect me against the two men. The same two men that… Gabriel had told me would protect me. What the hell was going on? Almost panicking, I jerked my head in the other direction, barely able to keep a scream from erupting from my parched throat.

I noticed Gabriel first, his massive body lounging on another seat across the wide aisle. And Moose. He was happily lying under the man's legs as if he didn't have a care in the world. I wasn't certain whether to be incensed or grateful. I couldn't seem to stop shaking, also realizing that the same two men who'd drugged me were chatting only twenty feet away.

From what I could tell, I was on a luxurious private plane. I was sick to my stomach as another wave of memories flooded in. Two men had attempted to break into my house, both with automatic weapons in their hands.

Then there'd been the sound of gunfire.

They'd been gunned down. They were dead. My God.

And I'd been taken.

One of the assholes noticed I was awake, rising to his feet and jostling Gabriel. I unfastened my seatbelt, still woozy from the effects of the drug they'd shoved over my mouth. My wrists hurt like hell. As I rubbed them, I wanted nothing more than to crawl away, to find some hidden compartment to shelter myself in. Somewhere in my mind, what little was left of my ability to rationalize everything that occurred, I knew that wasn't going to be possible.

Gabriel was right in front of me, obviously in full command. He was always going to be there. Even if I'd been able to escape the men who'd captured me, he would have scoured the ends of the earth until he'd found me.

Then my punishment would be that much worse.

I watched as the powerful man shifted in his seat, slowly turning his head in my direction. He made no outward gestures at first, but I could tell by the gleam in his eyes that he was thrilled I was awake. After brushing his hand over Moose's head, something that intrigued as well as disgusted me, he rose to his feet, giving almost silent instructions to one of his goons before easing down in the seat next to me.

Shuddering, I tried to keep from looking in his eyes, but as they'd done from the moment I'd met him, they mesmerized me, yanking me into another dreamy state of mind. How could one man have that kind of effect on anyone?

Wolf.

Lycan.

Loup-garou.

I shook my head, trying to shake away the awful visions. My nerves remained on edge, enough so I continuously smoothed my hand down one of the few skirts I owned, trying to rid my palm of the sweat beaded across my skin. My efforts failed the moment he shifted in my direction.

"You're awake. How are you feeling?" he asked in the same throaty voice that always sent flutters into my heart.

I felt the pulse in my throat more so than normal, the hard thudding making it difficult to swallow. "Fine. I'm just fine."

The bastard chuckled, as if anything about the situation warranted a light response. He'd kidnapped me, for God's sake, taking me away from my home and business. I could hear Moose's slight snores and tried to take comfort in the fact the bastards hadn't hurt the only creature that had mattered to me in a long time. But it was hard, so tough that I remained lightheaded, uncertain how to react.

"Drink some water, Coraline."

Every time he said my name, butterflies almost consumed my stomach. I hated myself for that fact as much as my forced realization I'd allowed the man to fuck me.

Not once but twice.

And I'd enjoyed it.

God. What was wrong with me? My rebellious side hungered to find something sarcastic to say, the statement meant to keep him on edge, but at this point nothing came to mind. How could it? I was in a private jet flying to God knows where, all because he'd insisted I was in danger. But I was. Wasn't I? The bastards who'd broken one of my windows had seemed intent on taking me as well, one of the nasty men lunging toward me, snarling the entire time.

Then they were dead.

Gabriel exhaled, the deep sound filtering into my ears. He reached down to the table in front of me, wrapping his long, elegant fingers around the bottle of water then cracking the plastic top. I don't know why I watched his movements like a hawk, but it gave me some crazy kind of comfort. Maybe the side of me trying to protect myself wanted to make certain he didn't spike the bottle with another mind-altering drug.

Although he positioned the bottle directly in front of me, I didn't bother moving. After a few seconds, I sensed his patience waning. He finally took my hand into his, rubbing the rough pad of his finger across my palm before forcing me to hold the bottle in my hand.

"You need to hydrate. The effects of chloroform can linger."

He issued the words as if someone else had done the dirty deed. Maybe that was the reason I snapped, but my mind finally cleared, enough so my usual rough edge returned. "What the hell do you care? You instructed those assholes over there to kidnap me. Did that give you some kind of jollies? I know you're a sadistic man, but since I didn't fall into your arms like some wayward young girl, did that push against your masculinity?"

My glare only caused his expression to turn to amusement. God, I wanted nothing more than to rip out his eyeballs.

"In case the drug affected your memory, let me refresh it for you. Two men broke into your house attempting to kidnap you. What they would have done once they brought you to their destination is something I doubt you would have enjoyed."

"And what the hell are you doing?" I could barely spew the words, my throat was so dry. There was no other choice but to gulp down part of the water. After chugging almost half, I tried to catch my breath.

He took a deep breath, holding it as if keeping me in suspense was just another modus operandi. "While it's true that you've been taken against your will, I assure you that it's to save your life."

I'd always reacted without thinking and tonight was no exception. I tossed the entire remainder of the water into his face, recoiling in horror as soon as I'd realized what I'd done.

Gabriel blinked several times, finally shaking his head. Within seconds, one of the goons offered him a cloth to wipe his face. All I could think about was how he had the two men trained like seals. He took his time wiping away the remnants.

Then he grabbed both my wrists, pulling them into one hand. His eyes narrowed as he leaned over, his breathing ragged. "Listen to me, Coraline, because I don't want to have to tell this twice."

His eyes were entirely different than before, just like what I'd experienced in the dreams, the hint of crimson surrounding his irises. I pressed my back against the seat, struggling to get out of his hold. There was no chance. He was far too strong.

"I've told you that there are some very bad people hunting for you. They found you. They wouldn't have stopped until they had you in their clutches. I won't tell you the horrible things they were planning on doing to you. Yes, I took you away from your home, but because I need to protect you and nothing else."

Nothing else?

He'd entered my life like a freight train, refusing to be denied.

He'd fucked me like a wild animal.

He'd… seduced me into thinking I could trust him.

And he'd had the fucking nerve to act like he gave a damn about my dog.

I yanked my hands again, still failing to budge them an inch. "Just who are you protecting me from?"

Gabriel tilted his head, searching not just my eyes but my very soul. "I will tell you when necessary. We will be landing in Chicago soon. Rest until then."

Chicago. At least I knew where the hell I was being taken. "What then? What do you plan on doing to me?"

The way he leaned over was possessive in nature, the damn smile curling on his upper lip sending a wave of shivers all throughout my body. When our lips were only centimeters apart, a part of me wanted him to kiss me. "That will be determined by how you behave."

Behave. He actually believed I would obey anything he asked? No, he commanded? Not a snowball's chance in hell.

"One thing you will be required to do is follow my rules." He issued the words as if they would entice me.

"What rules?"

"They will be explained to you once we arrive. I suggest you keep in mind that failure to do so will result in harsh punishment."

I resisted laughing in his face.

When I jerked my hands again, he let go, allowing me to get as far away from him as possible.

He kept the smile on his face as he moved out of the seat. "I'll have another bottle of water brought to you. I suggest you drink the entire contents."

His suggestion felt more like another demand.

I couldn't seem to take my eyes off him as he walked down the wide aisle, talking to both his men. While I couldn't hear what they were saying, I knew by the way the two men glanced in my direction that I was the topic of the conversation. I hated the way my body constantly reacted to him, something I was going to avoid again at all costs.

Moose suddenly woke from his slumber, his tail thumping before he rose to his feet, ambling in my direction. As I wrapped my arms around his neck, I did what I could to keep tears from forming. I refused to allow the horrible man to know he was getting to me. When I closed my eyes, burying my head against the top of my pup's head, a single tear fell.

So many questions formed in my mind, but not all of them had to do with Gabriel's sudden appearance in my life.

My mother had come close to begging me to return to Louisiana. She never did anything without a reason.

That's what I needed to find out before it was too late.

CHAPTER 9

oraline

I had no idea what time it was other than that it was late, likely in the middle of the night. I never wore a watch and of course the two beefy goons hadn't stopped long enough to grab my phone. In fact, I had nothing with me other than the clothes on my back. I remained as far away from Gabriel as possible, Moose positioned on the seat between us in whatever brand of SUV the men had left at the airport. While I could see views of Chicago out the window, all that did was continue to cause chills to race down my spine.

I'd heard almost nothing after we'd landed at the airport, other than Gabriel instructing one of them to whisk me away to the vehicle, shoving me inside as if bullets were flying. At least Moose didn't seem alarmed by the activity, trotting along behind me until safely nestled inside. Now I clung to him as if the big, happy dog would be my lifesaver.

We'd ridden in silence for at least fifteen minutes.

"I'm certain you're hungry," Gabriel said in a quiet voice.

I fisted my hands, digging my nails into my skin. "Not in the least, but I'm certain Moose is. I guess your... *men* didn't think about bringing his food or anything else he's used to."

When he sighed, I dared glance in his direction. He continued to stare out the passenger window, the interstate lights providing an excellent view of his chiseled and clenched jaw. He was growing frustrated with me.

Too bad.

"No, Coraline. My soldiers were attempting to save your life. However, point taken. We will stop on the way so you can get your dog what he needs."

"My dog has a name, which you've already heard more than once." Soldiers. He used the term as if he and his men were in the middle of a war. Maybe that's exactly the way they lived their lives.

Gabriel smirked as he turned his head, taking his time and rubbing the back of Moose's neck. "Yes, he does."

The three words were said with no inflection, but they seemed to mean so much to him.

"What's open this time of night, some dirty supermarket?" I knew I was pressing my luck, which is what I always did when I was nervous.

Chuckling, he leaned forward, providing directions to the man driving. When he sat back, he turned his full attention to me. "This is Chicago. I assure you that you can find almost anything you desire all hours of the day and night." Why was every word he issued dripping with innuendoes?

I didn't respond, returning my attention to the road. Maybe ten minutes later, the driver exited the highway, heading into a well-lit area. I craned my neck, finally noticing what appeared to be an outdoor mall. Sure enough, there was a pet store located within, the bright lights indicating it remained open. How in the hell would a man like Gabriel Dupree have any idea about pet stores?

After the driver pulled into a spot, he stared into the rearview mirror. "Do you want us to remain here, boss?"

"Yeah, that should be fine. I doubt we'll have an issue at this point." Gabriel exited the car, moving behind the SUV then opening my door. "Let's go."

"Moose is coming with us."

His reaction wasn't what I would have expected. "Of course."

My legs were shaky the moment I planted one foot on the pavement. Gabriel seemed to sense I'd yet to fully recover from being drugged, wrapping his arm around my elbow.

While I wanted to jerk it away, it was obvious I needed the support. Moose stayed by my side as we walked in. The garish lights were no different than in New York or Louisiana; however, the store appeared much larger. Maybe there was someone inside who could help me get away.

The near silence in the building was a clear indication that there were no customers this time of night. A knot formed in my stomach as true despair settled in.

"How am I supposed to buy anything? I don't have my wallet or any cash." I grabbed a cart as I waited for his answer.

"Purchase whatever you need, Coraline. I'm taking care of the bill." He started to head toward the register then stopped, shifting his full attention to me once again. "I think you know this, but if you try and ask anyone for help, you will only be putting them in danger."

So generous and so dominating. I shuddered just hearing his words.

I moved down the first aisle, trying to control my breathing. All I could think about was the last kiss, the way he'd captured my mouth.

The way he'd taken me roughly, exciting every cell in my body. I gripped the handle of the cart, using enough force that as I stared down at my hands, all I could concentrate on was how white my knuckles had become.

"Are you certain you're alright, Coraline?"

When the man dared to press his hand against the small of my back, I almost screamed at him to stop using my name. And to stop touching me. But the ugly truth was that I didn't want him to. I craved his touch, the way he made me feel deep inside. No. This was crazy. He'd kidnapped me against my will. He'd… maybe he'd saved my life.

Every move was perfunctory as I selected Moose's favorite dog food, allowing my captor to grab the forty-pound bag from my hands. Maybe that's the moment my rebellious side returned. Within a few minutes, I'd moved from one aisle to another, dropping treats, toys, and a new leash into the basket, so many items that the basket was overflowing. However, I didn't stop there. I headed straight for the dog beds, selecting the most expensive and largest one I could find.

Price was no object. Right? He would pay dearly for taking me away from my life.

"That should do it. Moose deserves to be comfortable, even in his captor's house." I glared at Gabriel, expecting him to remind me about following the rules.

He didn't.

Gabriel didn't say a word the entire time, even gently pushing me aside and rolling the basket toward the cash register. The young girl eyed us carefully as she rang up the items. I had a feeling she would have called the police if Moose hadn't jumped up on the counter, happily receiving the biscuit she'd offered him.

When we were safely nestled inside, the packages carefully positioned in the back, I couldn't rid myself of a cold chill. As the driver rolled out of the parking lot, I realized I was more exhausted than I'd been in my life. While I did my best to keep my eyes open, it became almost impossible. As I closed them, I felt Moose's head pressing against my thigh. All I wanted to do was curl up in bed, pretending this had never happened.

Maybe I was just dreaming. Maybe I'd wake up and...

Jerking awake, I almost immediately panicked. "What is..." Then everything came crashing back all over again. I was still in the back of the SUV, but it was parked in what looked like an underground garage. Only seconds later, I realized I was alone. Moose! I slammed my hand against the window, scanning the area. Moose remained right by Gabriel's side as he talked with one of his soldiers, the other moving toward them, shaking his head as he did so.

I was clearly able to see all three men were armed, casually discussing whatever the hell they found necessary in the middle of the night. After a few seconds, I couldn't stand it any longer, getting out of the vehicle.

Gabriel snapped his head in my direction, obviously dismayed I'd dared to exit without his permission. He issued a few additional words before walking in my direction.

His grip on my arm was entirely different than it had

been in the store, his fingers digging into my skin. "You should have waited inside."

"Why? Are there bad men hiding in the shadows?"

"Stop fighting me." He pulled me away from the vehicle, refusing to allow me any chance to pull away. When I noticed an elevator up ahead, I realized this must be where he lived. Maybe I'd expected a mansion somewhere or a full compound with soldiers lining the exterior. He thrust me inside, making certain Moose was right beside me.

"I don't plan on it."

When the doors closed, he turned to face me, smashing his hands against the cold steel wall. He crowded my space, lowering his head until whatever exotic aftershave he was wearing filtered into my nostrils. Where the scent had made me intoxicated before, this time it made me nauseated.

"I'm losing patience with you, Coraline. While I understand you're exhausted, uncertain of what the hell is going on, and obviously furious that I interrupted your life, it's time you accept my control."

"You make it sound so easy, Gabriel. As if I'm the kind of woman who wanted someone to invade her life. That's just not the case."

I hated the way he smiled with every statement of defiance I made, as if he knew some burning secret I was holding deep inside. "You seem to forget that I've seen the woman inside as well as every inch of her dazzling exterior. You can't hide from me. You will be punished for your infractions."

"What infractions? Acting pissed off because I was drugged?"

His breathing became labored, the guttural sound he made filling the space.

I darted my eyes back and forth, my lower lip quivering. When he dropped his head another two inches, I didn't realize until it was too late that I'd arched my back, brushing my lips across his. When I jerked away, he pressed his heated fingers against my face, flexing them open and holding me in place. He raked his gaze down my face to my neck before brushing his thumb across my lips.

"I don't want you," I whispered, no longer recognizing my voice.

"You're lying to me, my sweet Southern girl, but you'll learn soon enough that you can never hide anything from me. I will know."

When he exhaled, my legs quivered. I had a feeling he would have gone further if the elevator didn't slowly shift to a full stop.

Leaning back, he rubbed his knuckle under the same eye where I'd shed a tear, acting as if he was concerned about me. Then he took me by the hand, leading me into a corridor. The gray walls were barely illuminated by sconces, the shadowed glow giving an ominous appearance. The windowless atmosphere seemed perfect for a man of his... stature.

I should have guessed he'd take me to the end of the hall. Only the best for Gabriel Dupree. Right?

While I suspected he wanted a reaction to his glorious penthouse, I was too tired to care. I was surprised that all of the packages purchased at the pet store had been placed inside, even able to chuckle when Moose began digging to find a new favorite toy in one of the bags.

Gabriel locked the door behind us then proceeded to walk around me, removing his jacket and tossing it across one of the two leather couches. He unbuttoned his shirtsleeves, rolling them to his elbows before bothering to address me.

"This is my home, which means it's your home as well. You are free to move about the condo, but you are not under any circumstances to go outside that door without permission."

"What about walking Moose? He does need that a few times a day."

He tilted his head, closing his eyes, obviously prepared for my question. "I'll assign one of my men to expect your call on a daily basis and the reason."

"So, I'm going to be guarded at all times?"

"Yes, you are. Would you like something to drink?"

Every word since leaving the pet store was so businesslike, his personality even darker than I'd experienced in Thibodaux. "I... Sure."

He moved toward me once again, searching through the bags until he found the two bowls I'd selected. Then he hoisted the bag of dog food over his shoulder, giving me another stern look before walking away. Moose trailed behind him like a dutiful pup, not understanding that he was in the presence of true evil.

I folded my arms across my stomach, aching inside but I followed, determined to try to get some answers. When I walked into his kitchen, I was struck by two things. He was washing both bowls, then filling one with water. Next, he found a pair of scissors in one of his drawers, opening the dog food then grabbing a cup from his cabinet and filling the massive bowl to the rim. The amount of food was far too much, but I didn't want to stop him.

Actually, I enjoyed the way he'd adapted to Moose being around, even though I suspected he'd never had a pet before in his life.

What gave me even more pause was the fact his kitchen was... incredible. Colorful. Lived in. There were two vibrant pieces of art on the walls, the colors of magenta, scarlet, tangerine, and the most gorgeous cerulean blue creating a sensual environment. There were several small appliances as well as a tall pepper grinder in wood. Several of the cabinet doors were all glass, the items inside beautiful yet only some of them matching. There were even towels placed haphazardly on handles of the larger appliances.

Either he had messy help, or he really used the space, which I found difficult to believe.

He'd already placed the bowls on the floor, standing back and watching Moose's instant reaction with his hands on his hips. Then he grabbed two glasses from one of the cabinets, finding an open bottle of red wine under another. I was struck by how odd it seemed that he was comfortable in the space.

After pouring the two glasses, he merely slid one across the counter, chuckling softly.

"What's wrong?" His question seemed rhetorical, but I knew he meant from seeing my reaction.

"Do you cook?"

He narrowed his eyes before answering. "Yes, I do. Actually, cooking is one of the few things that relaxes me. Does that seem so strange to you?"

"Yes, it does. I would have thought a man of your obvious wealth would dine out almost every night."

After swirling his glass, allowing beads of wine to slide dangerously close to the rim of the glass, he took a sip before answering. Several things surprised me about the man, including the way he closed his eyes while tasting the wine, enjoying every moment of the flavor. He swallowed then walked closer, leaning against the counter.

"While I enjoy sharing a delicious meal with a beautiful companion from time to time, I find that most restaurants are overpriced for what they serve. In addition, it is often irresponsible for me to dine out."

"Irresponsible? Why?"

His eyes lit up as he laughed. "I've had a target on my head for years. I refuse to allow any innocent lives to be placed in danger."

The statement struck me as farfetched. "Interesting. Does that mean you have a conscience?"

"That remains to be seen. I suspect there are some who would call me the devil. Come. I think Moose can handle finishing on his own."

I found myself following him again, returning to the living room. While he sat down on one of the couches, I headed for the bank of windows, staring out at the Chicago skyline. It wasn't that much different than New York, just as dense and overpopulated. I finally took a sip of wine, surprised how good it tasted considering all I'd been through.

"Would you like me to make us a late dinner?" he asked a full two minutes later.

"I'm not hungry but thank you." Why was I thanking him? For what?

"You will need to eat tomorrow whether you're hungry or not."

"Don't treat me like a child, Gabriel. I've been taking care of myself for a very long time." While I heard the sharpness in my voice, I honestly didn't care if he punished me.

"Understood. Then don't act like one."

"Do you?" I asked as I swung around to face him. "How could you since you don't know anything about me? Anyone can find academic or employment records. Hell, my guess is you have enough connections to know how little I have in my bank account. But you don't... know me."

He sat on the edge of the couch, placing his glass on the table. "That is very true, but something I would like to change."

"Why, Gabriel? Why? You can have any woman in the world, yet you came to Louisiana to save my life. I don't get it. I just don't..." I allowed the words to trail off. I wasn't getting anywhere with the man.

"The why is irrelevant at this point in time, Coraline. I think we need to establish some ground rules."

"Why not?"

Exhaling, he gave me a stern look as if I'd already been a bad girl. "Are you going to listen to me?"

"Sure. Yes. I mean yes."

He folded his hands together, placing his arms on his knees. "While you might not believe I know you, I am well aware of your thoughts as well as your plans to try and escape. Doing so will endanger your life and you should know by now that there is nowhere you can go where I won't find you, especially in a city that you've never been to before. However, if you manage to find a way, I assure you that the kind of punishment you receive will be swift and very harsh. Do you understand me?"

"Yes, Gabriel. I do. Is there anything else you demand of me?" The thirty minutes spent at the pet store with another side of him faded away. He was nothing but a possessive bastard.

"You will do anything and everything I request."

"You mean that you demand."

There was no doubt I'd frustrated him. What did I care? He'd provided no answers to his actions. Maybe he never planned on telling me why I was his prisoner.

"Have it your way, Coraline. Undress."

"What?"

"I think you heard me." He grabbed his drink, easing back onto the sofa and crossing one leg over the other.

"You're such a son of a bitch."

"You do seem to know me. That being said, I'm going to spank you."

How could the man act like he cared about me one minute then resort to this? I wanted to refuse, but I had the distinct feeling he'd rip off my clothes, leaving me with nothing to wear. After placing the wine on the coffee table, a large slice of nerves kicked in as I pulled my shirt over my head, fighting to kick off my shoes at the same time. I hated the fact I suddenly felt shy around him. My reaction was silly. I closed my eyes, tossing the material then reaching for the button on my jeans.

I counted to ten then to fifty, trying to calm myself as I dragged the dense denim down my legs and to the floor. When I stepped out of them, I crossed my arms over my chest in some involuntary act of protection.

"Everything, Coraline."

The smoothness of his voice before had taken on an entirely different tone, darker and richer.

Hungrier.

The pulse thudded in my neck as I turned slightly, struggling to unfasten my bra. By the time I'd managed to remove the tight confines, his breathing had changed entirely. The sound wasn't just labored or ragged. There was a raspy quality to it that didn't sound human.

A lump formed in my throat as I opened one eye, making certain I hadn't fallen into a different kind of nightmare.

His eyes were mere slits, his chest rising and falling rapidly. I'd never seen such intensity in any man before from watching me undress. Gabriel acted like I was a feast being trussed on a silver platter.

Maybe that's all I was to him.

I couldn't seem to stop shaking as I lowered my panties, almost losing my balance because of the increasing nerves swarming my system. The bastard had placed his elbow on his bent knee, taking his time rubbing his index finger back and forth across his lips as he swirled his drink with the other hand.

"Turn around," he commanded.

"I'm not a toy or some stupid model."

"No, you are neither. You're much more important to me."

There was no reason for his words to strike me the way they did. Maybe the man did care for me. Nope. I wasn't going to believe it.

After doing what he demanded, I stood rigidly with my arms against my sides.

He took another two swigs of his drink before placing it on the table. When he stood, I sucked in my breath, watching in fascination as well as horror as he began to unfasten his belt.

"Turn around and place your hands on the window."

The commanding tone of his voice echoed in my ears. I stared at him for a few seconds before doing exactly as he asked, planting both hands on the slick glass. *No one can see. No one can see.* My thoughts didn't make me feel any better.

"Very good. Spread your legs."

Gabriel had walked closer, and I was able to see his reflection in the crystal clear glass as he slowly pulled the thick leather strap from his belt loops. My mouth was completely dry, my throat starting to close. I parted my legs, no longer able to look at him.

But I could feel him.

I could smell his desire as much as my own, the scent floating into the air between us. I was tense, every nerve in my body on edge, yet I still held some crazy kind of excitement as if I was going to enjoy this. I dared one more time to look for him in the glass, able to see enough of his reflection that I was forced to hold my breath. He ran the belt through his fingers for at least twenty seconds, caressing the leather.

My heart racing, I did what I could to brace myself for the horrible event, but the moment he swished the belt in the air, I couldn't hold back a ragged moan.

The cracking sound filtered into my ears, almost ringing although that was impossible. The shock of having him spank me like a misguided child allowed the first slap to fade away.

But when he issued a second then a third, my nerves exploded from a slight sting morphing almost immediately into utter blistering pain.

"Oh!" I screamed, my body folding toward the window. Panting, I lowered my head, immediately creating steam on the glass surface from my heated breath. As he smacked me four additional times, my legs started to give way. There was no describing the horrible sensations, pain that heightened into anguish.

After giving me two more, the bastard had the nerve to brush his fingers from one side of my bottom to the other. Did he really think caressing my skin would take away the discomfort?

"You need to listen to me at all times," he said quietly.

"Because you know better," I huffed, immediately regretting saying anything.

"Because I might be able to keep you alive."

The thought was more riveting than when he'd said it before, driving into the farthest reaches of my mind. What if he was right? What if men would continue hunting me down, determined to finish what they'd started? I closed my eyes, pressing my face against the cool glass as he continued the spanking, one hard smack coming after the other. Within seconds, my pussy was clenching over and over again, juice trickling down my legs.

The moment was just as insane as before, my desire overruling the horrible experience. I took shallow breaths, trying to clear my mind but it was no use. As I scratched my nails down the window, he cracked his belt across my upper thighs.

"God!" I screamed, unable to control my body. I kicked out, shifting back and forth. When he placed his hand on the small of my back, a sudden calm swept through me. His actions left me tingling all over, my need for him increasing. Nothing made any sense. A laugh bubbled to the surface as he brought the belt down several more times. At that point, the agony had turned into something else entirely.

I was wired, my body ripped by the electricity we shared. My nipples were hard as diamonds, my breasts aching. I wanted this man more than I would ever be able to explain. After at least five more, he crowded my space, rubbing his fingers up and down my spine.

"You will learn to obey me, Coraline. Doing so will simply take time." He leaned over, kissing the side of my neck. It was no use pulling away from him. He had me right where he wanted.

And yes, I craved more.

After caressing my bottom for several seconds, he ran his finger down the crack of my ass. I'd never forget the pain or the ecstasy as he'd taken me in my forbidden hole. No man had ever fucked me there. But I knew he'd do it again.

Sinful.

Delicious.

Amazing.

The three words played over in my mind as I continued to create steam across the window's surface.

Gabriel wrapped his hand around my hair, nipping my earlobe.

Then he pulled away, backing very slowly in his return to the couch.

I was caught off guard, biting back a whimper. While the pain lingered, that no longer mattered. I simply wanted him. His rough touch. His hot breath.

His wet kisses.

As crazy as it sounded in my mind, I needed the man.

"Turn around," he commanded as he sat down on the couch.

I did what I could to gather my breath, inching around to face him. Even the shadows couldn't hide his carnal expression. The man planned on ravaging me.

Then he beckoned me with a single finger. He looked like a famished man, ravenous to tear into something, shredding with his sharp teeth.

"I assure you that by following my rules, you will learn the true meaning of the word ecstasy."

Was he kidding? Did he expect me to buy that bullshit? My mind swooned all over again, two sides fighting deep inside. I wanted to hate him, but I wasn't certain I would be able to any longer.

Swallowing, I found myself obeying him, taking deliberate steps. When I was only a few feet away, he opened his legs, yanking me the rest of the way. I tingled all over as he took his time rolling the rough pads of his fingers up and down both legs. I was unnerved how incredible the sensations were, creating a wicked series of vibrations.

When he forced me onto my knees on his lap, I was forced to clamp my hands around his shoulders to keep from sliding off. He was rock hard, but I could tell he had other things in mind, at least for now.

Gabriel pressed his face against my stomach then licked around my bellybutton. I couldn't stop trembling, every nerve standing on end from his touch alone. He took his time, dragging his tongue back and forth across my skin, leaving me wet and aching.

Panting, I lolled my head, watching his facial expressions as they morphed into a darker side.

He dug his fingers into my hips, pulling me closer as he lowered his head. I pushed hard against his shoulders, everything starting to become fuzzy. When I felt his tongue swirling around my clit, I couldn't hold back a whimper, the effect instantaneous.

A nervous laugh bubbled to my lips, the sound ridiculous but with every swipe of his rough tongue, I was pushed into the most satisfying moment of bliss. The way he took his time sucking on my tender tissue put me in a spin of emotions. No man had ever licked me this way, learning what I enjoyed by the sounds of my breathing alone.

Stars in vibrant colors floated in front of my eyes. I could tell my nails were digging into his jacket as my pulse skyrocketed. Every guttural sound he made only fueled the explosive nirvana. I was dragged into a surreal moment, my body swaying even with his tight hold.

"So beautiful," he muttered, growling before burying his head into my wetness, licking ferociously.

"My... Yes, I..." Another nervous laugh left my throat as I threw my head back, studying the cathedral ceiling. I was lightheaded, every muscle tingling even more than before. There was something so erotic about the way he slid his hands around to my buttocks, kneading both before slipping his thumbs between my legs. That was almost all I could take. As soon as he pressed them just past my swollen folds, an orgasm swept up from the center of my core, blasting into me with enough force I bucked against him.

His hold only tightened. I wasn't going anywhere.

"Oh. My. God!" As the climax erupted like a tidal wave, he grunted like some wild animal, shaking his head back and forth. It was almost impossible to catch my breath as a single climax turned into a rolling wave of them, each one more intense than the one before.

"Come again," he demanded, switching the angle until he was able to thrust his tongue deep inside.

And I did, as if I couldn't ignore his commands.

The stars had turned into dancing shimmers trickling down, my heart hammering to the point echoes bounced from one side to the other. When I finally stopped shaking, I lowered my head, uncertain if I'd ever be able to think clearly again.

Gabriel brushed his lips back and forth across one leg then the other before lifting his head, his eyes nothing but dark pools. When he eased me off his knees, I was shocked how shaky I remained, still lost in the beautiful moment.

As I backed away, I slid my finger across the seam of my mouth, my body still quivering. He had such a powerful impact on me even though I'd wanted to rip out his eyes only moments before. When he wrapped his long fingers around his glass, a smile curled across my lips. The moment he brought the rim to his lips, dragging his tongue from one side to the next, I countered by sliding my finger into my mouth.

I didn't recognize the temptress in me, the realization I was sucking on my finger pulling me into another darkened state. There was dancing amusement in his eyes, and he lifted his glass in appreciation before crossing his legs. The man was obviously so comfortable in his own skin.

The thought brought me somewhat back to reality. What if he was some kind of shifter? Another wave of anxiety did as much damage as the electricity had just seconds earlier. I lowered my gaze, reaching for my wine then walking toward the window. Standing in front of a wall of glass felt filthy, although there wasn't a chance anyone could see me.

Dozens of other questions rushed into my mind but why bother asking him? He would only tell me points of information when he was ready. I leaned against the glass, taking several sips of my wine. I'd never felt so drained in my life.

I didn't realize Gabriel had approached until I felt him prying the wine from my fingers, hearing the sound of glass hitting glass. Then he scooped me into his arms, holding me against his chest.

"What are you doing?" I mumbled and pressed my hand against him.

"Taking you to bed."

I glared at him with as much raw emotion as I could muster.

"Alone," he growled.

As he walked up a flight of stairs, I was forced to loll my head against his shoulder. He seemed effortless in his actions, heading into a room and leaning over until he was able to turn down the bed. After gently placing me onto the sheets then covering me with a thick comforter, he stood back, staring down at me for a full thirty seconds before turning away.

"Take care of Moose for me, will you? He's really all I have left I care about. He's… my… baby."

CHAPTER 10

abriel

Her baby.

Coraline's request resonated with me more than it should. Within seconds, she was fast asleep, Moose slipping around me in order to jump across her legs. In his mouth was one of the toys we'd just purchased, the plush alligator almost as if he'd selected a symbol, providing me with a clear statement.

Don't fuck with my mommy dog or I'll eat you alive.

While he kept his eyes on the man standing over his mommy, his tail thumped in a perfect rhythm. Her protector. That's the role he'd assumed, although he was no match for the assholes who'd attempted to take her away from me twice.

I turned out the light and closed the door, heading down the stairs slowly, my thoughts drifting to the time spent in the damn pet store. As a laugh bubbled to the surface, I rubbed my jaw, forced to admit I'd enjoyed the experience, including the dog's excitement at receiving new toys.

The taste of her lingered in my mouth, her scent covering my face, filling my nostrils. She'd tasted of honey, only sweeter. I'd wanted more but could sense just how distraught she'd become. I dragged my tongue across my teeth, my cock aching to the point of madness. Goddamn, what the woman did to me. My chest tightened, making it difficult to breathe. I bucked forward, snarling as my beast rushed to the surface.

Take her.

Use her.

Mate with her.

The words burned into my mind, my wolf clawing at my insides, his hunger uncontrollable.

"Not yet," I snarled, pushing my hand against my chest, pain tearing through me, desire building all over again. Punishing her had created additional longing, my sadistic thoughts bridging the surface.

As I started to shake, I was shocked just how hard the rut hit me, forcing me against the wall. There'd been no warning, no pretense. I'd never experienced anything so powerful in my life. My body's reaction was a reminder that half of me had been forced to live as an animal, my primal needs overpowering any humanity I'd developed. All I wanted was to feast and fuck, my wolf prepared to refuse anything else.

I closed my eyes, fighting the effects. It took several minutes to get my urges under control. I took several gasping breaths, angry with myself. I was losing my ability to decide when to shift.

And when to take her.

Fuck. Fuck. Fuck!

However, there was no longer any doubt that she was my mate.

There was no turning back. Curse or no curse, she now belonged to me.

As I finished walking down the stairs, I allowed my anger to replace my desire. The bastards had gotten too close too quickly. I needed a clear head in order to focus on business as well as determining how best to deal with everything my father had told me. I also needed to think through what I was going to do with Coraline over the next few days. Bringing her with me had never been on the agenda, although I hadn't planned a damn thing about meeting her either. Now that she was in my possession, that's almost all I could think about.

Hissing, I grabbed my wine, heading toward the same spot where she'd been standing, still able to see her face in the reflection.

She'd looked at me with such repulsion, refusing to give in or realize she had no choice but to come with me. However, I wasn't the savior I'd claimed to be. There would be no fairytale ending or romance that we could hold onto. I'd read enough of her thoughts, had sensed her continuing fear. I was enraged at the circumstances, although my possessive side wouldn't have it any other way.

I also remained furious with my father, unable to understand why he'd handled the legend the way he had. Everything hinged on what I would learn when the information arrived.

If he remained a man of his word.

I brushed my index finger across my lips, still able to feel hers. Then I rubbed the tip roughly, moving it back and forth brutally until pain shot to my jaw. I wanted to feel something, anything. I needed to touch her sinewy skin as she writhed underneath me. I loved to feel her hot breath skipping along my skin as she moaned from the pure pleasure I was providing.

A deep exhale rushed up from the throat, draining the air from my lungs. I lifted my hand, watching in disgust as well as burning excitement as my muscles and bones changed, my knuckles popping then retracting, my fingers lengthening then becoming the size needed for massive paws.

That of a dog.

That of a wolf.

How I wanted my beast to be free to enjoy the darkness of night, the fresh scents of the forest.

And the hunt.

As my body began to shake, claws starting to pop away from my skin, I made myself close my eyes, doing everything in my power to shove aside the creature that had been forced on me. It wasn't working, my legs turning numb as the beast had the audacity to claw its way to the surface. A growl threatened to give me away, but I found it impossible to ignore.

My God, time was running out. After snapping my head toward the stairs, I clenched my fist, digging the tips of my claws into my skin until I was able to draw blood. Not yet. Not fucking yet. I stormed away from the window, doing everything I could to shove my wolf aside. His anger was as significant as mine, but I knew at some point his power would win out.

When I was finally able to get my beast under control, I gulped down the remainder of my glass of wine.

Then I reached for hers. At least alcohol soothed my bouts of rage, helping with my control. How long would that last? As I thought about what little I had learned about Coraline, I remembered one odd thought she'd had that I'd caught.

Her mother.

She was questioning why her mother had insisted on her return. My mate's curiosity was well founded and worth investigating. All in good time. Tomorrow it would be vital to establish a protocol of handling the woman I owned.

It was only a matter of time before another attempt was made to take her from me. This time I'd be ready.

Then the fuckers would pay.

* * *

Morning.

A rebirth.

The time when even the darkest spirits succumbed to their need for rest.

Sadly, I was even more on edge than I'd been the night before. My instinct continued to sweep through me, a reminder that time was running short. I'd left her one of my tee shirts, in exchange for the clothes I'd ruined. It would be necessary to purchase the items she needed soon enough.

Moose had found me in my office, bounding in as if he'd known me his entire life. In his eyes I could sense his intelligence, accepting that I was the alpha. I allowed him to hear a slight hint of my wolf's growl, which seemed to delight him. He pressed his head against my leg then clawed my thigh. The pup had a way of making me smile.

"Good morning, boy. How did you and your mama sleep?" His entire backside had wiggled as he'd approached, the little whimpers he'd made providing a moment of levity. When he moved in between my legs, I wasn't equipped to provide what the boy obviously needed. "I guess I'll need to take you out for a walk. Huh? I think you'd like that." When I scrunched the skin behind his ears, I sensed her presence.

Coraline stood in the doorway with her arms folded, a leash dangling from one hand, her face carrying the same defiance as the night before. At least she appeared well rested since several hours had passed.

"Have you owned dogs before?" she asked.

The question made me laugh. Soon, she would learn the truth as to why my parents had never allowed it. "I asked my father for one when I was seven. He told me that big boys didn't need props and that I should walk the world alone. Doing so would help build my resolve."

Her face fell. "That's… terrible. Just terrible. No wonder you turned out to be a…"

"You can say it, Coraline. Use whatever phrase you'd like. I assure you that it won't hurt my feelings."

"I couldn't care less about your feelings."

"Then why stop?"

She walked closer before answering. "While my parents were very strict, they allowed me the freedom of asking questions and experiencing almost anything I wanted as long as I accepted the responsibility for doing so. That included being able to speak freely around them. Do you know what that taught me? Respect. I assure you that when I have something to say that you need to hear, I will tell you." She clipped the leash in place, pulling Moose away purposely. "Now, what do I need to do in order to be able to walk my dog in this freaking city?"

"Why don't I walk with you?"

"Does that mean I can say no?"

I gave her a harsh look before moving toward her.

"Aren't you going to take your gun with you? Oops, darn. Mine must be in my purse somewhere in another state."

As I walked closer, I took the leash out of her hand. "While I have many enemies in this town, none of them are stupid enough to make an attempt during a busy morning in the heart of Chicago."

"Let me guess. They would rather sneak up on you at a restaurant, just like what happens to the mob in the movies."

"Coraline, no matter what you've read about my family, I run a very profitable and influential business here in Chicago. I've worked very hard to achieve success."

"So you're one of the good guys. I'll keep that in mind when you win another charity award. However, I'm certain the various news outlets would enjoy hearing how you kidnapped me. What about the rednecks from back home? Have they found their way to such a grand city?"

Rednecks. I found the word interesting for her to use. She was doing everything in her power to goad me. I refused to give her the satisfaction of a reaction. "There is no sight of them yet. But I assure you that they will come very soon. Fortunately, I will sense their arrival."

"See. What is that?"

"What are you talking about?" As we stepped into the elevator, she backed away from me.

"You say things like you'll know about something or you'll sense it. How? Are you superhuman? Are you from another planet?"

I laughed, enjoying the banter for a change. "Let's just say I've spent far too much time around unscrupulous men and women."

"I have no doubt you have."

Moose remained in front of her, wagging his tail and whining. She purposely looked away, stroking his head.

She'd expected that I was going to drag her onto the street. I did enjoy the look on her face when I walked with her out onto the third-floor atrium. She stopped short, slowly turning around, finally a look of happiness crossing her face. "You are full of surprises. Aren't you? This is gorgeous."

"This is actually one of the reasons I purchased the condo. I enjoy greenery, shrubs, and flowers. By the way, you can allow him off the leash."

"I didn't bring any bags with me to clean up afterwards."

Her casual nature created vibrations in my system. "They have pet waste stations located throughout the area. You'll see them."

"Now, I'm more than curious. Why don't you just purchase a house? You could have an actual yard with a garden. Butterflies. Birds. A dog." She walked further into the expansive room, heading toward one of the small bridges leading over a body of water.

"I've thought about it. However, I work long hours. The drive in would kill me, let alone I doubt an animal would thrive in my presence."

"Hmmm... You own a company, yet you follow normal rules of running an office?"

She had a lilt in her voice. "My partner and I own Dupree Enterprises, although it is a subsidiary of my family's corporation. To answer your question, I have ethics with regard to business. It's important that our employees see their managers and the owners working right alongside them, not cutting any corners."

"Hmmm... I'm impressed."

"I'll take that as a compliment."

After watching Moose for a few minutes, she turned to face me. "Let's recap the situation, Gabriel. You took me against my will, even though you had your men save my life from the same kind of assholes a wolf tore apart the night before. You insisted on leaving Louisiana quickly, which meant something else must have occurred that you haven't told me about. Now, I'm in another state with nothing to my name. No clothes. No toiletries. No phone. No money. What are you going to do with me? You owe me an explanation because I don't think you're just some sick wacko intent on cutting me into little pieces, using them as trophies. If you were, I doubt Moose would have bonded with you. Even worse, you have blue eyes the exact same color as the wolf that I brought into my clinic. Do you want to tell me how that's possible?"

Her tenacity continued to excite me.

"We'll take care of getting you everything you need this morning, except for a phone. I can't risk you telling anyone about where you are."

"I don't know anybody. I hadn't been in Louisiana long enough to make any friends and I doubt the few I've made in New York would give a shit. Yet, you already know that. Who else am I going to call? That stupid sheriff? Not a chance. And you ignored my real question."

Her suspicions were increasing. It was only a matter of time before I'd need to share what would soon happen to her and her life. I'd hoped to avoid it for at least a few days. "I'm no animal expert, but I do know that wolves have different color eyes just like humans, so what you experienced is possible. While that may seem like a coincidence to you, I have no other explanation."

As Moose came running in our direction, she shook her head several times. "Fine, but I don't believe in coincidences. I guess we'll just see if the wolf that protected me shows up in the middle of Chicago. Will you call it a coincidence then? What else happened in Thibodaux, Gabriel? Tell me. If you really want me to abide by your rules, then I need to understand why."

I thought about what I should tell her, if anything. There was no other choice. "My room at the hotel I was staying at was ransacked, the contents ripped apart."

She took a deep breath. "What you're saying is that they were obviously from the same group as the men who attacked me. Right?"

"I don't know for certain, but I suspect as much. What I do know is that whoever they are were sending a warning that I thought best to pay attention to."

"Funny. You don't strike me as the kind of man to back down to anyone, especially with your soldiers here. Let me guess. You have hundreds of them."

"Yes, you are correct. But I learned a long time ago that when you decide to go into battle, you make certain that you have all your resources available. I wasn't prepared in Louisiana."

She shook her head slowly. "Battle. While you think that I don't understand any of what is going on, you underestimate me. You might run a legitimate business, which is what all mafia families do these days, but underneath everything, you're a dangerous, ruthless man. That's something you've already admitted to me. Whatever business you have on the side—drugs, weapons, extortion, blackmail—that's why I'm here. Does my mother have something to do with this, or my father, wherever the hell he is? Am I payment for something? A terrible deed?"

"What an interesting imagination you have."

"Don't do that. Don't you dare do that."

Now I was getting more than just impatient with her; however, it was apparent I needed to find out about her ancestry. That might explain why she'd been targeted so quickly. "We're finished with this conversation, Coraline. That will have to do for now. Shower, then we'll take care of purchasing you everything you need, including additional clothes."

"What I need are answers as well as the truth."

"What you need is to accept that you now belong to me. There is no alternative, no ability to return to the life you led before. However, I will make certain you are well cared for."

"Oh, my God," she hissed. "You're serious. Well cared for? You are a true pig, not just a violent criminal. Come on, Moose. It's starting to stink in here."

As she gathered her dog, walking past me and heading to the elevators, another destructive instinct settled into my system, my senses on overdrive.

The person responsible for initiating the attack on my family was close. No matter what I had to endure, I would hunt the man down.

Perhaps the curse had left out several significant details.

Soon I would alter the legend.

The Dupree family would never be extinguished.

"Where are we going?" Coraline asked as she peered out the window of my Mercedes, appearing as uncomfortable as usual around me.

Her fresh scent lingered in my nostrils, the fragrance keeping my cock fully aroused.

"I know a women's clothing store you might like. From there we'll go to a drug store," I said casually as I glanced over. She'd remained silent after our conversation in the atrium, refusing to even look in my direction. While she continued to push my buttons, creating a carnal need even stronger than before, I'd managed up to this point to keep my emotions out of it. That alone could push me into a shift. I had to maintain a balance of sorts, unfeeling enough to manage my wolf while attempting to get her to trust me.

That was no easy feat.

"You think of everything," she muttered, obviously not impressed in the least.

As I pulled into the parking lot of a small but high-end mall, she laughed softly under her breath. My hand remained tightly woven around the steering wheel until I'd found a spot that would allow me to keep my eye on it while she was shopping. Her insistence that Moose come along for the ride could prove to be difficult to handle.

The rules would be discussed in their entirety when we returned.

"What about Moose?" she asked when she climbed out of the car.

"He should be fine in the car."

"Then the windows need to be partially rolled down. You're lucky it's not that warm. I won't allow him to stay in a hot car." She slammed the door, immediately walking a few paces away.

"Noted," I said under my breath then pressed on the window controls before cutting the engine. As I climbed out, I made certain my weapon wasn't visible as I scanned the parking lot.

Her expression remained one of amusement as I walked toward her, instantly taking her arm. "You're not wearing a suit. I'm surprised."

"As you said, I'm a man of surprises. I suggest you don't take very long."

"I'm an expert shopper. I gather you have a credit card."

I said nothing but gave her a single look, which forced her to look away.

"What's my limit?" she continued.

"Purchase what you need. I also recommend you select both casual and dressy outfits."

"For all the nights we're not going out? What fun."

Just before heading inside, I pulled her against the side of the brick building, keeping my voice low. "I've tolerated your hatred for me and your caustic mouth. However, you're going to behave while inside this location. Anything else won't be tolerated, including trying to solicit help. Remember what I said about innocent bystanders. You wouldn't want them to get hurt, now, would you?"

"No." Coraline's eyes opened wide, although I doubted that she was fully grasping the possible situation.

"Good." I threw open the door, continually scanning as we headed for the cash register.

"Can I help you?" the woman behind the counter asked, although I could tell by her tone that she couldn't care less.

I pulled my wallet from my back pocket, selecting my Centurion American Express card, flashing it in front of the girl. "I'm Gabriel Dupree. I would like for someone with absolute knowledge of your merchandise to help my friend exclusively in order to find everything she needs and wants. There are no limitations except for wasting our time."

Fortunately, the store clerk recognized both my name as well as the lack of spending limitations on my card.

She took it from my hand, fingering it lovingly. "Why, yes, sir. Can I say that it's an honor to have you in our store."

"Just take care of Coraline. She's very special to me." I glanced at her nametag, leaning over the counter. "And Margaret, I will not tolerate anything other than the best service you have. I hope I'm clear."

Margaret chewed on her lower lip as she nodded several times.

The smug look on Coraline's face was exactly what I'd come to expect. I walked away, moving toward the front entrance. There wasn't a woman inside the store who wasn't staring at me.

"I think you can stop being an asshole now," Coraline insisted, laughing softly under her breath.

Oh, the nasty, vile things I wanted to do to her.

After a few minutes, I walked outside, making certain Moose had settled before pulling my phone from my pocket. I'd yet to check in with either Alex or Bronco since returning, which wasn't like me. What had occurred with the Iceman might be a clear indication that the Brousseau family had enough influence to begin whittling away at all phases of our businesses.

"How's your vacation?" Alex asked in a chipper voice.

"You know I wasn't on vacation, and I've returned at least for the time being." If I honored my father's wishes, I would need to tell him soon enough that he would be handling a larger portion of the business. That would wait. There were still too many things were up in the air at this point.

"Hmmm… So soon, eh? I was getting used to being the big boss. I knew you were visiting your family. That doesn't always go well for me, so I didn't want to mention it."

"Any issues with the contracts?"

"You've been gone for three days, but no, everything is fine. I can hear anxiety in your voice. Is there something I should know about?"

Sighing, I continued pacing in front of the store. I'd lied to Coraline by indicating that I would sense if and when another band of the men who'd attacked her came into the city. What troubled me more than anything was that they'd been able to keep me from sensing their approach. Until they were in close proximity, I hadn't been able to gather their stench. How were they able to mask who and what they were? "We have a major contract that's yet to be signed. Alex, I need you to ensure that nothing will go wrong having our buyer sign on the dotted line."

"Sure, of course. I'm working with the attorney right now on the final changes that you and I discussed. What is really going on, Gabriel? I've never heard you this way."

"I have a bad feeling we're about to face a possible takeover."

Alex choked. "That's not possible. The stock hasn't been made public. The worst that could happen is the contract is pulled. Even then, we'll be able to regroup. It might take some time, but the business will survive."

"There will always be a way to tear us down, my friend. You need to keep that in the back of your mind." I had a feeling we hadn't heard the last from the reporter who'd accosted us at the gala. "Just call me if anything occurs. I should be in the office tomorrow."

"Will do. Stop worrying so much. We have this contract in the bag."

That's what I was worried about.

After ending the call, I returned to the store, finding both Coraline and Margaret near the dressing rooms. To my surprise, my mate was smiling, enjoying being treated like a queen.

She tilted her head, studying me as she held a stunning red dress in front of her. When I nodded, the warm flush creeping along her cheeks was like an electric shock penetrating my system. I was forced to back away, retreating to the safety of the outside. I took several deep breaths, clearing my lungs before contacting Bronco.

"Boss, Jesus. I'm glad you're okay but you sound like shit," Bronco said after whistling.

"I'm fine. What did Jackson tell you?"

"Only that you were attacked several times. What the hell?"

"Something with regard to my family and nothing more. Any trouble on the streets or with the other shipments?"

When Bronco hesitated, I knew my instincts had been right.

"We grabbed the toys and were able to retrieve the stolen merchandise from Emilio without incident. The man seemed eager to do so. And he supplied a list of assholes he'd promised sales to. I had them checked out. Funny thing is that most of those dudes have disappeared. Poof. Like they really never existed, but a least a couple of them had a trail I was able to follow. They left town with no notice."

I was barely able to keep my anger in check. We'd been played by Emilio. Perhaps he'd gone into business with another entity in an effort to throw us off.

Could that include someone from the Brousseau family?

"Find Emilio and bring him to the warehouse," I instructed. "We're going to have another chat with him, only this time bring a body bag."

"That's the thing, boss. He's also gone. In the wind. He left the shithole he's been living in with most of his crap still inside, but no doubt he left. Looks like in a real hurry too."

"I don't care what you have to do. Find him. Scour the ends of the earth if you have to but I want him."

"Sure, boss. I'll do what I can. What about the shipments?"

My instinct was working overtime, telling me that I should be prepared for some kind of sting operation. "I need you to find out all the information you can on the family of Coraline LeBlanc. They're out of Thibodaux, Louisiana. Dig deep on this one."

"Okay. What do they have to do with anything?"

"That I'm unsure of. Just find out what you can."

"On my list. I'll call you."

I could tell there was something else on his mind. "What else, Bronco?"

"There are some rumblings on the street. Nothing concrete, but I can tell people are nervous. I tried to talk to one of our informants, but the bastard has managed to avoid me like the plague."

My jaw clenched as I was forced to face an ugly truth. It would seem that the Brousseau family had managed to touch every aspect of my life in a destructive manner. That couldn't continue. "Which motherfucker refused you?"

"Josh. That ain't like him, boss. He's eager to earn a buck or two."

Josh. The kid was hooked on speed and anything else he could get his hands on. While I abhorred the use of drugs, he also had a handle on every criminal element in the city, specifically those who didn't belong. That had allowed me to interrupt arms sales in my territory without my authorization. That had also created new enemies. "I know where the fucker is. I want you to meet me there in two hours." As I relayed the location, my soldier laughed.

Bronco chuckled. "I'm looking forward to it, boss. At least Josh is a creature of habit."

"Yes. Yes, he is."

I ended the call then thought about the legend. I'd made friends in all walks of life, many who were academics given my charity work. Perhaps it was time to utilize their skills to try to dig deeper into this great legend. If my family was as important in the early nineteen hundreds as my father made them out to be, then there would likely have been something recorded in the history books regarding the feud between the two families.

After finding his number, I made the call. As I'd anticipated, I reached his voicemail. He was one of the most popular professors at the University of Chicago. "Luke.

It's been a long time, buddy. I missed you at the gala last week. Look, I need a favor. I'm curious about a legend, a curse that was placed on my ancestors over a hundred years ago. Something about a high priestess from the Brousseau family. See what you can uncover and if possible, as soon as you can. Thanks."

Bristling, I turned around to find Coraline standing in the doorway, several packages in her hand. While she had a slight smile on her face, her eyes told me another story.

She'd heard at least a portion of the conversation.

"Are you finished?" I asked.

"Yes."

"Then I'll complete the transaction." As I started to move past her, she pressed her hand against my arm.

"I don't know what the hell is happening, but if there's really a crazy curse about to destroy my life, then I deserve to know about it. But… I wanted to say thank you. Believe it or not, this was fun." She laughed nervously as if admitting it went against everything that she believed in.

Exhaling, my heart thudded against my chest from another surge of electricity. "I want you as happy as possible, Coraline. We will talk later."

"I hope you're not lying to me." She acted as if she wanted to say something else, but instead she locked eyes with mine.

In them I saw a recognition of my wolf.

As well as utter terror.

* * *

I'd left Coraline under Miller's watch. He had explicit instructions not to allow her out of the condo for any reason. There were no exceptions, including pretending her dog needed to be walked. The action had been taken care of before I left.

As I stepped out of my Mercedes, I checked the surrounding area. While considered a portion of my turf, East Garfield Park was also one of the most dangerous sections of Chicago, a place where violence had taken a significant toll. It was also ripe with the use of drugs, allowing Josh to get his hands on anything he craved. I knew his dealer, a savage asshole who'd challenged me once.

It had been a hard lesson for the scumbag to learn, but I'd had no additional trouble since then. However, the location I was about to enter indicated Josh was indulging in another one of his sick proclivities.

As Bronco climbed out of his Charger, he ran his fingers through his hair, hissing under his breath. He loathed coming to this part of town. I couldn't blame him. Even the stench was different than in our boroughs in the city. There wasn't a need for any discussion. He was well aware of my intentions. I only hoped Josh wasn't already strung out. Answers were needed.

I moved into the dry cleaners, Bronco trailing behind, the girl behind the counter barely paying us any attention. She was used to the comings and goings of a different kind of clientele. She'd been well versed in the art of silence. As I headed down the rickety stairs, I held my breath. The basement had been turned into a drug mecca, complete with several rooms where special clients could indulge in their fantasies. Josh had provided enough money to be considered one of the owner's top customers.

As I walked inside, the owner's eyes opened wide.

Ralph Stinson's name was unassuming. To anyone else, the man was nothing but a wiry accountant, boring in every way. Little did they know he'd killed at least a dozen people who'd fucked with him. I had to admire a man who could maintain two completely different personalities and professions without either colliding with the other.

Ralph jerked up from his desk, swallowing hard.

"Relax, Ralph. I'm not here to see you and after I leave, I was never here. Do you understand?" I shifted my gaze in his direction, allowing him to see just a hint of my wolf. "All I need to know is which room Josh is in."

"No question. You were never here. Last door on the right." Ralph immediately returned to his seat, shifting his attention to whatever work he was trying to accomplish.

Bronco mumbled behind me as we headed down the corridor. At least Ralph kept a clean establishment. That added to his credibility. I slammed my hand on the door, shocking the hell out of Josh and the naked woman in the middle of giving him fellatio.

She squealed as Bronco jerked her onto her feet, yanking her toward the door. "Get out of here, honey. Go home. Take a shower. Get clean. You'll live longer," Bronco huffed.

She didn't need to be told twice, grabbing her clothes and scampering away.

Even in the ugly lighting, I could tell Josh had paled. As he struggled to stand, I was able to sense he'd shot up with heroin but was somewhat coherent. I took two long strides, grabbing him by the throat and lifting his body several inches off the floor.

"Listen up, Josh. I don't like that you've been avoiding Bronco. In fact, that pisses me off. Now, we're going to have a nice discussion. If you cooperate, you can go back to your drug-induced haze. I think you know what will happen if you don't."

"Yes... Yes, sir," he struggled to say.

"Good boy." I let him down, wiping my hands on my trousers. I glanced around the room, shaking my head. How could people live like this? I hated my brother was in the business of supplying the same crap, but it was his choice to do so. Maybe things would need to change after

I took the helm. "You know almost everybody in this town. It would seem we have a bad apple trying to spoil the entire orchard."

"Wha… What?" he asked.

Snarling, I snapped my head in his direction. "There is a new player in town. He's obviously putting the fear of God into the neighborhood. I need to know who that is."

He swallowed several times, moving from one foot to the other. "I've heard the same shit but no names. I swear. And I've had no contact with them."

"Them. As in more than one?"

Nodding, he shot a quick glance in Bronco's direction. "Some freaking entity out of Alabama or Texas or something. Somewhere south."

"Louisiana?" I managed, my anger swelling.

"Yeah. Yeah! That's it. Don't know shit about them other than they are intimidating as hell. That's why I came here. Couldn't get my usual party favors off the streets. Nobody wants to sell shit right now." He shrank back after issuing the words, knowing how much I loathed a drug addict.

"How are they intimidating? Violence?"

Shrugging, he continued to shift, his nerves getting the better of him. "They don't have to resort to that. They use some kind of mumbo jumbo bullshit. That's what I heard, Mr. Dupree. I swear to God!"

I closed my eyes, almost laughing at the ridiculousness of the situation. "I believe you, Josh. What do they want?"

When he didn't answer, I came closer until there were only a few inches between us.

He looked away, shaking like a leaf. "I don't know for certain."

"Take a freaking guess."

When he lifted his gaze, there was real fear in his eyes, but not because of what I could and might do to him. Because of what he was about to tell me. "They're going to perform some sacrifice. You know, like slaughtering an animal, although my gut tells me they have something else in mind."

A sacrifice. The old ways of voodoo. "What are they trying to accomplish? Guess for me. You're a smart man."

"Getting to you. They won't stop until they have everything that belongs to you. Then…"

"Then?"

Josh dragged his tongue across his lips. "Don't kill me, okay? I just heard smack talk. I don't know if it's the truth."

"Continue or I will hurt you."

"Then," he managed. "Then they plan on exterminating you and your entire family."

CHAPTER 11

oraline

Nightmares.

I'd had them when I was very young, but the ones I'd experienced were never like the type that other kids talked about in school. Boogeymen in the woods. Creatures under the bed and hiding in the closet. Beasts clawing at the windows. Mine were indescribable, almost always the same. A suffocating three-dimensional cube that expanded in size as it chased me. The dream always ended with blood.

And my screams.

My mother had been advised by my pediatrician to take me to a specialist, but she'd been determined to handle my unclean dreams, as she'd called them, herself, touting her religion would help me. I'd been far too young to understand the chants and sayings she'd issued every night before I went to bed. All I knew is that after two months, they disappeared. Since then, I'd never had another nightmare involving the cube.

Other dark and demented dreams were something else. They'd started just after I'd entered puberty.

The cold shiver trickling through me was intense enough I held my arms, my entire body quivering.

I don't know why I was thinking about my childhood other than what I'd seen in Gabriel's eyes. Maybe I was losing all touch with reality, but I'd been able to see straight into his mind as well as a portion of his soul. The truth. His real identity that he did everything in his power to hide.

He was the wolf who'd saved my life. I was certain of it. Being born and raised in a small town in Louisiana, I'd been exposed to various beliefs about black magic and voodoo. Even though I knew there were still locals who believed in the religion, maybe I'd shoved my head into the sand in my assumption that the darker side of voodoo was no longer practiced, including the horrific sacrifice of animals. Maybe that's why I'd become a veterinarian in the first place.

I continued to stare out the window as the afternoon light began to wane, not really seeing anything but the thick clouds as they rolled in. Gabriel had left without saying anything other than he would return and I couldn't go to the atrium or anywhere else, no matter the circumstances. His attempt at protection was oppressive.

As I sipped my wine, the limited reflection in the glass allowed me to see just how comfortable Moose was in his surroundings. If I was right about Gabriel, no wonder my beautiful big baby boy was happy around the man.

They were from the same gene pool.

My God. What the hell was I thinking? That wasn't possible. The myth around Lycans was just like the horrible nightmares I'd experienced.

Impossible.

Then why couldn't I get it off my mind? I also continued to think about my fascination with werewolves that had stayed with me into adulthood. Hell, I'd watched every werewolf movie ever made more than once, had devoured every book. But werewolves and Lycans weren't the same. Lycans weren't forced to shift during a full moon. They could control when or if they did, maintaining their human form most of the time.

But what if Lycans lost that control, fueled by a hunger they couldn't explain? That would make them extremely dangerous.

"Girl. You *are* losing it." My God. How the hell would I know even if it was possible? Which it wasn't. A fantasy. Nothing more. Not real.

Yeah, keep telling yourself that.

I took another gulp of wine, almost finishing the glass. My heart pinging irregular beats and my hand continuing to shake, I walked to the open bottle I'd placed on the coffee table, refilling to the rim. Moose didn't bother opening his eyes, happily snoozing on the comfy bed. That alone seemed crazy to me. His life had been disrupted, but he was a happy boy.

What was I?

Disturbed.

Angry.

Confused.

Excited.

Every nerve in my body remained alive, tingling as if lit by a firecracker. All because of my extreme attraction and desire for the man who'd taken me away from my home.

Away from danger.

That was something I could no longer deny. Without Gabriel's help, the attacks would have been successful. There was no way of knowing whether they intended on taking me hostage or killing me. Was I afraid of Gabriel? Not really, but there was no doubt he was having difficulty controlling his anger.

As well as his hunger.

I returned to the window, searching for answers that I wasn't certain existed. Gabriel had been drawn to me, brought to the city in order to protect my life.

My thoughts returned to my mother. It should have been obvious much earlier in my life that she believed voodoo was a true religion, paying homage to the spirits that affected our lives on a daily basis.

Maybe I didn't want to think of my mother as different.

Yet she was.

As I was trying to wrap my mind around the connection and the reason that she'd insisted I return home, I heard noise, the sound of the door opening, muffled voices.

Gabriel was home.

Home. Would I ever be able to call another location home again?

He took his time walking into the room, not saying a word yet remaining just inside the doorway. I was able to see enough of his reflection to know he was pensive. I could swear I could hear his rapidly beating heart.

Even more terrifying, I knew what he was thinking, felt his increasing hunger.

He would soon devour me.

I took another gulp of wine, my nerves kicking in over my own intense cravings. Out of the corner of my eye I studied him as he walked toward his bar, making himself a drink.

Still silent, the only noise was the rapid beating of my heart echoing in my ears.

The quiet was killing me.

Moose suddenly detected Gabriel's presence, barking once then racing toward him, my pup's tail swirling as he squealed his greeting.

I should remain disgusted that Moose could even tolerate such a man, but I realized that my dog was super sensitive to all aspects of evil. That meant Gabriel wasn't a bad man. Yeah, right. I wanted to laugh, but the moment the two creatures shared was touching. When Gabriel whispered something to Moose, the pup reluctantly moved back to his perch on the dog bed, huffing as he almost immediately closed his eyes.

"How do you do that?" I asked, indignant that the man had so much control over my dog.

"Get him to obey? It's very easy, Coraline. Moose respects my dominance. I am the alpha after all."

"Which is something you expect from me."

There was that look that he gave me when he was frustrated as well as amused.

With a drink in his hand, Gabriel approached, his presence alone creating another wave of electric energy.

"Tell me about your mother."

I was shocked at his request. Why the hell would he need to know? "Why? She's moved on with her life."

"She lived in Louisiana for years, the same small town you returned to." He crowded even closer, his form becoming oppressive.

"Yes, she was born there. Why does that matter?"

"Because she is the reason you changed your life, returning to the dark place. You had a life in New York, the ability to advance in your career, yet you chose to leave it, which doesn't make any logical sense."

I laughed, more out of nervousness than anything else. "Why would you say that?"

"I don't really think I need to explain. You've been aware of the evil surrounding the city of Thibodaux your entire life, which is likely one reason that you purposely chose a university thousands of miles away. While you might have pushed the realization aside, somewhere in the hidden reaches of your mind, you were well aware of the atmosphere, men and women who believed in the old ways. You remained drawn to the area even after all these years. I find that… fascinating."

"Don't kid yourself. I hate the city, the small-town ways. I just…"

"Do you really? You have a connection to the old ways whether you choose to believe it or not."

My God. It was as if the man had been able to read my mind. "Old ways? You're talking voodoo." That's exactly what I'd overheard outside the clothing store. The curse he'd mentioned involved black magic. Suddenly, my throat felt constricted as I remembered something else my mother had told me.

"Beware of those who practice black magic, Coraline. They have evil in their hearts."

When he closed the distance between us, there was an extreme fire in his eyes, a heightened level of determination to unmask all the secrets I might hold inside. I turned to face him, barely able to keep my breathing on an even level. He was such a powerful man, igniting every desire as well as pushing me to the very edge of my sanity.

"Yes, Coraline. I'm talking about the darkest side of voodoo, often called black magic, the malicious counterpart of the true religion, an aspect some Cajun families still believe in practicing today. But you already know that."

"Are you suggesting my mother engaged in these practices?" I countered, tilting my head in some small act of defiance.

"That I don't know. But you do. Don't you, Coraline?"

Stop saying my name. Stop it! His near accusation pissed me off, although I couldn't deny the concept.

"No, she didn't. She believed in good things, allowing karma to take control," I insisted, although a nagging remained in the pit of my stomach.

"You're so certain."

"She told me that there were those who practiced the dark side of voodoo and they were evil. What does it matter if she did anyway?"

"Because you were brought back to Louisiana with a purpose in mind."

"What the hell purpose would that be?"

Gabriel took his damn time answering, pushing my frustration to the outer limits. "A sacrifice. You were supposed to be the sacrifice to the spirits so many of Jade's descendants believe in, which allows their world to remain safe from additional evil."

I glared at him, uncertain I'd heard him correctly. "Wait a minute. You honestly believe my mother would sacrifice me to... To what? Some crazy spirit she believed in? Are you out of your mind? My mother loved me. She would never do anything like that." I tried to turn away from him but found it impossible. The draw to him was even greater than before. My throat dry and my pulse racing, I could barely think clearly let alone move even a few inches. How had he managed to have this kind of effect on me?

"Do you deny the possibility?"

Why I found it difficult to refute immediately was beyond me. I remained stunned at his accusations, confused as to what he was getting at. Yet a portion of my mind knew there was some truth to what he was saying. My heart felt heavy, my mind almost a complete blur. "Why would she consider such a horrific act?" I was barely able to recognize my voice. That just couldn't be. Why warn me then bring me back? I rubbed my eyes, trying to make sense of anything.

"Because it's what she was taught to do. It's also likely she had no choice."

"She wouldn't do that. She was kind and loving."

He cocked his head, his eyes so damn piercing I was shoved into an altered state for a few seconds. Blinking, I forced myself to look away.

"As I said. It's possible she had no other choice."

"What the hell is that supposed to mean?" I was the one who moved within inches of him, arching my back as I continued my glare of rebellion. However, the smokiness of his eyes, the sound of his deep baritone had already pushed me into feeling out of control around him.

While I expected some sort of nasty retort, even a harsh reminder of his domination, he did little more than blow a swath of hot breath across my face, more out of frustration than anything else.

"It means that I must do everything in my power to protect you." As he lifted his hand, gingerly pressing his fingers against my face, the shiver running through me was ice cold.

I knew what he'd told me was true.

I was meant as a sacrifice to the very spirits my mother had told me were evil. While I didn't understand the reason why, nor did any of this make any sense, the connection between Gabriel and me continued to build. I felt safe just being near him.

"That can't be true. My mother was all I had, my father leaving us when I was barely two years old. I don't remember anything about him other than the limited details she shared over the years. We had no other family, no active support. She worked two jobs just to keep a roof over our heads." I wasn't certain anything I said would alter his damning accusation. I was cold inside, so damn cold, as if I would never feel warm again.

He was completely interested in every word I was saying, studying my face as he sipped his drink.

Suddenly, the wine had lost its taste. I moved away from him in a wide arc, placing the glass on the table. "She protected me, Gabriel. She loved me. Hell, she was my only friend for as long as I could remember. If you honestly expect me to believe that she's capable of doing something so… atrocious, then you're a fool."

My God, the man was insatiable. He inched closer, enough so I was able to gather a whiff of the drink he'd half consumed, the strong smell of bourbon as disgusting as the ugliness he'd just spewed.

Only I knew it wasn't a lie.

"You were lucky to have her, Coraline," he said quietly.

"But I'm just supposed to toss away that relationship. Right?"

"I didn't suggest that."

"Then what the hell are you suggesting?" When I turned around to confront him, the sickening realization that almost all I could think about was being in his arms washed over me. "She moved away. She's not here to hurt me."

"I never said she made the choice to ask you to return to your hometown."

I shook my head. "Then get to the point."

"The point is, Coraline, that there is a very powerful family who resides in Thibodaux. From what I've been able to learn, they've expanded to other southern cities, but the core group remains in the very town you grew up in. I've learned very little except they are extremely powerful, likely capable of requiring her full obedience. If she was spiritual, believing in the religion itself, that could have allowed them to control her."

"Control," I whispered, trying to remember everything my mother had told me. I hadn't wanted to learn. God, why hadn't I paid any attention? "What is the name of this family?"

"Brousseau. Have you heard of them?"

I wanted to say that I hadn't, but it was impossible to go anywhere without hearing the name, descendants owning several of the shops in town. My throat closed even more. "Yes, I've heard of them. How is it possible they can control someone's mind?"

"Come now, Coraline. Don't pretend you don't understand the capabilities. Voodoo is a powerful tool, damning if not handled carefully. From what I've been told, they are descendants of a very powerful voodoo priestess. She practiced the dark magic, ruling the area for several decades."

There was such determination in his voice that my throat almost closed. "What happened to her?"

"That I don't know. However, her entire village was torn apart somewhere around nineteen twenty. The perpetrators burned every building, killing all those who challenged them."

His haunting words kept the hard chill engulfing my body.

"Never trust an outsider, Coraline. Never. Their only intent is taking you away from me."

My mother's words from so many years before rushed into my mind.

"How do you know this? Why does it matter?" I managed, my voice barely a whisper.

He moved toward the window, polishing off his drink and remaining quiet. The aura around him was as electric as his personality.

"Talk to me," I demanded, inching closer. While I reached out to touch him, needing a boost of his power, I pulled my hand away, uncertain why he was telling me the story.

"As a boy growing up, I was told of the legend of the priestess, my father making certain I knew that her power had lasted well beyond her death."

I bit my lower lip, the knot in my stomach increasing.

"Only a few days ago, my father called me to Baton Rouge as well as my other brothers to relay more regarding the story he'd told us as children, the very one his father told him. The same one that had been passed down through the generations." He swirled the ice in his glass, the clinking sound creating another wave of jitters deep inside. "It would seem the legend he shared is more involved than he originally led us to believe."

"I don't understand why your father found it so important."

He kept his heated gaze pinned on me as he inched closer. "You see, my ancestors had Jade Brousseau's entire family and all those who believed she was a true goddess murdered. She was tied to a stake, just like so many of the others, left to burn until they were sent to hell. However, she survived and after doing so, she placed a curse on the Dupree clan."

"A curse," I repeated, goosebumps popping along my arms. I thought about things my mother had told me about her special religion, as she liked to call it. As I tried to concentrate, I was able to remember snippets of conversations. She'd mentioned more than once that the spirits never forgot any harm that befell them. I hadn't asked what she was talking about. I'd always thought her words were meant as a lesson, a reminder to be good.

"One so powerful that it changed every descendant born after that moment. At least according to my father," he continued.

A tense moment settled between us. I was terrified to ask about the changes.

Wolf.

He's a beast, a killing machine.

As if reading my mind, a smile curled on his upper lip. I'd felt the same sensations only hours before outside of the clothing store.

"Do you believe your father?" I whispered.

He stared into his glass before sucking on one of the ice cubes. When he turned to face me, his eyes were entirely different. Darker.

Redder.

He placed the glass beside mine, twirling it before lifting his arm, sliding the tip of his index finger down the side of my face. I felt every muscle tense, yet his action was gentle, a tender reminder that he wasn't going to hurt me.

"Who are you, Gabriel Dupree? You've saved my life for no reason that could make any sense to me. Who the hell do you think I am to you?" As usual, he didn't answer me right away, but his damn eyes continued to penetrate mine, keeping the butterflies in my stomach active as hell. "Tell me, dammit. I need to know. I deserve to know how I fit into this insane legend."

"Yes, you do. You are my fated mate, the only woman who can begin to put a stop to the tentacles of this curse."

His words reverberated in my mind, renewing dark visions that I'd only seen once in my life, but I'd never forget the revolting images. "What? What are you talking about? How could I play any role of importance?"

"Because the children of the purest bloodline must mate during the year of the two blue moons or thousands of innocent humans will perish."

I couldn't breathe, couldn't feel my arms or legs. I struggled to get away from him, only finding myself drawn closer and closer, as if he already had a hold on me, controlling my actions as well as my heart. No. No fucking way. I managed to back away, only to be yanked against him all over again. "Don't, Gabriel. I can't believe this. I won't. I'm not who you think I am."

"As I said. You belong to me. That fate you were born with. You have no choice in the matter, Coraline."

"Stop saying my name!"

"It's useless to try and get away from me."

Who the hell did the bastard think he was kidding?

I slammed my hands against him, breaking free from his clutches.

He jerked me back in position, his eyes narrowing as his chest heaved.

"You can't fight me, Coraline. You feel the strong connection, the burning need that we had from the second we met. Your desire is unlike anything else you've ever felt, the cravings becoming more intense, never leaving your mind."

"No. I can't want this. I have a life. I don't want you."

"Yes. You. Do."

The moment I tilted my head in another crazy act of rebellion, he gripped my jaw, pulling me onto my toes. As he threw his arm around me, tightening his hold, what little was left of my rational side attempted to push him away. Within seconds, I knew it was no use, the hunger I'd experienced before only increasing, shoving aside all intentional thoughts.

His breath sounds were irregular as he lowered his head, issuing a series of low, husky growls. If they were meant to terrify me, his attempt failed. He brushed his lips back and forth across mine before darting his tongue inside.

Within seconds, I was overwhelmed with the very need he'd accused me of having all along. Everything around me seemed to fade away, although the haunting words were never far from my mind. Just being in his arms was so powerful, enabling me to surrender in a way I hadn't been prepared for. I clamped my hand around his shirt, tugging as if I wanted him even closer.

Did I?

Could I dare believe what he'd told me?

Another rush of images floated into my mind one after the other, every one of them startling. The attacks, the way the wolf had stared at me. Then there were the words the last asshole had spewed off just seconds before gunned down by Gabriel's men.

"Your death is just the beginning."

I was lost in the vacuum surrounding me as the actions of the man holding me became more savage. He thrust his tongue inside my mouth, the kiss becoming an all-consuming moment of passion. Lightheaded, the way he ground his hips against mine only added to the yearning that was already out of control. He was so hard, throbbing against my stomach. All I could think about was having his thick cock buried deep inside my pussy.

When he broke the kiss, biting down on my lower lip, several moans floated between us. Very slowly he backed away, although his hand remained firmly locked around my jaw.

"As I said. You are mine," he breathed.

"My God. You are the wolf who saved me. Aren't you?"

Gabriel continually rubbed his fingers across my face, his nostrils flaring. "Yes."

His definitive answer terrified me, enough so I slammed my hand against his chest. That only made him jerk me even closer, until our bodies were molded together.

"Don't fight me, Coraline. Our connection is too strong," he said in a ragged whisper. "The need will never be satisfied."

The way he was talking was insane.

Or was it?

"Why? Tell me why," I insisted.

"Because we were always meant to be together."

"That's not possible."

"Isn't it? Are you certain about that?"

At that point, I wasn't certain about anything, especially about the man holding me in his arms or the notion that I belonged to him. When he fisted my hair, yanking my head to an angle, I reacted on instinct, raking my nails down the side of his face. The growl he issued this time was primal in nature, the sound reverberating in my ears.

"Then show me," I demanded, still shaking like a leaf.

He cocked his head, taking several rapid breaths. "You already know the truth. You recognized me from the clinic."

"That was an animal. I was mistaken."

"Do you remember what you said just before closing your eyes after you removed two bullets from my chest?"

Not only was his voice mesmerizing, but the question also sparked a shiver, one that oozed down my spine in slow motion. "No."

"Yes, you do. There's no place like home."

Perhaps he was expecting a reaction, but I was frozen. Hell, I was paralyzed as the true reality settled in. While I couldn't understand how it was true, there was no denying the unsettling fact.

He gave me no time to react, crushing his mouth over mine. There was no desire to fight him off any longer, no feeling of anxiety, just a burning need that refused to be denied. A hunger unlike before shifted into my system, my pussy lips already swollen, my nipples aching to the point of intense pain.

His hold on me continued and as he shifted his other hand down the length of my back, squeezing my bottom, my breath was stolen. The rush of electricity only ignited the fire between us, one burning so hot that it threatened to consume us both.

I pulled at his shirt, determined to touch his naked skin. I wanted nothing more than to feel the explosive heat just before it seared my skin. The kiss was brutal, his tongue dominating mine. I was no longer able to think clearly but it didn't matter. We were two beasts, our destinies forged years before.

Every sound he made only further embroiled my senses, sending a wave of vibrations dancing down the back of my legs. I continued ripping at his shirt until I was able to slide my hand underneath. The moment I touched his heated skin, I moaned into the kiss.

His body stiffened from my touch, his chest heaving. His grip on my face tightened, his fingers digging into my skin as he held me, sucking on my tongue. I was weak, my legs shaking. There was no doubt I would have fallen if he hadn't been holding me.

Stars floated in front of my eyes, the pitter-patter of my heart keeping me lightheaded. When he yanked on my hair, breaking the kiss and exposing my throat, several whimpers slipped past my lips. The deep rumble in his chest shifted to his throat. I closed my eyes as he slowly lowered his head, breathing across my skin before dragging his teeth down the length of my neck.

I was breathless, shivering to my core. Every action he took was possessive. He wanted my full surrender.

And I was no longer certain I could deny him.

"Show me," I insisted.

He closed his eyes, lowering his head as his breathing became even more labored than before.

"Show me," I whispered, uncertain I'd even uttered the two words.

Pulling away, he tossed his head back and forth, unrecognizable sounds rolling up from his chest. "No."

"Trust me, Gabriel. I need to know the truth."

"Be careful what you ask for, Coraline."

He fisted his hands, smacking them against his legs, the growls continuing.

Then he lifted his head, opening his eyes.

All the books I'd read, the movies in vivid color hadn't prepared me for the kind of truth real nightmares were created from.

My captor.

My lover.

My mate…

CHAPTER 12

oraline

"Are nightmares real, Mama?"

My mother took a deep breath, finishing drying her hands and tossing the towel onto the kitchen counter. "Come with me, Coraline."

She led me out our back door and into the yard, moving quickly toward the edge of the forest. When she stopped, she placed her hands on my shoulders. "Tell me what you see in the trees."

"Nothing."

"Use your imagination, sweet child. Close your eyes and tell me."

I did as I was told, shutting my eyes and trying to figure out what she was getting at. Then a series of images formed right in front of me. I reached out, trying to touch the closest tree. "It's green. Lots of sticks."

"Excellent. What else?"

I wiggled my nose, the smell like the nasty eggs that Mama boiled in water. I could swear I saw eyes. "Mama. There are creatures!"

"Yes, child. What do they look like?"

"I dunno. Scary."

"Tell me about their eyes. It's okay, baby girl."

Huffing, I didn't want to play this game any longer. When I tried to turn away, she pushed me even closer. I knew I had to obey. "They're red. All red. Is that possible?"

As she pulled me around to face her, she stroked the side of my face. "You can open your eyes now, baby girl."

When I did, I smiled because I could tell she was pleased. "Is that possible?"

She hunkered down, taking both my hands into hers. "Do you remember that I've told you that very bad men do exist?"

I nodded several times.

"There is much evil in this world, people who will stop at nothing to take what they want simply because they believe they have a right to do so. But the creatures in those woods are much more dangerous; however, they are your friends. You need to remember that, Coraline. If you ever see a beast with red eyes, promise me you'll consider the creature a friend."

"Okay, Mama. I promise."

The memory swam up from nowhere, one I'd hadn't thought about before. Now I knew why she'd warned me.

And I wasn't afraid of the beast standing in front of me. A friend. Her comment was interesting.

My instinct told me he meant no harm. Perhaps he never had.

My mother had been terrified that she could be used by her own people, forced to obey some unspeakable command. Had she managed to break free from the powerful hold after doing their bidding? Or had she actually brought me here for another reason?

"What does this mean, Gabriel? You've said I'm your mate. How can that be? I'm human, completely human." I felt awkward just saying the words.

As he walked toward me, I involuntarily stepped back.

He reached out, tilting his head as his nostrils flared. His eyes were no longer crimson rimmed in gold, returning to the same beautiful blue both he and his… wolf carried.

"I wish I had all the answers, Coraline, but I don't."

"The curse turned your family into wolves."

"Yes, which I've known about since I was a child. What I didn't know was the second and more damning portion."

When he moved closer this time, I didn't back away, instead listening as he told me a horrible story about exactly what would happen if he and his brothers didn't secure their fated mates as well as the reason for why I'd been attacked. While I wanted to believe I'd fallen into some kind of horrible nightmare, my thoughts shifted back and forth to the memory with my mother by the forest. Why had she warned me if her tales of creatures in the forests hadn't been true?

And why was I drawn to him in such an unexplainable manner?

Gabriel cupped both sides of my face, his chest heaving from his labored breathing. Every sound he made was carnal in nature, his nostrils flaring as the electricity roared from every cell in his body directly into mine. I was struck by the increased sensations, every one more powerful than they'd been before.

"I will protect you with my life when necessary."

I believed him. While nothing would ever make any sense again, I knew the man... the beast was telling me the truth.

"What if you can't?"

"Trust me." Every move he made deliberate, he lowered his head, inhaling as he brushed his lips across mine. "I'm going to mate you now."

Mate.

As he captured my mouth, pulling me onto my toes, my thoughts reverted to lessons I'd taken in animal behavior, including mating rituals. He wasn't just mating with me. After all, he'd called himself an alpha. He was knotting me.

A swarm of emotions rolled through me as the kiss turned into a roar of passion. He slipped his hand around to the back of my neck, digging his fingers into my skin as he brought me closer. There was no way of getting away from him. I slammed my hands against his chest, the heat becoming explosive between us as his actions became more aggressive.

Lightheaded, when he forced me into a slight arc, my stomach was pushed against his groin. The feel of his throbbing cock added to a rush of excitement, my desire nothing more than a wildfire of need. There was no explanation for the way I was feeling, the almost desperate longing that had overwhelmed me.

While a small part of me still wanted to pull away, the sinful woman inside craved his rough touch. Everything was surreal, my ability to understand what was happening between us gone. All I knew is that nothing would stop him from taking me.

Using me.

Tasting me.

Knotting me.

He dominated my tongue, all the while issuing low and throaty growls. The sound seemed to float all around us as if amplified by some unseen force. I could no longer think clearly, my pulse racing. The taste of him was sweet yet tangy, his scent more intoxicating than ever. I was thrown by my inability to see clearly, although a part of me no longer cared. He'd awakened the same kind of carnal need he'd been experiencing, one so desperate that nothing was going to stop us.

When he finally pulled away, his breath skipping, he darted his eyes back and forth.

Then he smiled and narrowed his eyes, sucking down air. With no further hesitation, he dragged me into his arms, using long strides as he exited the room. He moved up the stairs taking them two at a time, slamming his hand against my bedroom door, storming into the room and dumping me onto the bed. Even after he turned on a single light, shadows remained in the room. Were they a reminder of things to come?

Mate.

I couldn't get the word out of my mind or the meaning.

I jerked up onto my knees, struggling to catch my breath as I stared at him. I'd never felt so free or alive in my life, as if I'd been let out of a cage that I'd been placed in so long before.

"One day I won't be able to protect you, Coraline, but someone more powerful will take my place."

Why so many things my mother had told me came rushing into my mind I would never know, but the pieces of the puzzle started to fit together. She hadn't brought me home to sacrifice me. She knew Thibodaux was where the alpha would find me, the only person who could protect me against true evil.

While it was likely I'd never find the answer as to why I'd been chosen or how Gabriel and I were connected, there was no chance of ignoring what had been right in front of us.

Gabriel tossed his coat then yanked his shirt over his head, pitching it into the far reaches of the room. As he slowly started to unfasten his belt, he cocked his head, a sly and filthy smile crossing his face. "I suggest you undress. I don't think you want another round of discipline."

I remained on my knees, fighting to grab then toss my shoes, never taking my eyes off him. Another dazzling series of vibrations skittered down my spine as I tugged the dress over my head, swallowing before tossing it across the room. I'd changed clothes, choosing the same red dress he'd approved of in the store. I had no idea why I'd selected it, even going without a bra.

To tempt him?

To submit to him?

The realization that a little of both was the truth made me shiver. He'd already broken through several walls, peeling me free of the thick armor I'd had my entire adult life. Was this man the reason I'd never truly hungered for someone else? Had I always been destined to belong to him? The truth was almost as terrifying as a lie.

"Mmmm..." he muttered then pushed his hand between my legs, fingering my pussy through the thin lace. "You're wet."

"Yes."

"And hungry."

"Very."

He poked a hole through the material, driving his long digit past my swollen folds. I threw my head back, moaning as I closed my eyes. I almost laughed as he ripped away my thong, exhaling raggedly before thrusting several of his fingers deep inside. I bucked against the thick invasion, riding his hand for several seconds.

"You are such a bad, bad girl, Coraline."

"Yes," I panted, trying to focus but finding it almost impossible.

"But you are all mine now." A dark chuckle rushed up from his throat as he pulled his hand free, the expression he wore ripe with lust. He rubbed his slickened fingers around first one nipple then the other before pinching and twisting my hardened bud until I cried out in pain. "I will teach you to surrender fully and without hesitation."

His words alone tickled my senses, the anguish pushing me closer to a moment of ecstasy. When he pulled away, I whimpered.

"What do you want, Coraline?" he asked as he backed away.

"I don't know."

"Yes, you do. Tell me." While he smiled, I could tell he wasn't taking no for an answer.

"Fuck me." I was surprised at the crude words I used, but they obviously delighted him, his eyes shimmering in the dim lighting.

I inched to the edge of the bed, pulling his hands away.

Chuckling, he allowed me to finish unbuckling the thick piece of brass, his chest rising and falling as his hunger continued to increase. I dragged my tongue across my lips, teasing him as he peered down at me with half closed eyes. Every sound he made was barbaric in nature, adding even more fuel to the fire threatening to consume my system.

I no longer comprehended my actions as I tugged at the thick strap, my bottom still aching from the spanking I'd received the night before. When I'd freed his belt, he took it from my hands, rolling it under his nose and taking a deep whiff. Then he dangled the strap down my shoulder, sliding the end between my breasts.

His eyes were almost unrecognizable, the golden flecks around his irises drawing me in. The larger-than-life man was allowing me to slide past his armor, the one that had protected his wolf his entire life.

Cocking his head, he flicked the strap from one breast to the other, his entire face lighting up from sadistic thoughts I was clearly able to read, desires that should terrify me.

They did just the opposite.

I'd never been so wet or hot before, my pussy quivering as much as my legs were trembling. While he continued to toy with me, I dared to try to slide my fingers under the material of his trousers, tugging them past his hips.

He delivered a single smack of the belt against my bottom then wagged his finger. "You aren't in control."

I was forced to watch as he stepped into the shadows to finish undressing. I'd never felt so hungry for a man in my entire life, every muscle tense.

As he came forward, his actions were more like a predator than a man. Every muscle in his body was sculpted, chiseled to utter perfection. I was even more mesmerized than before, still fighting to control my breathing.

There was something different about him as he crawled onto the bed, hovering over me as he pushed me into the middle and onto my back. He allowed his gaze to travel down from my face to my legs then brushed the tips of his fingers along my thigh to my stomach as he slowly brought his eyes to mine.

He was enjoying studying the woman he'd claimed. Even the way he pulled my legs apart was possessive. I could still hear his ragged breathing as he shifted his torso over me, remaining on his palms and lowering his head, allowing his hot air to dance across my face.

Shuddering, I lifted my legs, wrapping them around his hips. My actions pleased him, his smile turning carnal. Everything about him was different, although I couldn't put my finger on why or how.

The combined scents of our desire were an intoxicating narcotic. I felt insatiable, unable to control my needs. When he lowered his body until his cockhead was pressed against my pussy, I lost all patience, slipping my fingers around his thick shaft. He growled his approval, never blinking as I pushed the tip just inside.

I could tell there was no holding back, no ability for the man to control his actions. When he plunged the entire length inside, a scream erupted from my mouth. His cock continued to swell, my muscles struggling to accept. Every sound he made was that of a true savage and as he plunged hard and fast, I pressed my knees against him, clinging to his arms.

I reveled in the moment, the sheer bliss that became overwhelming. The man was filling me completely, stretching me wide open. We were nothing but animals, brutal in nature. I tossed my head from side to side, shocked how different the sensations seemed. Powerful. Intense.

Altering me forever.

Gabriel continued pounding into me, his deep growls huskier than before. There were no words spoken, no need for romance.

This was nothing but primal fucking.

And I loved every second of it.

Lights sparkled in front of my eyes, my breath finally stolen as an orgasm ripped through me without notice. I jerked up, digging my nails into his arms as the wave swept up and down, leaving me speechless.

"Good. Yes," he muttered, his voice no longer Gabriel's. "Come again."

It was as if his command couldn't be denied. Within seconds, the single orgasm blew up into an explosion of passion.

"Yes. Yes. Yes. Yes!" My scream was bedraggled, every cell in my body surging with energy. I couldn't stop shaking as the climax continued. When it finally subsided, leaving me exhausted from the raw ecstasy, I raised my arms over my head, wallowing in the moment.

He lowered his head, biting down on my nipple, the combination of pain and continuing ecstasy making me lightheaded all over again.

When he started to pull away, I gasped, clamping my hands around the comforter as I struggled to lift my body to further entice him.

An indescribable look remained on his face. I could swear his features had changed, altered because of his wolf. A low hum rumbled up from his chest just before he turned me over, yanking me onto all fours. He fisted my hair, holding me in place before driving his cock back inside.

From this angle, I could feel how much his cock was throbbing. My muscles clamped and released several times, pulling him in even deeper.

He raked his fingernails down my back then began to power into me, the force enough that I would have been shoved against the bed had he not been holding me in place. For a full minute, maybe longer, all I could concentrate on was the sound of our brutal fucking, skin slapping against skin.

"All mine," he muttered, his cock swelling even more as he thrust like a frenzied man.

"Uh. Uh. Uh. Uh. Uh," I managed, clawing the bedding, every color of the rainbow rushing in front of my eyes. Nothing could be this pleasurable.

The change was incredible, pushing me to an entirely different level of nirvana. I couldn't stop tingling, my heart now hammering against my chest as a true understanding settled in. He wasn't finished expanding. Soon his tip would be bulbous.

And there would be nothing I could do to break our connection.

As another incredible orgasm began to sweep through me, the pressure continued to build, the electricity surging to another level.

I threw my head back with a ragged scream just as his body began to shake violently. This would change everything between us and while I had no full understanding of what was happening, I knew that from this point on, he would own me.

Every. Single. Inch.

When he issued a roar, the sound filled the room as he erupted deep inside, filling me with his seed. I closed my eyes, dropping my head.

Then I began to shiver as another series of visions popped into my mind.

Visions of violence.

Visions of bloodshed.

And visions of death.

* * *

Just being able to snuggle in a warm bed was surprising. The fact Gabriel had stayed by my side even more so. I was able to gaze out the floor-to-ceiling window as I remained nestled in the crook of his arm, admiring the glow of the tall buildings surrounding us. While Moose had ventured into the room, he remained on the floor, something he never did with me. Maybe he knew better than to crowd the space of the alpha.

I laughed softly at the thought, still trying to process our intense round of fucking.

"How did you know the pet store would be open?" I asked, determined to talk about anything but the damn curse. I still couldn't fathom what he'd told me was the truth, even though I was forced to realize that there were things on this earth that couldn't be explained.

"A woman I cared for had a dog."

His answer was succinct, without any emotion. I jerked my head up, resting my chin on his chest. "What happened?"

Gabriel shifted on the pillow, easing his arm behind his head. "She wasn't interested in a serious relationship with an unscrupulous man."

"Your business?"

"There are always people around me who have no issue attempting to use any weakness against me. Jasmine was no exception. She was approached by two Feds in her office, asking her questions about my business. She almost lost her job because of it. We hadn't been as close at that point, my long hours and what she called a lack of integrity getting in the way."

"I'm sorry."

He chuckled. "Don't be. I'd never expected our relationship to last, even if her Great Dane enjoyed my presence."

"She didn't understand the real reason why the dog liked you. Did she?"

Sighing, he looked down at me, squeezing me against him. "No. No one can know what I am. My entire family has taken great measures to hide our true nature."

I sat up, tugging the sheets around me. "What happens now?"

He kept his eyes on my face as he brushed his fingers down my arm. "Now, I hunt down the people responsible."

"Why, if we're now both safe from this curse?"

"Because I believe there's more."

"I don't understand."

"I'm expecting something from my father in the morning. If what he said is true, there is a third part to this curse. I'm certain of it."

"Meaning what?"

"Meaning they will continue to come after us until they avenge the murder of their people."

Exhaling, I gripped his hand, rubbing my thumb across his palm. "Then I'm going to ask my mother to fill in the blanks. I think she had a foretelling. It wasn't about sacrificing me. It was about protecting me."

He studied me for a few seconds, his eyes full of hunger all over again. "Then why bring you to the one place the family has the most power?"

"I don't know, but I am going to find out. That is if you'll allow me a chance to talk with her."

As he shifted his hand to my cheek, rubbing gently, I sensed his concern increasing. "If what you've told me is true, contacting her could place her life in danger."

"Maybe so, but she owes me an explanation."

"How can you get in touch with her?"

"I have no idea where she is, which might be on purpose, but she always carries her cell phone with her. I know her. Please let me make that call."

I heard the sound of his phone ringing and pulled away. He was always conducting business.

He growled his disapproval then eased from the bed, padding around to the other side. "Bronco."

He turned away from me, moving closer to the window to ensure I wouldn't hear him. As he did, I thought about the last time I'd seen my mom on a cold, dreary day in January, which had been the only time she'd visited me in New York. I closed my eyes, remembering the laughter we'd shared over lunch, her words of praise over my recent job promotion from sub grunt to grunt. I chuckled.

That had been over two years before. I could still see the way she'd beamed, even giving me a special gift, a necklace she'd known I'd admired from her collection.

I wasn't certain I'd ever see the beautiful piece of jewelry again. It was likely the little cabin I'd grown up in had been destroyed, burned to the ground. I held my arms, trying to avoid another round of shivers.

Another memory suddenly popped into my mind, something I'd forgotten all about.

It was the last thing she'd said to me before stepping on the plane.

"You've been the greatest joy of my life. You are very special, and I've done everything in my power to protect you from the monsters. Never forget just how important you are. Remember when I'm gone that everything happens for a reason. Karma has a way of making things right, even if her decisions on how we can't often understand. One day you won't be able to fight your destiny. I only pray it will happen before it's too late."

While I'd thought her words were nothing more than her typical spiritual passages, trying to further encourage me to continue fighting for my career, now I began to wonder. She'd known all along this moment was coming. She protected me, but from the truth. I hadn't been ready to ask the right questions.

Now I was.

I got out of bed, dragging my dress from the floor and sliding into it. As soon as Gabriel got off the phone, I would do what it took to convince him to allow me to talk to her. My mother knew more than she'd told me.

A few seconds later, I could see Gabriel had ended the call. He remained staring out the window. A sickening feeling oozed into my system.

"What's wrong?"

When he turned to face me, advancing slowly, a strange series of thoughts entered my mind. It was like I was reading his. A tragedy. What?

"Gabriel. Answer me."

He closed the distance, taking several deep breaths before answering. "I asked one of my soldiers to check on your family history. He was as thorough as possible, although your mother did what she could to hide her identity by taking your father's name."

I wanted to be angry with him but that's the kind of man he was given the number of enemies he faced. "That's nothing new, Gabriel. They were married for a short period of time, and she kept his name. What other horrible things did you find?" I hated the defiance in my voice but a part of me continued to unravel.

"Were you close to your father?"

Exhaling, I tried to keep the anger out of my system. "Are you kidding me? He didn't want us and left when I was very little. There were no birthday cards or Christmas presents. I don't think there was any financial support either. I told my mother the day I turned thirteen that I never wanted to hear his name mentioned again. I never have. Why?"

"He died several years ago, cardiac arrest."

While I was taken aback, I had no real feelings for a man I'd never really met. "I'm not certain what I'm supposed to say or why it would matter. All I care about is my mother. She's the only family I have."

A sickening feeling shifted into me, a wooziness that almost doubled me over.

"I think you're right in that she made every attempt to protect you," he said quietly.

"Because?"

"Because of what importance she believed you had in this game of revenge."

Swallowing, I tried to control my nerves as I walked closer, studying his eyes in the shadows. "As your mate."

"Yes…"

"Why are you telling me this? What does it matter now?"

He took my hand, squeezing my fingers. "My Capo had men hunt down your mother with my brother's help. Sadly, she was easy to find given the fact she did keep her cell phone active."

I could tell by his actions, his angry yet stilted words, that something had occurred. "What did they do? What? Tell me!"

"I'm sorry, Coraline, but your mother was already dead."

CHAPTER 13

abriel

Coincidences.

The word no longer existed in my vocabulary. Coraline's mother's murder had been meant to send a message to the followers of the voodoo religion.

Don't fuck with them.

Not only had Bettina LeBlanc done everything in her power to protect her daughter, she'd also managed to bring the two of us together, thereby starting an end to the curse. I didn't need the reason why at this point, although I knew that could come into play later.

I stood by the window in my home office, having been there for almost two hours. The sun had risen, vivid colors crisscrossing the sky. However, I sensed tumultuous weather was on the horizon, as if the force of nature was providing a dynamic backdrop to the events that my gut told me were going to escalate. I had a very bad feeling in the pit of my stomach, too many questions unanswered. While a part of me had hoped that by mating with her there would be some kind of significant change, my rational mind had told me otherwise.

I sensed Bronco's presence and took a deep breath. What he'd found out about Bettina had been vital to a further realization that the Brousseau family had gone underestimated for far too long, my father's lack of disclosure to blame.

"I came as soon as I could, boss," Bronco said as he entered the room.

After checking my watch and realizing it was only a little after seven, I sighed. I didn't need my keen instincts or senses to tell me that today would be difficult. The foreboding feeling hadn't left me since his call.

"What else have you found out about Emilio?" My instinct continued to tell me the little prick had been a significant part of this game the Brousseaus were playing.

"He was sighted at a motel just outside of town. I wasn't certain what you wanted me to do with him."

"I have no doubt the man was paid to betray us. We need to find out the name."

Bronco nodded. "Then maybe we pay him a little visit."

I moved closer to my desk, placing my hands on the surface and leaning over. "This time, the bastard is going to talk."

"I'll be ready," he said, a grin crossing his face, although it was short lived. He walked closer, appearing more uncomfortable than I was used to. "I've heard some disturbing rumblings on the street."

"Such as?" There were always rumors floating in the dark realm, most of which could be ignored.

"That reporter has been supplying information to the Feds."

Exhaling, I did what I could to hold any real reaction. While it wasn't something I hadn't anticipated, the timing was horrific. "Any details?"

"Nothing worth mentioning, but I think you should be concerned."

"We may need to handle this reporter as well, but not now. Let's see how it plays out. Anything else?"

He glanced over his shoulder as if worried someone would be listening. Then he moved to the other side of my desk. "I don't mean to question you, boss, but several of the soldiers are questioning why business has been interrupted. I've tried to brush it off, but their concern is increasing."

I shook my head, a deep rumbling growl trying to rise to the surface given my wolf's increasing anger. "It will all be dealt with soon, Bronco."

"If you don't mind me asking. How? I know you well enough, boss, to realize you're under a lot of stress. It has to do with the woman. Right?"

My Capo knew better than to question me, but he'd been loyal with every aspect of my business as well as the family secret. "There is a darkness surrounding my family, Bronco, a curse placed by a powerful queen of dark voodoo."

He huffed, biting back a laugh when he noticed I was serious. "Okay. What does that mean exactly?"

"That means that every aspect of my empire is being challenged and that will continue. Coraline must be protected at all costs. That's even more important until I'm able to figure out who's behind the various sabotage events. Make certain you have soldiers by her side at all times."

After sucking in his breath, he nodded. "You can count on me, boss. I'll keep an eye on Emilio until you're ready to confront him."

"Yes. You do that. If he tries to run, do what's necessary to prevent him from doing so, but I want him left alive." At least for the time being.

"Understood. I'll have round the clock protection for Ms. Leblanc."

"Excellent. Thank you, Bronco." He knew he'd been dismissed, giving me a nod of respect before walking out. Emilio would provide answers one way or the other.

I couldn't completely take my mind off Coraline. To see the way that she'd reacted last night to the knotting had been… delicious. I could still feel her writhing body underneath mine, the heat she'd exuded more powerful than before. I fisted my hand, trying to curtail my hunger. What I did find interesting is that I'd had no desire to shift and feast during the last twenty-four hours. I could only imagine that had to do with my connection to Coraline.

Hissing, I pounded my fist against my desk. Everything was unraveling, stripping me of full control. That couldn't continue. I noticed the screen on my phone popping to life seconds before it rang, surprised as well as pleased that Luke had taken the time to return my call.

"You are an early riser," I said, half laughing.

"And you know school is in session. If I don't get to my office by six every morning, I don't have any time to myself," Luke answered. While he usually had a positive tone in his voice, this morning's call seemed entirely different.

"You have answers for me?"

He exhaled, the sound exaggerated. "I'm no expert in this culture, Gabriel. The university isn't keen on lessons around black magic."

"But I know you, my friend. You have interesting pastimes."

"Okay, so you do know me," Luke said before bursting into laughter. "Look, you're from Louisiana. You've heard all the stories about the prominence of voodoo a century ago. That isn't the case today, or at least I thought so."

"Meaning?"

"Meaning that there is still a small but active subculture that practices the dark art, but you mostly hear about it involving tourists. Practitioners make a good living off their small shops and tarot card readings in New Orleans, Baton Rouge, and other destinations."

"But? There's more," I said, more than just curious as to what he'd learned.

"They keep to themselves, some still living in small communities. As you might imagine, they certainly don't like people sticking their noses in their business. You are right that there was some mention about what happened to several of these communities starting over a hundred fifty years ago. I found a book containing a single article regarding one small town in particular that was burned to the ground, only to have a resort pop up two years later."

"My family's involvement?"

Luke huffed. "The Dupree family ruled the area, including most of law enforcement at the time and probably the newspapers. I suspect that's why there are very few articles. What isn't documented is anything about this curse you mentioned, although I am intrigued by it."

I knew that Luke had dug deep in his investigation. "I'm not certain what to believe."

"Maybe we can have lunch at some point, and you can tell me all about it." The lilt in his voice had returned. "Or a golf game. It's been far too long."

"It has, my friend. We'll pick a date. Is there anything else you found useful?"

"There was a mention in another source about a scientific occurrence. Two blue moons? I haven't found any corroborating evidence, including anything from astrologers or the science community, but I find it curious that it was mentioned in not one but two older books on voodoo."

"Interesting."

"Maybe that's the reason for global warming," he chortled.

"Yeah, maybe."

"Oh, I did find a fascinating ancestry tree on the Brousseau family. While I can't say for certain it's official, it might be something you're interested in seeing."

I allowed a smile to cross my face. "You bet I'd like to see it."

"I'll see what I can do about sizing it in order to email the file to you."

"Excellent. I appreciate you returning my call, Luke." Everything was coming to a dead end. If the information my father had promised didn't arrive today, I would give the man a piece of my mind. Then I would send soldiers to retrieve it from his hands.

"No problem, buddy. Remember to call me."

I didn't like being shoved into a corner and that's exactly what this situation was beginning to feel like. I held the phone in my hand, debating how to play out the rest of the day. What had to occur was the contract signing. The last thing I needed was an interruption in Dupree Enterprises.

Alex's phone rang several times, although it didn't go to voicemail. When he finally picked up, the exasperation in his voice raised my hackles.

"What the hell is going on, Gabriel?" Alex barked, the noise in the background almost drowning out his call.

"What are you talking about?"

"I think you need to turn on the television. There are at least eight reporters here. Hold on. Let me get the fuck inside the building. No comment. Do you hear me? I said no comment."

"What do you have to say against the accusations levied on Dupree Enterprises?"

"Did you know Gabriel Dupree was supplying weapons to other countries?"

"Are you a part of Mr. Dupree's underground world?"

The questions came fast and furious from the background, every word fueling my rage. In my mind I saw blood. I would crush the reporter's windpipe with one squeeze of my hand. I began to pace the office, cursing under my breath.

"Thank God the building is still almost empty."

I knew he was stepping into the elevator, could tell he was fuming.

"If I had to venture a guess, I'd say that contract with the Barton Group will never happen, Gabriel. Do you know what kind of a loss that will mean?"

I knew exactly what kind of a loss that would mean. "We'll salvage it."

"Uh-huh."

The connection dipped to almost nothing, the two minutes of silence trying my patience.

When I heard a door slam, I took a deep breath.

"Jesus. Fucking. Christ," Alex snarled. "They were waiting for me to arrive. Do you mind telling me what the hell is going on?"

I thought about how to answer him. When I didn't right away, my partner jumped in again.

"Is there any truth to the fact you're selling guns to fucking foreign countries? I knew you had another business on the side. I'm not fucking stupid, or maybe I was for ignoring the situation. I deserve an answer, Gabriel. I am not going down with you on this one."

"I'll tell you what's necessary when I arrive at the office."

He laughed, the sound bitter as hell. "Good luck getting in. Unless you're freaking Superman, they're going to try and detain you. The fuckers are everywhere."

"I'll be there as soon as I can."

"Yeah, well, you might want to change your mind."

"Meaning what?"

Alex mumbled under his breath. "I could be wrong, but it would appear a couple of unmarked cars just arrived. Oh, goody. Maybe it's the Feds."

"Don't say anything at this point, Alex. And if they don't have a warrant, do not let them in."

"It would appear you've been through this before. You and I are going to need to talk about our continuing relationship, unless we're both in prison and it won't matter."

He ended the call abruptly. I'd never seen the man so rattled in all our years together. Perhaps I should have prepared him for the possibility of being questioned. I moved toward my bookshelf, pulling away the panel hiding one of my highly secure safes. As I tugged out another weapon as well as some additional ammunition, I sensed her presence.

My woman.

My lover.

My mate.

I was almost overwhelmed with desire, my wolf awakening. After doing everything I could to push him back into his cage, I took my time getting everything I needed before turning to face her.

Coraline walked in slowly, her arms crossed. She was pale, the news from the night before taking a significant toll. While Moose trailed behind her, she immediately flattened her hand, directing him to sit, which he did.

She studied the smaller weapon I had in my hand, remaining quiet as I strapped the leg holster against my calf. Then she walked closer.

"What's going on, Gabriel?"

I cupped her cheek, disturbed how cold her skin felt to the touch. "Nothing for you to worry about."

Snarling, she purposely took a step away, avoiding my hold. "That's not good enough. I'm smack in this middle of your world at this point. I've now lost almost everything that mattered to me. I deserve to be told what the fuck is going on and what you're planning."

"Be careful asking questions, Coraline. My world is complicated."

"Your world involves two distinct factions, both of which are ruthless, but there's more that's troubling you today. Maybe I'm just losing my mind, but I can read a portion of yours. There's more danger. Are the police involved?"

I wasn't surprised our connection was getting stronger, but I was indeed troubled that she would learn more than she should be required to handle. "It would appear the FBI has arrived at my office, likely prepared to pepper me with questions. I will need to handle the situation."

"This has everything to do with the Brousseau family and their curse. Doesn't it?"

"That's what I'm going to find out. While I'm gone, I'm expecting a delivery from my father. Maybe he'll help to provide some answers. That should be the only time you're interrupted."

"Interrupted. I live such an exciting life." Her defiance had returned, obviously a mechanism protecting her heart. She'd said almost nothing after hearing about her mother, turning away from me and shedding a few tears in private. Then she'd stared at me, condemning me for her mother's murder.

I couldn't blame her. However, I could avenge her mother's death and I would.

"I don't need to remind you that you are to stay right here. Do you understand me?"

A wry smile crossed her face. "Of course. Where the hell would I go at this point?"

Hunger. While my father had warned his sons that hunger would get out of control, he'd never taken the time to discuss deeper emotions. I was falling hard for the defiant woman with the sassy attitude and mischievous smile. My feelings weren't just centered around keeping her safe or with my carnal needs.

She was very special, a beautiful reminder that there was more to life.

No one was going to take that away from me.

"Just answer me this. Do you care about me or is this all about saving your family?"

Her question was like a knife cutting through me. As soon as I advanced, she moved behind Moose, holding him by the collar. "You need to trust me, Coraline. I will never intentionally place your life in danger. I'll return as soon as I can. We may need to get out of the city for a while."

"That's not what I asked you, but I guess I got the answer that I was looking for. I'm just your possession disguised as your mate. At least I know where I stand."

I moved toward the door, hissing under my breath. I couldn't leave her this way. My pulse quickened just thinking about her, needing her. "I've never been good at expressing my feelings to anyone. You are my mate, Coraline. Neither science nor history books will explain why. However, I don't need anyone to tell me how I feel; the thunderous need surging through my veins, the kind of hunger that no food will satisfy. I cannot live without you, nor do I want to try. You are everything that matters to me, and I will die in order to protect you." The words burned my throat, my loins aching to have my cock buried inside of her.

Her soft laugh was full of despair, creating a wave of energy that tensed my muscles.

"My mother used to say that there was nowhere on this earth where I could run to get away from my destiny. Maybe the same is true for you, Gabriel."

I drank in her perfume, holding it in my nostrils for a few precious seconds. Then I headed toward the door to my office. Her mother was right. The time of reckoning had come.

* * *

While I'd managed to avoid the majority of the press, moving into the underground garage through the second opening, I knew it was only a matter of time before the bastards hunted me down. I'd left explicit instructions with Jackson to block out anyone attempting to come to the penthouse, even assigning two additional soldiers outside of the building. The assholes would find a way to try to grab their fifteen minutes of fame.

"Do you want to tell me what the fuck is going on, Wallace? The Feds are investigating Dupree Enterprises? That's unacceptable," I snarled after pulling my car into my private space. I had the prosecuting attorney under my thumb, able to find some fairly unscrupulous activities with gambling in his past. That had ended a good portion of the investigations stemming from whatever flavor of allegations were thrown my way.

"You know neither I nor my office can control the Feds. They do exactly what they want when they want," he answered. It was good to hear a hint of fear in his voice.

"I don't need to tell you how damaging it would be for my company to be placed under scrutiny. Find out what is going on and stop it."

"I'll do my best, Gabriel, but it's out of my jurisdiction."

"I don't think I need to remind you that your reputation is at stake. I doubt that pretty little wife of yours would want to find out about all the money you've stripped out of your bank accounts."

"Damn you, Gabriel."

Laughing, I ended the call, shoving my phone in my jacket pocket. I would be able to count on his assistance. As I headed toward the elevator, I had an uncanny sense that I was being watched, but not by anyone involved with law enforcement. Before entering the cold steel box, I allowed a deep and husky growl to echo in the space. Maybe a warning would provide me with some time.

As expected, the Feds had arrived. I could smell their odor from the moment I entered the suite. The receptionist had already arrived, her face pensive.

"Good morning, Mr. Dupree. There are some men in Mr. Drummand's office. They've been asking where you are."

"Don't worry about it, Betsy. I'll handle it. Just keep everyone away for the time being and hold all phone calls."

"Yes, sir."

I took long strides down the corridor, throwing open the door to Alex's office. My partner lifted his eyebrows as soon as I walked inside, moving away from his desk.

The assholes turned around immediately, sneers on both their faces.

"Gentlemen. Do we have an issue?" I asked, keeping a smile on my face.

"As I was explaining to your partner, there have been certain accusations made that require answers," the taller agent said. There was something odd about his demeanor, enough so I remained on edge.

"First of all, I need to see identification," I stated, glancing from one to the other.

The two of them glared at each other before bothering to pull out slick black thin wallets, both opening them at the same time. I snagged the closest, inspecting the badge carefully. I'd seen enough of them in my time, which allowed me to identify a bogus ID in less than twenty seconds. From what I could tell, they were authentic.

I inspected the other then moved to Alex's bar area, pulling a bottle of water from the refrigerator and twisting the cap. "Do you have a warrant, Agents Spencer and Reynolds?"

They gave each other another look.

"We thought you'd want to cooperate, Mr. Dupree," Agent Reynolds answered. There was far too strong of a gleam in his eyes as if they were catching a prized marlin. While there was nothing associating to my other business inside this office, their investigation was only beginning.

That continued to piss me off.

"While my partner and I have nothing to hide, I certainly do like standard protocol. Don't I, Alex?"

Alex could tell where I was going, nodding in agreement. "Mr. Dupree is right. We have important business to handle today. If this is just a fishing expedition, then I think it's best we contact our attorney."

"If we are required to get that warrant, which we already have enough evidence to do so, not only your entire day will be interrupted but your lives as well. I think that's something you need to keep in mind," Agent Spencer added.

I walked closer to the man, never blinking. "Are you threatening us, Agent? Because if you are, I'll do what it takes to have your badge."

"That's not a threat, Mr. Dupree. That's a promise," Agent Reynolds stated, his tone full of confidence.

I took a few seconds to enjoy the cold water. "Here's the thing, gentlemen. I don't like being threatened. As you might imagine, I've been forced to deal with the experience on several occasions. I assure you that the outcome wasn't pleasant. I suggest you hand me your cards. I'll have our attorney contact you to make an appointment." I lifted my water bottle, giving them another wide smile.

The look they shared this time was unrecognizable. That didn't trouble me. What did was that they weren't bothered in the least by my demands. When they both reached for and grabbed their business cards, I nodded toward Alex's desk, observing their behavior as they performed the action. Both Alex and I remained quiet as they scanned the office again then left, softly clicking the door as they closed it.

Alex exhaled, moving immediately to yank their cards off the desk. "We need to talk."

I headed in his direction, cocking my head. For the first time, I could see fear in his eyes. "Alex, you and I have been partners as well as friends for a long time. You are well aware who my father is and that my brothers and I are following in his footsteps. I've worked very hard to separate the two businesses and I've been successful up to this point in doing so."

"Gabriel, I don't need a lecture on you or your family. I've looked the other way for years because I've enjoyed working with you. However, I also have a family to consider."

"I will make certain they are protected."

"Against what? Being arrested? Not a chance. Are you going to make certain they have a tidy sum every month while I wallow in prison for crimes that I had nothing to do with? Or are you talking about enemies who might be prepared to annihilate everything in your world?" He opened his eyes wide only seconds later. "You are actually talking about both. My God. The power and influence you think you have is just..."

His words trailed off, but his concerns remained. "Yes, to both, but it won't come to that. Especially any issues with law enforcement."

"Jesus. You can't promise me that. I know how this game works. Guilt by association. It's already happening, Gabriel, whether you like it or not."

"Meaning?"

"Meaning just before those bastards stormed into my office, I had a call from Mr. Barton himself. Oh, he was very good about being apologetic for terminating our relationship, even trying to tell me that they'd had some recent financial blows, but I could see through his cloud of bullshit. You can only imagine what's going to happen with some of our other clients. We could be ruined." Alex glared at me, the pulse in his neck throbbing. "Why the hell didn't you tell me? Why? I thought you trusted me. I'm your damn partner, for fuck's sake."

Fuck. I'd gotten so far behind the eight ball that the Brousseau assholes had already unleased their wrath. "The FBI has nothing, Alex. If they did, they would have had a warrant in their hands."

"Maybe so, but they will be back. I need some time to think about what I'm going to do and whether or not I can continue with our partnership. It's nothing against you, Gabriel, but I'm not the kind of man you are. I prefer for my family not to worry about whether I'll be gunned down in a dark alley one day. Things will change if and when you ever fall in love. All the money, the power. None of it means shit without them."

"Take whatever time you need." I allowed a vision of Coraline to shift into my mind. Perhaps this was the first time I could fully appreciate what he was saying.

Alex seemed surprised that I didn't fight him on it. His expression softened as he grabbed his keys off his desk, heading for his office door.

"I do trust you, Alex, more than I can the majority of people I have in my life. I'm certainly not a good man, not like you are, but I do have integrity. I kept you in the dark for this very reason. You don't know anything about my other world so you will never have to lie. I will respect whatever decision you make."

Sighing, he rubbed his eyes then cocked his head over his shoulder. "Don't let anyone tell you you're not a good man, Gabriel. I've seen you when you're around children, animals. Hell, anyone who needs help. You'd give the shirt off your back. That's the reason I was able to tolerate what little I knew about your other… business. I'll call you in a day or so."

When he walked out, I glanced down at the two agents' cards he'd left, fingering one then the other. It was past time to flush out the identities of those involved in this bogus attempt at destroying the Dupree dynasty.

A bad taste remained in my mouth about the recent visit. As I dialed Wallace again, I held the cards up to the light. They were identical to every other one I'd seen. "Wallace. I have two names for you I need checked."

"Sure, I can do that. So far, I can find nothing tangible with regard to an investigation, but I have a call into a buddy of mine at the bureau. Maybe he'll drop a hint or two." Wallace seemed exasperated.

"Call me as soon as you know anything concrete."

"Will do."

I stood at the window staring out at the bright sunshine. Seconds later, a sick sense of knowing settled in.

Danger.

My mate was in dire peril.

Everything in my world was spiraling out of control. This was just the beginning. They were destroying us from within, waiting to strike until we were so distraught that we could miss their planned attack. I tried to walk through the various possibilities, realizing that while I was the main target at this point, the incidents would escalate around my brothers.

The second my phone rang, I yanked it from my pocket. Wallace was already returning my call. "Let me guess, the asshole agents don't exist."

"Oh, they exist, but first of all, they were from different departments. More important, they're dead, both killed in the line of duty last year," Wallace stated.

"A fucking ploy. And the investigation?"

"Well, according to my buddy, one doesn't exist. Somebody has a grudge against you, Gabriel. I suggest you be very careful."

"Yeah, I'll do just that."

As I raced down the corridor, I immediately grabbed my phone, dialing Jackson. He needed to get Coraline the hell out of the building and to a safehouse.

My blood curdled.

The call went straight to voicemail.

CHAPTER 14

 orty-five minutes earlier

Coraline

I'd always believed I was a rational person, capable of knowing the difference between fantasy and reality without issue. I was no longer certain of anything at this point. I touched the side of my face, still able to feel the tingle from where he'd placed his fingers.

Gabriel.

After saying his name over and over in my mind, I tried to shove the burning desire to be close to him away, even if I knew it was going to be impossible. My body ached all over from the incredible round of sex the night before. I'd felt so close to him, as if we were a couple. A laugh erupted from my mouth. We weren't in a relationship. We were in a mating cycle, one that would cool down. Then again, I had no clue.

I was also stuck in a nightmare, one that would be difficult to awaken from. My mother was dead. Dead! She'd been taken from me. Why? She'd defied some descendants of people who'd been murdered long before any of us were born? Or because she'd refused to give in to their demands? My emotions were all over the place, my mind reeling from far too many questions.

Then Gabriel had left me alone.

Again.

Suck it up.

Even my inner voice hated my ridiculous behavior. Hot one minute because of raging desire and ice cold the next. Mix in a few tragedies and what do you have?

Disaster.

A wolf. I'd seen his eyes.

"God," I muttered, still sick inside, but I made a promise to myself. The assholes who'd taken her life would pay.

After pouring food into Moose's bowl, I remained in the kitchen with the coffee cup in my hand. It was my favorite place in the house, the only room that had a sense of warmth. I leaned against the counter, studying the space, still able to feel his aura. Had Gabriel meant what he'd said? Was I more than just a possession to him?

I closed my eyes, tingling all over, his scent remaining on every inch of my skin. Even as I smiled from the memory of our passion, tears slowly began to fall. I'd only shed a few of them before, likely from falling into shock.

My mother was gone.

I wanted so to believe she'd done everything in her power to protect me, including from my own father. I managed to put the cup on the counter then dropped my head, allowing myself to sob. Moose nuzzled against my leg, whining then jumping on the counter when I didn't respond by petting him.

"I'm sorry, buddy. It's just… I don't know what to believe any longer. At least I have you." My baby barked once, forcefully pushing his muzzle against my stomach. I wrapped my arms around his head, unable to stop shaking.

"Ms. LeBlanc."

The voice came out of nowhere. After yelping, I jerked my head up, immediately reaching for one of the knives in the butcher block. Moose growled then issued several big boy barks.

"Whoa. It's okay," the man said as he held up his hands, swallowing hard as he stared at Moose. "Remember? I'm Jackson."

"It's all right, Moose." I continued to hold the knife as I glared at him. "What do you want?"

Moose took a step forward, sniffing the soldier. I could tell the man was nervous of a black lab. Hmmm...

"Moose, let him be." The pup finally huffed, returning in my direction. The poor guy looked relieved.

"To see if you needed anything. And to let you know a package arrived for Mr. Dupree. Nothing to be nervous about."

The man's voice was pleasant, not at all what I'd expected or heard up to this point. "No, I don't need anything."

He gave me the kind of look that I wouldn't have expected out of a killing machine. Empathy as well as respect. The combination was fascinating. After nodding, he turned to leave.

"Would you like a cup of coffee, Jackson?"

Surprised, he glanced over his shoulder at the door. That's when I realized just how much respect Gabriel's men had for him.

"Don't worry. It'll be fine with Gabriel." I pulled a cup from the cabinet as well as the basket of coffee pods for the Keurig. "Really."

His face softened. "I'd love one. Thank you very much." After he selected his choice, I popped it into the machine then pulled the cream from the refrigerator, pushing that and the sugar in his direction.

"How long have you been working with Gabriel?"

"Since I was eighteen."

"Did he force you into employment?" I asked, curious as to if he would answer.

He laughed, the sound genuine. "God, no. It was more like he made an offer I couldn't refuse. He caught me trying to break into his car. I thought he was going to beat the crap out of me, but he could tell I was starving to death. Hell, I weighed maybe eighty pounds."

"Jesus. Why?"

When I placed the cup in front of him, his eyes lit up. He took his time dumping six teaspoons of sugar along with a hefty amount of cream. I said nothing to him, realizing this simple gesture meant the world to him.

"Because I was living on the streets, eating out of trashcans and dumpsters. I'll never forget the day. Cold and snowy. My fingers were numb, but I was being tested by a gang. They were going to let me hang with them if I could steal the car. I was pretty good with electronics, so I had the door open when Mr. Dupree came out of nowhere." He laughed then took a gulp of his drink, not even caring it was steaming.

I could swear the man was eating his first bite of caviar from his reaction. "I'm sorry, Jackson. I don't know what to say."

He shrugged, offering me a huge smile. "Trust me. It was the best day of my life. Mr. Dupree took me to a restaurant and allowed me to eat everything I wanted. I was small, but I could eat a pile of food. He didn't complain about the bill or how much time I'd taken. Then he took me to buy some clothes. It was the first time in I don't know how long I had jeans that fit me. After that, I ended up in his home for two weeks, I think."

"Really?"

His eyes twinkled again. "Yeah. He gave me two choices. Clean up my act and work for him or he was going to take my ass to the police station. You know which one I chose. I've been loyal ever since. He's treated me real good."

"I'm really glad to hear that." There was a genuine adoration of the man, which gave me another perspective.

"He even made me get my GED. Forced me to study. The man hounded my ass too." He laughed, took a gulp and hunkered down. "I didn't mean to hurt your dog, Ms. LeBlanc. I'd never do that." He tentatively held out his hand.

"You didn't hurt him, Jackson. He was just being protective of me. Thank you for saving me in Louisiana."

Moose took deliberate steps in his direction, bypassing the man's hand and licking him up the length of his face.

I bit back a laugh seeing Jackson's response. He jumped back as if he'd been bitten, dropping and breaking the mug.

"Damn it. I'm sorry, Ms. LeBlanc. I'm just clumsy." Jackson scrambled to pick up the pieces, cutting himself while doing so.

"Whoa. It's okay. It's just a cup and you didn't do anything wrong." He allowed me to help him to his feet. I found the trash, waiting as he dumped the broken pieces then yanked his wrist under the faucet.

"That was stupid of me. Just stupid." Jackson laughed when I did, thankfully a little more at ease.

"I think Moose enjoyed it. Why don't I try and find a Band-Aid?"

He pulled his hand away, shaking his head. "Nah. It's fine. Just a scratch. Besides, I need to get back to my post. I'll pay for the cup if you want."

"Don't be silly, Jackson. It's just a cup." I forced a paper towel into his hand, giving him a stern, almost motherly look. What an odd moment.

After nodding awkwardly, he backed out of the kitchen. I glanced down at Moose, shaking my head. There were so many things about Gabriel that surprised me. Maybe I could actually start to like the man.

My mate.

I dumped the rest of my coffee, moving through the condo as I thought about the delivery. What kind of information could his father have sent that would matter? My curiosity getting the better of me, I headed for the front door. There was no package, which likely meant it had been put in Gabriel's office.

The plain brown wrapping usually indicated a service had been used. When I walked closer, I realized it had been couriered. While I knew that Gabriel would be pissed, I had to find out what the hell was going on. After listening for any sounds that he'd returned, I took a deep breath. I'd accept whatever punishment he wanted to dole out. Fine.

The wrapping was easy to remove, the plain white box providing no indication of the contents. When I opened it, I wasn't necessary surprised to find what looked like a very old photo album. It had been well maintained, but the pages had already yellowed.

I held it gingerly in my arms as I moved to one of the chairs, sitting down and opening it slowly. The first were grainy, almost unrecognizable pictures, the sepia color starting to fade. They had to be from the late eighteen hundreds. I scoured my memory banks. The first camera had been invented in the eighteen eighties. As I flipped through several more pages, I began to see a pattern in the photographs.

As well as a story.

In Baton Rouge.

In New Orleans.

In the Bayou.

My instinct told me that it was a telling of two families, both considered powerful. I found myself devouring every picture, feeling the same emotions from what was being depicted. As the two cities began to flourish, the smaller communities vanished.

As I neared the end of the album, the last few photographs were both stunning as well as horrifying.

They were of men and women burned at the stake, their faces depicting their agony. Children were crying at their feet, so many of them dragged away by men.

And the last picture was of several mass graves.

All caught on camera…

A wave of emotion swept over me, enough so I had to bend at the waist, my stomach in knots. I closed the album, fighting to breathe as I reached over, returning the album to the box it had come in.

As a single piece of yellowed paper floated down from the back, I watched it go all the way to the floor. When I had the courage to reach for it, I realized just how fragile the piece of paper was, the old parchment unprotected. I pulled it into the light, barely able to decipher the writing. Whoever had written the words had obviously been under duress or elderly.

December twenty-sixth, nineteen hundred and twelve

My child,

It is with a heavy heart that I must write you about the death of your sister. She gave her life trying to protect so many others. Monsters came into the village, destroying everything. They burned us at the stake, stealing our babies from us.

As night fell, the last of those who'd fought against the evil tyranny finally succumbed, taken to be with the spirits who would protect their bodies from further harm.

Trust me, my sweet boy. Their deaths will not be in vain.

I have placed a curse on the entire family responsible, a spell so powerful they will succumb to a kind of evil that they will not recover from.

Let it be known that anyone born of Dupree blood will pay for their bloodshed, the animals refusing to hear the cries of so many. Given their beastly actions, they will learn what it's like to live as creatures of the night. All descendants will be born as wolves, forced to feed their hunger. And if they live and continue thriving, they will face two blue moons in the distant future. On that day, the firstborn sons of the pure bloodline will be forced to hunt for a mate. But that isn't all they will face.

As I read the conclusion of the letter, tears slipped past my lashes, my heart aching for all those who were murdered.

Then I comprehended the curse wasn't over, the last words of Jade Brousseau sealing a fate that would change my life forever.

Gasping, I struggled to my feet, the room spinning. I managed to return the letter to the album, but I had to get some damn fresh air. My throat was closing, my entire mind a blur.

"Come on, Moose." I raced to the front door, gasping for air. Who gave a shit about his leash? When I threw it open, I barely noticed Jackson out of the corner of my eye. "Don't try and stop me, Jackson. I just need some air. I'm going to the third-floor atrium to walk Moose." I raced down the hall, slapping my hand on the button, the door opening immediately.

Moose panted, pushing hard against my legs as I backed into the elevator, until to keep from sobbing like some child. No. No! This was crazy. Nuts. A curse that…

And it would force…

I couldn't think clearly, nor was I certain I wanted to at this point. The reality of what we were facing was too much to endure. As I wiped my eyes, Moose tried to comfort me, but it was no use. I closed my eyes, reliving the horror that I'd seen. The ping of the elevator made me jump, but when I walked into the atrium, at least a slight sense of peace slipped into my system, even if it was going to be short lived. I walked toward the other end, looking over my shoulder several times. Jackson should be on my heels any time. I slid into an area that was hidden by trees. At least I'd be able to grab a few minutes to myself.

"Go play, boy. Just stay close," I mumbled the words, forcing myself forward. The serenity of the atrium was exactly what I needed. Maybe being here would clear my mind, allowing me to think this through.

I was organized, a plotter. I closed my eyes, ridding my mind of the horrible photo album. "Think. Think."

My mother had mentioned my destiny dozens of times in my life. If her intention was to keep the curse from happening, she'd known that she'd have to lure me back home. That checked all the boxes in my mind since Gabriel's family was close.

But didn't she know that the horrible event had occurred somewhere in the Bayou? Maybe that's why she believed in the spirits, honoring those who had died. But why? Why save the descendants of a murderous family?

Something else had happened all those years ago. There had to be another story. My gut churned from the thought.

"You're very distraught. Is there anything I can do?"

The unrecognizable voice shocked me. I'd heard nothing, including the man's approach. I immediately sucked in my tears as I opened my eyes. While there was nothing terrifying about the man, I was no fool. Looks could be deceiving.

"I'm sorry. I thought you were crying. I didn't mean to scare you," he continued.

"You just startled me." I darted a look to see if I could find Moose. I was shocked Jackson wasn't dragging the man to the ground. The stranger looked pleasant enough, his shaggy dark hair almost covering his eyes. While at least ten years older, he had a youthful air about him.

"I can tell," he said, laughing. "I just come up here to take a break from work. At least I get to work from home, right? Although it's not all it's cracked up to be. I'm not lucky enough to have a dog like you."

At least my mama had taught me how to perceive the danger around me. As soon as he mentioned my pup, I backed away, immediately darting around to the side and heading toward the elevator.

When the mysterious stranger stepped out of nowhere, the grin on his face could only be described as evil. In his hand was a gun.

I skidded to a stop, eyeing the four men who were headed in my direction. My God. I'd walked into a trap.

"What the hell do you want?" I demanded, remembering I'd seen another elevator on the other side of the atrium.

"Such a caustic mouth for such a beautiful woman. As far as who I am. *Je serai ton sauveur.*"

He would be my savior. Like hell he would. "Get away from me."

"I'm afraid I can't do that. You're far too important."

As Moose rounded the corner, barking and growling, the asshole lifted his hand, aiming his weapon at my baby.

"No!" I screamed, lunging forward.

Pop!

"I'm so glad to meet you, Coraline. Your mother told me so much about you."

* * *

Gabriel

The two men who'd been assigned to remain outside were dead, both shot in the head. The fact I'd been too late exposed a weakness that I couldn't tolerate.

As I raced out of the elevator, Bronco and Miller following, the same intense series of sensations remained.

Rage.

Terror.

Revenge.

I had the Glock in my hands, inhaling as soon as I was in the hallway. I was able to gather a scent that hadn't been here before, the strong testosterone indicating a male, a stranger.

"Fuck, boss," Bronco yelled from behind me.

Jackson had slid to the floor, his hand placed against his chest, his shirt soaked with blood. Rage unlike anything I'd ever known rushed into me.

"Stay with him. I have to find Coraline." The damn door to my condominium was unlocked. I knew within seconds that she wasn't inside. While there was no sign of a struggle, I doubted she'd left of her own free will. I glanced into my office, snarling the moment I noticed the contents on my desk. I flipped through a few of the pictures, sick at the sight of them. When I noticed the single piece of paper, I yanked, almost ripping it in two. I quickly read the damn letter, realizing instantly that if Coraline had looked at the contents, she could have been upset.

I unfolded the last corner of the letter and immediately my skin began to crawl.

It was the name of the person that Jade Brousseau had sent the letter to. A growl rose from my throat as my wolf began to surface. I couldn't allow a shift to happen, not until she was safe.

When I returned outside, Bronco looked up at me. There were tears in the man's eyes.

"I don't know, boss. I don't think he's going to make it," Bronco said.

"I called 9-1-1," Miller added.

"He *is* going to make it." I crouched down, touching Jackson's face. His eyes were still not dilated, but he was having even more difficulty breathing. "You're going to be alright. Just rest." I pulled his weapon from his hand. He'd seen the asshole coming. "Do you know who it was?"

"Na… No. Some… asshole. Atrium. Go. Save her."

Atrium.

"Get him to the hospital, Miller. Bronco, come with me."

I should have known she'd gone there. Was it possible she was safe from whatever had occurred?

The moment the doors opened on the third floor, my blood turned to ice. The scent of a gun being shot lingered in the air, strong enough for my keen senses to pick up. There was more.

Blood.

"Go that way," I directed to Bronco, moving in the direction of the stench. I found the reason why in less than a minute. Moose had been shot. Oh, God. I could tell by the sight of trampled plants that there'd been a scuffle. When I knelt down, I pressed my fingers against his neck. Thank God, he had a pulse.

Moose opened his eyes and stared into mine, his imploring, but at least he was able to thump his tail. I detected the stench of at least five assholes, all of them men.

"Just rest, little buddy. I'm looking for your mama." I patted his legs before rising to my feet, moving toward another section. There was no one else in the atrium, but they hadn't been gone for long. That much I knew.

When Bronco came forward, shaking his head, I slipped my weapon into my holster. "She was taken."

"What the hell happened to the dog?" he asked.

"I guess he got in their way."

"What the hell is going on, boss?"

I turned in a full circle. "Is Emilio still hunkered down?"

"From what I've been told. No visitors either. He's hiding out."

"First, we get help for Moose. Then we are going to have a nice visit with Emilio. This time, he will tell us everything he knows. Then he'll face the full penance of his actions."

CHAPTER 15

 abriel

Revenge.

That's what I wanted even though I knew it was the reason my family's life had forever been altered. However, I didn't give a shit whether the spirits would haunt me forever. I would find Coraline, and I would bring her home.

As I pulled into the parking lot of the veterinary hospital, Bronco exited immediately, scanning the location in case we'd been followed.

"You're good, boss," he said as he opened the rear door, stepping away as soon as he did so.

"Stay out here." As I gathered Moose into my arms, I could see such sadness in his big brown eyes. There was far too much bloodshed. When I walked inside, she was waiting with a gurney by her side. While a smile crossed her face, she was pensive. "Hello, Jenny." I'd kept tabs on the only other woman I'd cared about, finding it odd that she'd quit her high paying advertising job, returning to the work she'd done to support herself through college. "Your new profession suits you."

"What happened, Gabriel?" As she helped two male techs gets the pup on the gurney, I pushed aside memories of the past.

"He was in the wrong place at the wrong time. You need to take care of him. He's a very special dog."

"Yours?" she asked.

"No. He belongs to someone very special." I held my breath as he was taken behind a set of doors, my heart remaining heavy.

Jenny nodded. "I understand. We have the best team here. I'll stay with him tonight. Should I call you?"

"Please do." When I started to hand her my card with my private line, she pressed her hand against mine.

"I still remember your number. I'll let you know."

"Thanks." Sighing, I waited until she'd retreated behind those same doors before heading outside, tossing on my sunglasses. "It's time. You drive. I have a phone call to make."

"Is the dog going to be alright?" Bronco asked.

"He damn well better be."

As I dialed my father's number, I had a feeling what to expect from him.

"Son. I was expecting your call."

"You knew all along the damn Fontenot family was involved in this curse. They are descendants of the Brousseaus."

"Yes," he said quietly. "But I didn't know until recently. I was sent the pictures from the album I sent starting several months ago. One a month. Then the letter with the curse arrived a day before I called you. The Fontenots are the strong-arm portion of the Brousseau family. While they don't practice the old ways of black magic, they don't need to. They are dangerous in their own right."

Of course they were. They'd challenged our hold on Louisiana as well as Florida for years. However, we'd thought of them as little more than an annoyance up to this point.

"They've taken Coraline. Why didn't you tell me mating with her wasn't my only obligation to fulfill this bloody curse?"

"Would you have followed through if I had?" he asked, half laughing after doing so.

I thought about his question. "No."

"I thought if you were lucky enough to fall in love, then maybe it wouldn't be a burden."

Laughing, I stared out the window, watching the world float by, a world where others had no idea that monsters lurked in the shadows, waiting to consume flesh and blood. "I have fallen in love with her, but I refuse to turn her."

"Then the Brousseau family will have won."

"Put the extended family on notice. I will need their help. I have a feeling she's been returned to the Bayou."

"You're probably right. Call me when you find out for certain."

"I assure you that I will." I almost tossed the phone when I ended the call.

"What the hell, boss?" Bronco barely managed.

"We are facing an enemy unlike anything we've ever seen before. That means a good portion of my soldiers will learn my true identity." I turned my head, allowing him to see a slight change in my eyes.

While he shifted in his seat, also twisting his hands around the steering wheel, he had no expression on his face. "That won't bother any of them, boss. We'll remain loyal."

We would see.

Fortunately, the drive wasn't long; I had doubts I would have been able to control my wolf. He wanted his own taste of revenge, something I was determined to allow. If Emilio thought hiding out in a seedy little motel was going to save his life, he was dead wrong.

I thought about the photo album as well as the ploy with the Feds. The play had been one of the best I'd experienced, causing the downfall of my reputation as well as allowing them to take Coraline without incident.

I didn't waste any time exiting the vehicle, bursting into the room. Emilio immediately backed away, attempting to reach for his gun.

"I wouldn't do that if I were you, Emilio."

Bronco closed the door behind us, merely standing guard in front.

"I gave you a chance, one that would have saved lives. You failed me again. You do know what that means."

Sweat immediately slid down both sides of his face. He shifted his gaze back and forth, the terror in his eyes more intense than usual. "I couldn't help you, Mr. Dupree. They would have killed me. I'm here because I think they want me dead anyway."

"The Fontenots?"

He seemed surprised I knew. "Yeah, Tony. He's the fucking asshole leader right now. Horrible bastard."

I almost laughed. It was apparent that despite my reputation, he feared what Tony would do far more than I. "Interesting." I clamped my fist around his shirt, easily able to lift and toss him onto the bed. Then I leaned over, sliding the weapon from his pocket and into mine. "I'm going to ask you once, then I'm going to start shooting, but there won't be any kill shots, at least not yet. Do you understand?"

At least he had the good sense to nod in affirmation.

"Excellent. I need to know where they would take a very good friend of mine."

"I don't know. I swear to God. They didn't tell me shit."

I placed the barrel of the gun just above his right knee. "I don't have time to waste, Emilio. One last time. Where is she?"

"I honest to God don't know."

Now the fucker was sweating profusely.

Although I moved the weapon away from his leg, when I fired a single shot, he jerked back, letting out a howl and pitching down on the bed. Sighing, I wasn't entirely certain I was going to get anywhere and that truly pissed me off. "Am I just wasting my time here?"

When he didn't respond right away, I yanked him by the shirt again. He was panting from fear. At least he knew what I was capable of.

"There's a place… a burial ground in the Bayou. I promise you that I don't know the exact location. I just heard one of the assholes talking about it."

I shifted my attention to Bronco. "Why don't you go to the car? Contact the pilot. We're headed to Louisiana."

Bronco shifted his gaze to Emilio then nodded before exiting the room.

I slowly returned my attention to Emilio, patting him on the opposite leg. He flinched, whimpering as he fisted the comforter. "I'm sorry, Mr. Dupree. I never wanted this to happen."

While every indication gave me the sense that he was telling the truth, he still needed to learn a valuable lesson, one I hoped this time he wouldn't forget.

As I started to shift, he was mesmerized.

Until my claws formed, breaking through the tips of my nails.

Then he threw his head back and screamed.

* * *

The Bayou. While it existed all around Baton Rouge, the boggy terrain was the densest around Thibodaux.

Returning to the godforsaken place angered my senses. However, as soon as I stepped out of the rented Jeep, I was able to indulge in her sweet scent.

As well as the stench of her terror.

At least she was still alive.

Other vehicles moved into position within seconds. I was almost surprised to see all three of my brothers had arrived with a hefty contingency of their soldiers. They'd been advised of the existence of the photo album as well as the letter sent to the great-great-grandfather of Tony Fontenot. They knew what was at stake. They'd also experienced other difficulties with further attempts at sabotaging their businesses. It was time to draw a line in the sand.

With blood.

There were also other Dupree descendants who'd joined the effort, most of them remaining in the shadows of the forest, some already making the transition into wolves. What remained troubling was our inability to sense the perpetrators. Perhaps that was one aspect of the curse Jade had made certain to use in order to keep her thousands of descendants safe.

Luke had sent me the email he'd promised, although I'd had little time to spend on deciphering the names. However, it was clear the Brousseau tree branched off into several factions. While it would appear a solid number of the original family members had remained alive after the massacre, their numbers had been significantly diluted.

That didn't mean they didn't carry a powerful gene, one provided by the voodoo priestess. They had certain advantages over our family, which had enabled them to become so destructive. And they'd been able to prepare for the year of the two blue moons.

"What the hell are we doing here?" Marcel asked.

"Saving our future," Christoff answered.

While darkness was settling in, the limited light hadn't hindered our abilities. We could see clearly into the forest, although I knew both the rough terrain as well as the blackened skies would impede our soldiers' efforts. After taking a deep whiff, I realized that the smaller animals had fled, aware that a battle was about to ensue. Smart little creatures.

As requested, several of the soldiers had brought powerful lights with them, although they'd been instructed to keep them dark until given the orders otherwise.

"Are you certain we should shift?" Sebastian asked after he flanked my side.

"We have no other choice if we want to defeat them," I snarled.

"And save your mate," Marcel said, his tone continuing to remain furious.

I narrowed my eyes as I looked at him. "Do you now believe what our father told us?"

He hesitated, scanning the woods. "I'm no longer certain what to believe. We have far too many enemies at this point."

"Which means we can't let our guard down at any time," Christoff hissed then pulled his assault rifle in front of him. "We kill anyone who attempts to get in our way."

While I wasn't interested in starting an all-out war, I would do whatever was necessary to get my mate back. After taking another deep whiff, my gut told me we had no time to waste. If our intel was wrong, the location centered in another part of the Bayou, our attempts at ending the first stage of the battle would be lost.

That couldn't happen.

"It's time." I moved out first, heading in the direction where my wolf guided me. As we moved into the thicker part of the forest, the ground squishing beneath our feet, the stench of mold and decay became more appalling. I could hear several of the soldiers mumbling, unaccustomed to the bog. They would soon learn how to navigate or perish to the other murderous creatures who owned a good portion of the area.

Poisonous snakes.

Alligators.

Mountain lions.

I continually scanned the area, every sound penetrating my eardrums. We'd gone well over a mile when I heard what sounded like voices. I threw out my arm, stopping those closest from continuing.

Sebastian moved around me, taking two additional steps. Then he turned to face me, his eyes already glowing. "Less than half a mile."

"Yes…" I snarled under my breath. I moved down the line of men, providing details about what I wanted them to do, which included spreading further into the outlying perimeter of the forest to enable us to encircle as much of the area as possible.

Then the full push was on.

As we raced forward, the voices of our enemy became much clearer. There were at least two dozen of the bastards just ahead, likely more in the surrounding trees. I had no doubt they were prepared for our arrival. Just waiting for the massacre to begin.

Within seconds, the stench became stronger, a dim glow in the distance drawing my attention. A fire.

They were planning on sacrificing Coraline just like their ancestors had been. I started to run as did the others. Within seconds, gunshots rang out, several bright lights turned in our direction. They were attempting to outmaneuver us.

I got off several rounds, taking down at least four of their men. Then my wolf refused to ignore his needs. As the transformation began, I sensed my brothers were also succumbing to their hunger. Pain ripped through my body, forcing me to the ground. I was gasping for air, every sound becoming more intensified, every smell enticing my beast.

When my claws were freed, I pawed the ground, able to gather Coraline's scent with ease. And I could read her mind. She was terrified, struggling with the bindings keeping her immobile. I sprang forward, my body finishing the last of the transition, racing through the forest as I issued low, husky growls. I was calling all the others, preparing them for the fight ahead.

A series of screams and anguished cries floated into the night sky, the sound like sweet music. Panting, I shifted from one side to the other, picking off several enemies before they had a chance to fire a single shot. But there more, so many of them, the attack well planned.

I was forced to ignore the horrible cries, trying to connect mentally with Coraline. She needed to stay calm in order to survive. The forest reeked of blood, the coppery scent fueling the drive, my need to feed. But now wasn't the time.

"There's so many of them," Sebastian relayed, our mental tether fully in place.

"Find my mate," I instructed, powering forward.

"Go. Go. Go!" Christoff added, suddenly within inches of me. A flash drew our attention, one of their soldiers taking aim and firing.

Christoff lunged toward the man, his actions pushing him in front of me. Even though the bullet hit him square in the chest, he didn't falter, reaching the terrified man and within seconds, tearing him apart. When he fell to the ground, I bounded in his direction.

"Go," he instructed. *"I will heal."*

And he would, the shot just missing his heart. I let off another howl then broke through a line of trees. The sight in front of me drove my rage to the extreme.

Coraline was tied to a pole, the thick rope wound all the way to her ankles. Beneath her was a heaping pile of brush, beside her a lit torch, the flame licking toward the heavens.

I took several deep breaths, waiting as dozens of my people moved into a circle, all with weapons pointed in their direction. The standoff would end with a significant loss of life, but as with all battles of this kind, the loss of life was necessary for continued evolution.

"Be careful, brother," Marcel said, his wolf gleaming in the firelight.

"Find the leader. The bastard is here," I instructed to every creature then padded forward, stopping only yards away from the horrific scene. Coraline was struggling to take

deep breaths, her eyes full of fear. *"Look at me, Coraline. I am here."*

I couldn't be certain whether our mating was enough to connect our minds. When she slowly lifted her head, her gaze finding mine, I gave her an exaggerated nod. Her resilience was strong, a smile crossing her face.

"How?" she asked in her mind, although I sensed she was finally able to understand.

"Because I am Lycan."

She seemed to take comfort in my answer, holding her head high.

"Well. Well. Well. I expected you sooner."

The voice came from behind the pylon but within seconds, the asshole moved into the light. He was a large man, at least six foot five, his blond hair glowing in the torturous light.

I clawed the ground as a response, inching closer. The men flanking his side immediately raised their weapons. I was surprised most of them were filled with terror. They hadn't been told what to expect. While our soldiers were mystified, it was obvious rumors had given them partial information on who and what we were.

"There are at least two more lines of their men behind him," Sebastian communicated as he inched closer.

"We will go through them all," I said, growling afterwards.

"You need to survive," Marcel scoffed.

"I assure you I will, brother. This is just the beginning." I took careful steps toward the obvious leader, realizing from what limited information I'd found on the Fontenot family that the man standing in front of me was Tony Fontenot, the prince of his father's crime syndicate, the man ready to take over given his father's ill health. Two powerful families with dangerous pasts.

"I'm sorry. You can't talk, but I know who you are," Tony said then laughed, causing all the men surrounding him to do the same. "I'm Tony Fontenot, but I guess you already knew that. You're nothing if not prepared for your enemy. Or were you this time?" He dared to brush his fingers across Coraline's arm before walking closer.

She recoiled, hissing after he walked away. "Bastard."

"Breathe, Coraline. Don't provoke him," I said, swinging my head in her direction.

Her questions increased, but she remained quiet.

"Did you enjoy the little shows I put on? The questions. The accusations. I particularly enjoyed tipping off the reporter. Too bad he interrupted that fabulous charity event. But I got to see it all up close and personal."

I hadn't been able to detect the bastard's presence at the event. Christ.

"Anyway," he continued. "As you can see, I'm prepared to sacrifice your beloved mate. I was hoping you'd arrive in time to see the glorious event. By the way, I just want to point out that we outnumber you. There is nothing you can do about it. My only hope is that in the process, the entire Dupree family will be exterminated. You see, I knew all four of you would come to save the day, which only leaves that disgusting brother of yours in prison. I have special plans for him."

There was no time to waste. As I commanded the others in my mind, I leapt off the ground.

In the melee that followed, hundreds of shots were fired. I felt every blow that wolf members of my family were forced to endure, some of the bullets issued killing blows. While our attack was savage, Tony managed to yank the torch from the ground, lighting the aged wood. As flames erupted, Coraline screamed, fighting with the rope holding her in place.

No longer did anything matter except for saving her. I lunged over the flames, my sharp canines piercing the rope. It took several seconds to chew my way through. As the bindings startled to unfurl, my mate fought, knowing her life depended on it. When she managed to free her arms, dragging the rest of the rope away, she reached out for me.

"Gabriel!"

"Trust me. Jump on my back. You can do it." I only prayed she continued hearing me. When she followed my command, pistoning her body away from the killing flames and grabbing onto my back, I threw my head toward the

blackened sky and bellowed. The smoke was thick, the acrid stench rushing all around us. She clung to me, digging her nails into the scruff on my neck as I bolted away from the fire. The pelting gunfire continued, screams erupting from every corner, but nothing would stop me from saving her.

I raced through the forest, able to lose the assholes following me within minutes. When I finally breached the other side, I sensed her exhaustion as the adrenaline flow that had kept her from panicking faded away. I slowed then finally stopped, allowing her to slip to the ground.

A single whimper escaped her mouth as she crawled away from me, her eyes never blinking. She took several deep breaths then struggled to rise to her feet, holding her arms as she scanned the darkness.

"Why do I know what you're saying? How?" she asked, her voice breathless.

While no danger remained close, I took my time scouting the perimeter before moving closer. I cocked my head, studying her intently. A trickle of fear remained in her, but her curiosity continued to increase.

"Because you're my mate." I could easily tell she understood, a slight smile crossing her face, even though her eyes continued to show she was drifting into shock. I moved closer until we were only inches apart.

Every move she made tentative, she reached out, finally stroking my muzzle. "Gabriel."

"Yes."

The wind had shifted, pushing the stink of blood and death away. As I lifted my head, staring at the full moon, I knew in the bowels of my being the war between the two families was just beginning.

* * *

Two days later

There was a somber aura in my father's house even though nothing had changed since my last visit. A knowing had settled in, a realization that the fight we were facing would continue to be bloody as hell, far too many lives lost. While we'd proven we were a force to be reckoned with, the curse remained active.

I barely tasted the drink in my hand, the liquor doing little to calm my nerves or the now constant hunger burdening my system. My brothers seemed to be experiencing the same subtle yet powerful emotions that we hadn't been able to ignore.

"Tony Fontenot hasn't been found," our father said as he continued to stare out the window of his office. He hadn't moved in several minutes, barely touching his drink.

"The area in the Bayou has been cleaned," Sebastian said more in passing. Of all of us, he seemed the least affected, even handling business while a combination of our soldiers had been commanded to scour the kill zone for any evidence.

Exhaling, I took another sip, the burn in the back of my throat enough to rile my wolf. "He must be found."

Pops laughed, shifting a quick glance in my direction. "He won't surface again until necessary."

"He's hiding with his tail between his legs," Marcel chortled.

"There was no winner in the recent battle, brother," I chastised. "Too many lives were lost because we were caught off guard."

"Then what the hell do you suggest we do?" Christoff asked.

I thought about his question. There was no easy answer. "We prepare and you hunt for your mates." While I'd searched for the reporter, he'd disappeared, but there was evidence he'd been removed by someone else. Tony had taken steps to eliminate any loose ends.

Sebastian laughed. "I asked the question before. How the hell are we supposed to do that?"

"You keep your damn eyes and ears open. Allow your wolf to come to the surface but learn to control him," Pops ordered then turned around to face us. "The Fontenots cannot command an inch of our turf. Do what you need to in order to keep that from happening. And for God's sake, find your mate, Sebastian."

His command was clear, his chest heaving. He walked closer to the group of us, finally placing his hand on my shoulder. "The enemy will retreat for a short period of time, which will allow us to repair the damage they've done. But make no mistake. They will return with a vengeance."

The words finally seemed to settle into all of us. I took a deep breath, longing to get the fuck out of Louisiana. However, there was one last task before I would be able to coax Coraline from leaving.

I would return to her house in search of answers for the reason behind her mother's murder as well as why the spirits had chosen her was important to the woman I'd sworn to protect.

I owed her that, even if she refused to accept the final portion of the terrible curse. I'd yet to tell my father about her decision for fear he would retaliate in some manner in order to protect the family.

I loved her.

Not just as my intended mate, but as a man longing to spend the rest of my life with her. While the future might not be cast in stone just yet, I would find a way to continue sharing the joys of our passion.

Even if it meant eventually losing my life.

CHAPTER 16

abriel

Fear.

It continued to resonate in Coraline, enough so she was wringing her hands. As I reached over, I expected her to flinch. She'd yet to relax, unable to completely process what had occurred only days before.

"Did you call about Moose?" she asked as I pulled the Jeep down the same road where she'd first been attacked.

"He's doing well."

"Don't lie to me, Gabriel. That's all you've said for three days."

Exhaling, I gently placed my hand on her knee, squeezing more for comfort than anything else. "I'm not lying, Coraline. He's in good hands, recovering without issue."

She slowly turned her head in my direction. "He's more important to me than you understand."

"You don't have to explain." The tension between us was unsettling, but the last thing I wanted to do was push her. As I neared the house her mother had sold her, I sensed her anxiety increasing. "Are you certain you want to do this?"

"I have to know what those monsters did. Besides, I need to know why my mother never told me the truth."

"Remember that the truth can be more harmful than the fiction."

Coraline laughed. "In this case, you're wrong."

As I pulled in front of the house, it was easy to see someone had invaded her privacy. The door remained slightly ajar, the front blind twisted. When she leaned forward, shaking her head, I reached for my weapon before killing the engine. "Stay here until I come for you."

"Do you really think one of those assholes remains inside?"

"It's entirely possible."

"I don't care any longer. I'm angry enough I'll kill them with my bare hands." She bolted out of the Jeep, heading for the front door.

I moved behind her, unable to detect any sign of human life. She hesitated before pushing open the door. As we'd both expected, the place was in disarray, furniture turned over, various objects tossed around the room. She remained quiet as she walked through the house, barely touching anything except for a single dog's toy, tossing it and watching as it landed on the kitchen table.

"She must have left me something. Anything," she whispered. "I'm going to find it."

As she moved through the house, I kept my distance even though I searched the various rooms in case there was anything tangible with regard to future plans. From what I could tell, the bastards had only meant to threaten her by disturbing her life. She was methodical in her search, looking in every drawer and closet, cursing under her breath when she found nothing except for a necklace. Huffing, she seemed relieved, clutching the piece in her hand. I allowed her to walk away, giving her some time, yet I remained on edge.

I found her minutes later staring up at small opening to the attic.

"Help me," she said, her tone demanding. When I didn't respond at first, she snapped her head in my direction, her eyes pleading. "Help me."

As I pushed aside the thin piece of plywood, dragging the rickety stairs into position, she remained pensive.

"Let me do this," she said in such a whispered voice that I could tell just how despondent she was.

I backed away, allowing her to climb the stairs. Every part of me craved being by her side. While she wasn't fragile, her entire world had been turned upside down. I couldn't imagine how difficult it was for her to accept what was expected of her.

My patience was gone after a few minutes, forcing me to head into the attic. She sat cross-legged in front of a trunk, the only thing positioned in the small space. Without uttering a single word, I moved beside her, hunkering down. In her hands were several photographs, including family photos. It was obvious the baby being held in the woman's arms was Coraline, the man to the right completely uncomfortable with the picture being taken.

There was also an open letter that rested next to her knee.

After a few seconds, she acknowledged my presence.

"It would seem my father was a distant relative of the Brousseau family. As my mother writes in this letter, he was given a special gift, the ability to cast a spell over a woman in order to woo her to have his child." She laughed. "She explains that she learned only after giving birth that her husband had lied to her, but she kept what she'd found a secret, raising me as if we were a normal little family. At least she came to her senses, tossing him out. By then she'd developed a life in Thibodaux, fearful what would happen if she tried to leave."

I took the piece of paper off the floor, scanning the contents, the letter written only four weeks before. The contents of the letter indicated the Brousseau family had groomed several individuals the same way as they had her father, rewarding them for luring unsuspecting women into their lairs. It was likely her mother was murdered for what she'd learned.

The last paragraph was the most damning.

Her mother had already been impregnated by another man, someone she'd fallen in love with, the man killed just because he was in the way.

"My mother had secrets," she stated with no emotion. "But she fell in love. She knew the man was special, meant to be a significant part of ending the curse. She must have been heartbroken at the loss of the man she loved, which is what allowed her to be lured by my father in the first place. Then she accepted what had happened. She knew if she didn't, my life would be in danger every day." Coraline laughed bitterly, finally turning her head in my direction. "I am your intended mate."

Her statement was definitive, but the sadness in her eyes remained. "She loved you," I struggled to say.

"Yes, she did." She opened her hand, fingering the small necklace she'd found. Without telling me its significance, she placed it around her neck, patting the small cross after doing so.

"I can't force you to accept this destiny. This is your home. I don't wish to force you to leave."

"Do you love me, Gabriel?"

"Yes." I was able to answer without hesitation.

Her lower lip quivered, yet there was a twinkle of hope in her eyes. "Then this isn't my home. My home is with you, the man I've fallen in love with."

She couldn't know how much her words meant, or the sentiment around them. While I had no full understanding of what the future would bring, I knew that it was possible to build a life together.

Somehow.

Some way…

* * *

Coraline

Two weeks later

"In business news, Dupree Enterprises, an innovator of highly sought after computer technology, has been awarded a multimillion-dollar exclusive contract with the Barton Group, the leader in providing home electronics."

I stood in front of the television, watching the evening news with keen interest. Gabriel had been so worried about reestablishing his relationship with the owner of the company on the news that he'd lost several nights of sleep.

"You didn't tell me you signed the contract with Barton," I said in passing as I sensed his presence. While he remained quiet, a trickle of shivers skated down my spine, my breath skipping. When he walked closer, easing my hair away from my neck, the feel of his hot breath forced my nipples into full arousal. "That's not fair."

"Who said anything in life is fair?" he mused before issuing a single growl, lowering his head and pressing his lips across my already heated skin.

I closed my eyes briefly, enjoying the quiet moment, my hunger increasing with every passing second. "Bad boy."

"Yes, one big, bad wolf," he murmured then slipped a glass of champagne over my shoulder. As he dangled it in front of me, I noticed something sparkly in the bottom.

"What have you done?"

"My baby deserves treats."

The single bark from across the room indicated Moose thought Gabriel was talking about him. We both laughed, Gabriel immediately beckoning for the pup.

Moose was only too happy to bound closer, his tail swirling in circle after circle. The thought of almost losing him remained heavy on my mind.

"You're going to get him excited," I managed, my voice barely a whisper.

"I was hoping to get you excited."

I pulled away on purpose, shuddering to my core. After watching the two of them interact for a few seconds, I peered into the glass. There were two diamond earrings. The man had been showering me with gifts for a solid two weeks.

Wolf.

The word was never far from my mind. While the nightmares had abated, my thoughts had remained intact. What had happened was more than just a nightmare. Still, I'd been lucky to find the love of my life, although a small part of me still believed I should have pushed him away. However, I knew in my heart that wouldn't have lasted, my resolve giving in. Our connection was far too strong, increasing every day.

The fact I could read his thoughts, communicate without speaking remained a mystery as well as a shock, but being able to know what he was thinking often came in handy. Especially when he thought I was being a disobedient little woman. I licked the rim of my glass, biting back a laugh. Just to see him with Moose was a sheer joy. I was grateful every day that my pup had almost fully recovered.

I was happy, more so than anyone could believe, but a tension remained between us, the last jagged knife edge of the curse. He'd yet to approach me with a discussion, but I could tell he was thinking about it more and more. The first blue moon was in little over a month, his hunger continuing to increase. While he'd been able to control it most of the time, I'd known every time he'd left our bed, foraging in the darkness for food.

He'd provided no details and I hadn't asked for them. Still, the thought of being forced to turn into a... creature was horrifying, even if I'd be allowed to remain human the majority of the time. I took a sip of champagne, almost laughing at the way the bubbles tickled my nose. In the beautiful waning light of the glorious sunny afternoon, the jewelry sparkled, giving me a series of quivers.

He'd brought me to his house in the Hamptons, the structure more like a mansion. However, he was right in that we both needed respite as well as privacy. We'd also needed time together, to learn about each other and to allow Moose some kind of normal life after all he'd been through.

As Gabriel walked toward me, a twinkle in his eyes, I could easily tell what he had on his mind, and it didn't have anything to do with our special connection.

His cock was rock hard, throbbing against his jeans.

I just realized what he was wearing and couldn't help but laugh.

"What's so funny?" he asked as he closed the distance, towering over me given my bare feet.

"You. I've never seen you in jeans before."

"Hmmm... I am a man of many layers."

"Uh-huh. And you're full of hot air."

Without hesitation, he whisked the glass from my hand, taking long strides then planting both on the bookshelf. Laughing, I raced away from him, darting around the couch. His grin remained as he moved from one side to the other in his attempt to reach me, but I was too fast for him.

Then he jumped over the couch, yanking me into his arms. As he fisted my hair at my scalp, dragging me even closer, my heart hammered against my chest. He had a way of doing that to me.

"You should know by now you can't get away from me."

"You sure about that?" I asked as I palmed his chest.

When he let off a series of growls, my pussy clenched and released. God, what the man was able to do to me.

"I'm certain," he muttered then captured my mouth. I adored the taste of him, the way he felt in my arms. He was so strong, so alive and energetic. The electricity roaring through us like a freight train only increased with every day, my desire explosive.

As he thrust his tongue inside my mouth, a quiet resolve fell over me. While I missed what I'd built in my life, I couldn't imagine spending a day without him. I questioned my reasoning every day, including whether or not it was the curse talking, but my heart told me otherwise.

The letter and pictures my mother had left barely began to scratch the surface of why she'd allowed herself to be used. Although I suspected that her belief in the religion as opposed to the black magic of voodoo was the reason. Still, I had a feeling there was so much more to the story, something that might never be revealed. I would learn to live with that eventually.

I wrapped my arm around his neck, fingering his hair. The way his cock was pressing against my tummy kept shivers dancing all the way down to my toes. However, I was feeling particularly mischievous this evening, more so than I had since our arrival.

When he broke the kiss, nipping on my lower lip, I gave him a hard shove, able to break free then dash toward the door. I managed to make it halfway up the stairs before he snagged me, easily tossing me over his shoulder.

"I thought you knew better than to tease and disobey me," he said in a husky voice.

I pounded on his back, unable to keep from laughing as Moose stood in the doorway, barking up a storm. He'd learned how playful we were together, enjoying the family time almost as much as chasing the ball on the beach.

Even if it was freezing outside.

I should have known Gabriel was up to something, his jovial mood entirely different than normal. When he took me into the kitchen, thumping me down on the table, I did everything I could to scramble away.

But it was no use.

He pressed down on the small of my back then yanked my dress up to my waist. The single snap of his fingers indicated he'd ripped another pair of panties from my body. The man owned me at least a dozen pairs.

"Let go of me."

"Not going to happen until you learn to obey me."

"But I've been a good girl."

"Right. You backtalk me constantly. You refuse to follow orders. That alone means you deserve a harsh spanking." The lilt in his voice was so damn sexy, the change in him entirely different than I'd expected.

I looked over my shoulder, realizing he'd shoved a wooden brush in his pocket. He'd been planning this all along. "You are such a bastard!" I teased.

"So you've told me before. Keep your position or I will start again."

When he brought down the brush, I cringed from the sound alone. While the pain was intense, I bit back any sound, refusing to give in.

"Bad, bad girl," he huffed then delivered so many in rapid succession that I lost count.

"Ouch! That hurts like hell."

He leaned over, crushing his weight against mine. "Spankings are supposed to hurt, my woman."

"Your woman, huh?" I barely managed to get the words out of my mouth before he started again. The heat and anguish continued to build as well as the dazzling sensations swept through me like a firestorm, the scent of my raging desire undeniable. When he wouldn't stop, I whimpered on purpose, trying to gain some level of sympathy.

He wasn't buying it, smacking me again and again.

Finally, I gave in, pressing my face against the cool wood of the table. He seemed to sense my resignation, slowly lowering the dreaded brush only inches from my face before leaning over again. "I'm going to devour you, my mate."

He pulled me into his arms, jerking me off my feet. Gasping from his roughness, I wrapped my legs around him, giving him a sly smile as I immediately reached for his button and zipper. The grin on his face was adorably evil, pushing me into a heightened level of bliss.

When I finally freed his cock, my mouth watered, hungry to drain every drop of cum. But he was having none of it, walking me toward the table once again. As he eased me onto the edge, I stroked the base of his shaft, pumping as I twisted my hand, creating a wave of friction.

"Mmm... Be careful what you do, little girl."

"I don't want to be careful."

His upper lip curling, he impaled me with the entire length of his cock, filling me instantly, my muscles aching as they always did from the intensity of our sex.

"Oh..." Gasping, I clung to his shoulders as my pussy clenched around the thick invasion.

"Mmm... Yes. You're so tight."

I gazed into his eyes, realizing the glow around his irises had changed as they always did when we made love. A strange but settling emotion passed through me, a peace that I hadn't felt before.

He pulled almost all the way out, teasing me as he smiled. When I bucked my hips, tempting him, he pounded hard and fast, driving me almost instantly to the point of a mind-blowing orgasm. I was shocked how quickly my body responded, the climax rushing through me faster than a tidal wave.

"Oh. Oh. Oh!" I threw my head back, slapping my hands on the table, stars floating in front of my eyes.

Every thrust was more brutal than the one before, his needs increasing. Even though I could tell he was doing everything to control his desire, I couldn't help myself and squeezed.

His eyes flew open, a series of growls coming from deep within him. When he couldn't hold back any longer, he erupted deep inside with a loud roar toward the heavens.

A few seconds later, he laughed, his eyes closed as he lowered his head. "Such a naughty girl."

I said nothing, swallowing hard then issuing the words I'd never thought I'd say. "Turn me."

He didn't respond at first. Then he opened his eyes, searching mine. "You don't know what you're asking."

"Yes, I do."

"There is no going back."

"I know, but if I don't then I'll lose you. I can't allow that to happen. I do love you, Gabriel. I don't know why or if I should, but I do. Now, you must trust me. I know what I want and what I'm asking."

He remained rigid then pulled away, adjusting his trousers as he turned around. "Your life will forever be changed."

"It already has been. Turn me."

I would never forget the look in his eyes as his beast rose to the surface for a few seconds. Maybe they would haunt me for the rest of my life. Maybe I'd learn to hate seeing them, but I knew what I was asking was the right thing.

My mother had been right.

This was my destiny.

The night was gorgeous, not a cloud in the sky, the stars brighter than I'd ever seen them. While still cold, I felt an incredible warmth inside, as if my entire body was electrified. Just standing with my feet in the sand, the rolling waters of the ocean crashing against the shoreline was amazing. But the three-quarter moon was the star of the show, almost close enough I could reach out and touch the giant orb. There was almost a distinct blue hue that was more pronounced than the night before.

"Are you certain?" Gabriel asked, as he had several more times since the day before.

"Yes."

He cupped my face, brushing his thumb across my cheek. The way his eyes shimmered continued to fascinate me. He'd warned me of what I'd experience, the pain that I'd be forced to endure when shifting for the first few times. He'd also described the hunger and what it would be like.

While I wasn't capable of completely understanding, I knew I would never be alone.

As he backed away, removing his clothes, I couldn't take my eyes off him. I'd seen him as his wolf, as well as dozens of others. They were majestic creatures, unlike the stupid depictions in the movies. However, I'd yet to see him shift.

I braced myself, uncertain of my reaction, holding my breath as the transformation began.

The ground beneath my feet vibrated, his howls echoing in my ears. I swallowed several times, my heart racing when he dropped onto all fours. While I felt a moment of fear, I knew he would never hurt me. I found myself moving closer, finding the experience incredible, although the horrible sound as his bones broke, the agony spilling across his face sent butterflies into my stomach.

When he stopped moving, only then did I take a step away, struggling to control my breathing.

Gabriel slowly lifted his head, staring at me with such intensity. He was a glorious wolf, his ebony fur still shimmering in the darkness.

"Are you alright?" he communicated, sending tingles down my legs.

"Yes," I said out loud. "I'm fine."

He padded closer, coming within a few inches, waiting for me to run away instead.

I slowly lowered to my knees, now able to see him at eye level.

"I will always protect and love you, Coraline."

"I know." When I could feel his hot breath skipping along my skin, I closed my eyes and shifted my head, exposing my neck. With every passing second, I grew more and more lightheaded.

There was no way to describe the sensation as his canines broke through my tender flesh, but within seconds, an odd yet amazing feeling of euphoria engulfed my system. As quickly as the incident had occurred it ended.

Then I heard his intense howl. He was making a statement as well as a threat.

His family wouldn't be fucked with.

Anyone who tried would face his wrath.

Gabriel

"Handle it, Bronco. That fuck isn't going to back out of our deal. If he gives you any additional trouble, do what you need to."

"Will do, boss. Damn assholes. The shitass rumor about wolves has really gotten people scared," Bronco huffed.

I snorted even though I remained pissed. Three regular customers had attempted to back out. That wasn't going to happen. Since returning to normal business activities, the fear was no longer regarding the Fontenot family or their fake curses they'd attempted to use. It was regarding the ugliness swirling around man-eating monsters searching through the forests. While my soldiers had remained loyal, I'd seen the looks in their eyes the first time they'd been in my presence since the attack in the forest.

Fear.

Blatant fear.

They had no way of knowing since I'd turned Coraline that my hunger was far easier to control.

"Business is business, Bronco. Make certain the pig understands that."

Bronco laughed. "My pleasure. By the way, I'm real glad Jackson is going to be alright."

"I am as well." I ended the call, shoving my phone into my jacket pocket.

"How's Jackson?" Coraline asked, as she had every day.

"He'll make a full recovery."

"I'm so glad. He is a special guy, and he adores you."

"And how would you know that?" I asked, half laughing.

She shrugged, giving me a mischievous look. "I know things."

"Uh-huh. That's what I'm afraid of."

"Trouble in paradise?" she asked.

I'd debated taking the call with her in the car but given the shit that was going down, I'd had no other choice. Just returning to Chicago had been a necessity. "Nothing I can't handle."

"What about Alex?"

Exhaling, I turned to face her, seeing a glimmer in her eyes. She had a way of putting me in a better mood just with a simple smile. "He's hanging around."

"Even after all the rumors?"

I couldn't help but laugh. "What sane person actually believes there are such things as werewolves?"

"Loup-garou to be exact."

"Hmmm… It seems you've been spending far too much time on the computer."

"Perhaps. What about this asshole from Louisiana?"

Tony had still yet to surface, likely given he'd lost a significant number of his soldiers. However, he'd sent word to cease all acts of revenge, even though I knew that would only continue for a matter of time. He was licking his wounds, preparing for the next attack. "The family members and their soldiers are being controlled."

"Which means we're all still in danger."

I pulled her hand to my lips, dragging my tongue across her knuckles.

"Be careful. You're driving. Where are we going anyway?" she asked, her skin glowing. She was wearing the earrings I'd bought her, something she did often. She'd yet to shift, although I saw no rush in forcing her to do so until her hunger bridged the surface. However, she was even more beautiful.

"A surprise and do not ask or I might have to pull over and give you a spanking in the middle of the car."

"No, you wouldn't."

"Don't tempt me."

She laughed, the lilt floating through the Mercedes. Instead of the spanking, maybe I'd just fuck her instead.

A quiet settled between us until I took an exit off the highway. Then she sighed.

"They will come after the family. Won't they?" she asked.

"Yes, in time, but we will better be prepared."

When she turned her head, a single tear slipped past her lashes. "I hope so."

"Trust me, my beautiful mate. No one will ever hurt you again."

"Except you," she said, laughing to break the somber mood. After I made a few turns, she sat up in her seat, staring out the windshield. "Confess. What is this surprise?"

"Such impatience." The smile remained as I turned down the last street. "We're going to search for a house. I found one I think you'll like close to this neighborhood."

"Seriously? What about the condo? I thought you loved it there."

"It's cold and impersonal. Plus, there's no yard for Moose to play in or our children."

"We're having children?" she teased.

"Ten at least."

"Not a chance in hell."

When I pulled into a parking lot, she frowned. "Funny-looking house."

"I never said the house was the only surprise. Did I?" When I parked the car, she groused under her breath, climbing out when I did. When I pulled a wad of keys from my pocket, she cocked her head.

Then when she finally noticed the sign next to the door, she gasped. "What have you done?"

"You lost your clinic when we left. I know how much you miss your practice. I thought it was only fair to purchase you a new one." As I unlocked the door, I studied her reaction.

The moment she walked inside, she squealed. Then she threw her arms around me. "This is amazing."

"So are you."

"Thank you. This means so much to me." She pressed her lips against my cheek then backed away, acting like a kid in a candy store as she moved through the various rooms.

Tonight I'd ask her to become my wife, to share a life with me in all aspects. I loved her. I'd never believed I was a man capable of feeling anything, but Coraline had changed my life. While danger would always lurk in the shadows, the curse hanging over our heads, our family had only grown stronger.

The legend would be retold to our children, and in my mind, I knew there was yet another portion to go through. Somehow, we would endure.

Because we were creatures of the night, predators who would stop at nothing to protect our family.

Werewolves.

Lycans.

Loup-garou…

The End

AFTERWORD

Stormy Night Publications would like to thank you for your interest in our books.

If you liked this book (or even if you didn't), we would really appreciate you leaving a review on the site where you purchased it. Reviews provide useful feedback for us and our authors, and this feedback (both positive comments and constructive criticism) allows us to work even harder to make sure we provide the content our customers want to read.

If you would like to check out more books from Stormy Night Publications, if you want to learn more about our company, or if you would like to join our mailing list, please visit our website at:

http://www.stormynightpublications.com

BOOKS OF THE BENEDETTI EMPIRE SERIES

Cruel Prince

Catherine's father conspired to have my father killed, and that debt to the Benedetti family must be settled. Just as he took something from me, I will take something from him.

His daughter.

She will be mine to punish and ravage, but when she suffers it will not be for his sins.

It will be for my pleasure.

She will beg, but it will be for me to claim her in the most shameful ways imaginable.

She will scream, but it will be because she doesn't think she can bear another climax.

But when she surrenders at last, it will not be to her captor.

It will be to her husband.

Ruthless Prince

Alexandra is a senator's daughter, used to mingling in the company of the rich and powerful, but tonight she will learn that there are men who play by different rules.

Men like me.

I could romance her. I could seduce her and then carry her gently to my bed.

But that can wait. Tonight I'm going to wring one ruthless climax after another from her quivering body with her bottom burning from my belt and her throat sore from screaming.

She will know she is mine before she even knows she is my bride.

Savage Prince

Gillian's father may be a powerful Irish mob boss, but he owes a blood debt to my family, and when I came to collect I didn't ask permission before taking his daughter as payment.

It was not up to him… or to her.

I will make her my bride, but I am not the kind of man who will wait until our wedding night to bare her and claim what belongs to me. She will walk down the aisle wet, well-used, and sore.

Her dress will hide the marks from my belt that taught her the consequences of disobeying her husband, but nothing will hide her blushes as her arousal drips down her thighs with each step.

By the time she says her vows she will already be mine.

BOOKS OF THE MERCILESS KINGS SERIES

King's Captive

Emily Porter saw me kill a man who betrayed my family and she helped put me behind bars. But someone with my connections doesn't stay in prison long, and she is about to learn the hard way that there is a price to pay for crossing the boss of the King dynasty. A very, very painful price…

She's going to cry for me as I blister that beautiful bottom, then she's going to scream for me as I ravage her over and over again, taking her in the most shameful ways she can imagine. But leaving her well-punished and well-used is just the beginning of what I have in store for Emily.

I'm going to make her my bride, and then I'm going to make her mine completely.

King's Hostage

When my life was threatened, Michael King didn't just take matters into his own hands.

He took me.

When he carried me off it was partly to protect me, but mostly it was because he wanted me.

I didn't choose to go with him, but it wasn't up to me. That's why I'm naked, wet, and sore in an opulent Swiss chalet with my bottom still burning from the belt of the infuriatingly sexy mafia boss who brought me here, punished me when I fought him, and then savagely made me his.

We'll return when things are safe in New Orleans, but I won't be going back to my old home.

I belong to him now, and he plans to keep me.

King's Possession

Her father had to be taught what happens when you cross a King, but that isn't why Genevieve Rossi is sore, well-used, and waiting for me to claim her in the only way I haven't already.

She's sore because she thought she could embarrass me in public without being punished.

She's well-used because after I spanked her I wanted more, and I take what I want.

She's waiting for me in my bed because she's my bride, and tonight is our wedding night.

I'm not going to be gentle with her, but when she wakes up tomorrow morning wet and blushing her cheeks won't be crimson because of the shameful things I did to her naked, quivering body.

It will be because she begged for all of them.

King's Toy

Vincenzo King thought I knew something about a man who betrayed him, but that isn't why I'm on my way to New Orleans well-used and sore with my backside still burning from his belt.

When he bared and punished me maybe it was just business, but what came after was not.

It was savage, it was shameful, and it was very, very personal.

I'm his toy now, and not the kind you keep in its box on the shelf.

He's going to play rough with me.

He's going to get me all wet and dirty.

Then he's going to do it all again tomorrow.

King's Demands

Julieta Morales hoped to escape an unwanted marriage, but the moment she got into my car her fate was sealed. She will have a husband, but it won't be the cartel boss her father chose for her.

It will be me.

But I'm not the kind of man who takes his bride gently amid rose petals on her wedding night. She'll learn to satisfy her King's demands with her bottom burning and her hair held in my fist.

She'll promise obedience when she speaks her vows, but she'll be mastered long before then.

King's Temptation

I didn't think I needed Dimitri Kristoff's protection, but it wasn't up to me. With a kingpin from a rival family coming after me, he took charge, took off his belt, and then took what he wanted.

He knows I'm not used to doing as I'm told. He just doesn't care.

The stripes seared across my bare bottom left me sore and sorry, but it was what came after that truly left me shaken. The princess of the King family shouldn't be on her knees for anyone, let alone this Bratva brute who has decided to claim for himself what he was meant to safeguard.

Nobody gave me to him, but I'm his anyway.

Now he's going to make sure I know it.

BOOKS OF THE MAFIA MASTERS SERIES

His as Payment

Caroline Hargrove thinks she is mine because her father owed me a debt, but that isn't why she is sitting in my car beside me with her bottom sore inside and out. She's wet, well-used, and coming with me whether she likes it or not because I decided I want her, and I take what I want.

As a senator's daughter, she probably thought no man would dare lay a hand on her, let alone spank her thoroughly and then claim her beautiful body in the most shameful ways possible.

She was wrong. Very, very wrong. She's going to be mastered, and I won't be gentle about it.

Taken as Collateral

Francesca Alessandro was just meant to be collateral, held captive as a warning to her father, but then she tried to fight me. She ended up sore and soaked as I taught her a lesson with my belt and then screaming with every savage climax as I taught her to obey in a much more shameful way.

She's mine now. Mine to keep. Mine to protect. Mine to use as hard and as often as I please.

Forced to Cooperate

Willow Church is not the first person who tried to put a bullet in me. She's just the first I let live. Now she will pay the price in the most shameful way imaginable. The stripes from my belt will teach her to obey, but what happens to her sore, red bottom after that will teach the real lesson.

She will be used mercilessly, over and over, and every brutal climax will remind her of the humiliating truth: she never even had a chance against me. Her body always knew its master.

Claimed as Revenge

Valencia Rivera became mine the moment her father broke the agreement he made with me. She thought she had a say in the matter, but my belt across her beautiful bottom taught her otherwise and a night spent screaming her surrender into the sheets left her in no doubt she belongs to me.

Using her hard and often will not be all it takes to tame her properly, but it will be a good start…

Made to Beg

Sierra Fox showed up at my door to ask for my protection, and I gave it to her… for a price. She belongs to me now, and I'm going to use her beautiful body as thoroughly as I please. The only thing for her to decide is how sore her cute little bottom will be when I'm through claiming her.

She came to me begging for help, but as her moans and screams grow louder with every brutal climax, we both know it won't be long before she begs me for something far more shameful.

MORE MAFIA AND BILLIONAIRE ROMANCES BY PIPER STONE

Caught

If you're forced to come to an arrangement with someone as dangerous as Jagger Calduchi, it means he's about to take what he wants, and you'll give it to him… even if it's your body.

I got caught snooping where I didn't belong, and Jagger made me an offer I couldn't refuse. A week with him where his rules are the only rules, or his bought and paid for cops take me to jail.

He's going to punish me, train me, and master me completely. When he's used me so shamefully I blush just to think about it, maybe he'll let me go home… or maybe he'll decide to keep me.

Ruthless

Treating a mobster shot by a rival's goons isn't really my forte, but when a man is powerful enough to have a whole wing of a hospital cleared out for his protection, you do as you're told.

To make matters worse, this isn't first time I've met Giovanni Calduchi. It turns out my newest patient is the stern, sexy brute who all but dragged me back to his hotel room a couple of nights ago so he could use my body as he pleased, then showed up at my house the next day, stripped me bare, and spanked me until I was begging him to take me even more roughly and shamefully.

Now, with his enemies likely to be coming after me in order to get to him, all I can do is hope he's as good at keeping me safe as he is at keeping me blushing, sore, and thoroughly satisfied.

Dangerous

I knew Erik Chenault was dangerous the moment I saw him. Everything about him should have warned me away, from the scar on his face to the fact that mobsters call him Blade. But I was drawn like a moth to a flame, and I ended up burnt… and blushing, sore, and thoroughly used.

Now he's taken it upon himself to protect me from men like the ones we both tried to leave in our past. He's going to make me his whether I like it or not… but I think I'm going to like it.

Prey

Within moments of setting eyes on Sophia Waters, I was certain of two things. She was going to learn what happens to bad girls who cheat at cards, and I was going to be the one to teach her.

But there was one thing I didn't know as I reddened that cute little bottom and then took her long and hard and oh so shamefully: I wasn't the only one who didn't come here for a game of cards.

I came to kill a man. It turns out she came to protect him.

Nobody keeps me from my target, but I'm in no rush. Not when I'm enjoying this game of cat and mouse so much. I'll even let her catch me one day, and as she screams my name with each brutal climax she'll finally realize the truth. She was never the hunter. She was always the prey.

Given

Stephanie Michaelson was given to me, and she is mine. The sooner she learns that, the less often her cute little bottom will end up well-punished and sore as she is reminded of her place.

But even as she promises obedience with tears running down her cheeks, I know it isn't the sting of my belt that will truly tame her. It is what comes next that will leave her in no doubt she belongs to me. That part will be long, hard, and shameful… and I will make her beg for all of it.

Dangerous Stranger

I came to Spain hoping to start a new life away from dangerous men, but then I met Rafael Santiago. Now I'm not just caught up in the affairs of a mafia boss, I'm being forced into his car.

When I saw something I shouldn't have, Rafael took me captive, stripped me bare, and punished me until he felt certain I'd told him everything I knew about his organization… which was nothing at all. Then he offered me his protection in return for the right to use me as he pleases.

Now that I belong to him, his plans for me are more shameful than I could have ever imagined.

Indebted

After her father stole from me, I could have left Alessandra Toro in jail for a crime she didn't commit. But I have plans for her. A deal with the judge—the kind only a man like me can arrange—made her my captive, and she will pay her father's debt with her beautiful body.

She will try to run, of course, but it won't be the law that comes after her. It will be me.

The sting of my belt across her quivering bare bottom will teach Alessandra the price of defiance, but it is the far more shameful penance that follows which will truly tame her.

Taken

When Winter O'Brien was given to me, she thought she had a say in the matter. She was wrong.

She is my bride. Mine to claim, mine to punish, and mine to use as shamefully as I please. The sting of my belt on her bare bottom will teach her to obey, but obedience is just the beginning.

I will demand so much more.

Bratva's Captive

I told Chloe Kingstrom that getting close to me would be dangerous, and she should keep her distance. The moment she disobeyed and followed me into that bar, she became mine.

Now my enemies are after her, but it's not what they would do to her she should worry about.

It's what I'm going to do to her.

My belt across her bare backside will teach her obedience, but what comes after will be different.

She's going to blush, beg, and scream with every climax as she's ravaged more thoroughly than she can imagine. Then I'm going to flip her over and claim her in an even more shameful way.

If she's a good girl, I might even let her enjoy it.

Hunted

Hope Gracen was just another target to be tracked down… until I caught her.

When I discovered I'd been lied to, I carried her off.

She'll tell me the truth with her bottom still burning from my belt, but that isn't why she's here.

I took her to protect her. I'm keeping her because she's mine.

Theirs as Payment

Until mere moments ago, I was a doctor heading home after my shift at the hospital. But that was before I was forced into the back seat of an SUV, then bared and spanked for trying to escape.

Now I'm just leverage for the Cabello brothers to use against my father, but it isn't the thought of being held hostage by these brutes that has my heart racing and my whole body quivering.

It is the way they're looking at me…

Like they're about to tear my clothes off and take turns mounting me like wild beasts.

Like they're going to share me, using me in ways more shameful than I can even imagine.

Like they own me.

Ruthless Acquisition

I knew the shameful stakes when I bet against these bastards. I just didn't expect to lose.

Now they've come to collect their winnings.

But they aren't just planning to take a belt to my bare bottom for trying to run and then claim everything they're owed from my naked, helpless body as I blush, beg, and scream for them.

They've acquired me, and they plan to keep me.

Bound by Contract

I knew I was in trouble the moment Gregory Steele called me into his office, but I wasn't expecting to end up stripped bare and bent over his desk for a painful lesson from his belt.

Taking a little bit of money here and there might have gone unnoticed in another organization, but stealing from one of the most powerful mafia bosses on the West Coast has consequences.

It doesn't matter why I did it. The only thing that matters now is what he's going to do to me.

I have no doubt he will use me shamefully, but he didn't make me sign that contract just to show me off with my cheeks blushing and my bottom sore under the scandalous outfit he chose for me.

Now that I'm his, he plans to keep me.

BOOKS OF THE DARK OVERTURE SERIES

Indecent Invitation

I shouldn't be here.

My clothes shouldn't be scattered around the room, my bottom shouldn't be sore, and I certainly shouldn't be screaming into the sheets as a ruthless tycoon takes everything he wants from me.

I shouldn't even know Houston Powers at all, but I was in a bad spot and I was made an offer.

A shameful, indecent offer I couldn't refuse.

I was desperate, I needed the money, and I didn't have a choice. Not a real one, anyway.

I'm here because I signed a contract, but I'm his because he made me his.

Illicit Proposition

I should have known better.

His proposition was shameful. So shameful I threw my drink in his face when I heard it.

Then I saw the look in his eyes, and I knew I'd made a mistake.

I fought as he bared me and begged as he spanked me, but it didn't matter. All I could do was moan, scream, and climax helplessly for him as he took everything he wanted from me.

By the time I signed the contract, I was already his.

Unseemly Entanglement

I was warned about Frederick Duvall. I was told he was dangerous. But I never suspected that meeting the billionaire advertising mogul to discuss a business proposition would end with me bent over a table with my dress up and my panties down for a shameful lesson in obedience.

That should have been it. I should have told him what he could do with his offer and his money.

But I didn't.

I could say it was because two million dollars is a lot of cash, but as I stand before him naked, bound, and awaiting the sting of his cane for daring to displease him, I know that's not the truth.

I'm not here because he pays me. I'm here because he owns me.

BOOKS OF THE CLUB DARKNESS SERIES

Bent to His Will

Even the most powerful men in the world know better than to cross me, but Autumn Sutherland thought she could spy on me in my own club and get away with it. Now she must be punished.

She tried to expose me, so she will be exposed. Bare, bound, and helplessly on display, she'll beg for mercy as my strap lashes her quivering bottom and my crop leaves its burning welts on her most intimate spots. Then she'll scream my name as she takes every inch of me, long and hard.

When I am done with her, she won't just be sore and shamefully broken. She will be mine.

Broken by His Hand

Sophia Russo tried to keep away from me, but just thinking about what I would do to her left her panties drenched. She tried to hide it, but I didn't let her. I tore those soaked panties off, spanked her bare little bottom until she had no doubt who owns her, and then took her long and hard.

She begged and screamed as she came for me over and over, but she didn't learn her lesson…

She didn't just come back for more. She thought she could disobey me and get away with it.

This time I'm not just going to punish her. I'm going to break her.

Bound by His Command

Willow danced for the rich and powerful at the world's most exclusive club… until tonight.

Tonight I told her she belongs to me now, and no other man will touch her again.

Tonight I ripped her soaked panties from her beautiful body and taught her to obey with my belt.

Tonight I took her as mine, and I won't be giving her up.

BOOKS OF THE DANGEROUS BUSINESS SERIES

Persuasion

Her father stole something from the mob and they hired me to get it back, but that's not the real reason Giliana Worthington is locked naked in a cage with her bottom well-used and sore.

I brought her here so I could take my time punishing her, mastering her, and ravaging her helpless, quivering body over and over again as she screams and moans and begs for more.

I didn't take her as a hostage. I took her because she is mine.

Bad Men

I thought I could run away from the marriage the mafia arranged for me, but I ended up held prisoner in a foreign country by someone far more dangerous than the man I tried to escape.

Then Jack and Diego came for me.

They didn't ask if I wanted to be theirs. They just took me.

I ran, but they caught me, stripped me bare, and punished me in the most shameful way possible.

Now they're going to share me, and they're not going to be gentle about it.

BOOKS OF THE MONTANA BAD BOYS SERIES

Hawk

He's a big, angry Marine, and I'm going to be sore when he's done with me.

Hawk Travers is not a man to be trifled with. I learned that lesson in the hardest way possible, first with a painful, humiliating public spanking and then much more shamefully in private.

She came looking for trouble. She got a taste of my belt instead.

Bryce Myers pushed me too far and she ended up with her bottom welted. But as satisfying as it is to hear this feisty little reporter scream my name as I put her in her place, I get the feeling she isn't going to stop snooping around no matter how well-used and sore I leave her cute backside.

She's gotten herself in way over her head, but she's mine now, and I protect what's mine.

Scorpion

He didn't ask if I like it rough. It wasn't up to me.

I thought I could get away with pissing off a big, tough Marine. I ended up with my face planted in the sheets, my burning bottom raised high, and my hair held tightly in his fist as he took me long and hard and taught me the kind of shameful lesson only a man like Scorpion could teach.

She was begging for a taste of my belt. She got much more than that.

Getting so tipsy she thought she could be sassy with me in my own bar earned Caroline a spanking, but it was trying to make off with my truck that sealed the deal. She'll feel my belt across her bare backside, then she'll scream my name as she takes every single inch of me.

This naughty girl needs to be put in her place, and I'm going to enjoy every moment of it.

Mustang

I tried to tell him how to run his ranch. Then he took off his belt.

When I heard a rumor about his ranch, I confronted Mustang about it. I thought I could go toe to toe with the big, tough former Marine, but I ended up blushing, sore, and very thoroughly used.

I told her it was going to hurt. I meant it.

Danni Brexton is a hot little number with a sharp tongue and a chip on her shoulder. She's the kind of trouble that needs to be ridden hard and put away wet, but only after a taste of my belt.

It will take more than just a firm hand and a burning bottom to tame this sassy spitfire, but I plan to keep her safe, sound, and screaming my name in bed whether she likes it or not. By the time I'm through with her, there won't be a shadow of a doubt in her mind that she belongs to me.

Nash

When he caught me on his property, he didn't call the police. He just took off his belt.

Nash caught me breaking into his shed while on the run from the mob, and when he demanded answers and obedience I gave him neither. Then he took off his belt and taught me in the most shameful way possible what happens to naughty girls who play games with a big, rough Marine.

She's mine to protect. That doesn't mean I'm going to be gentle with her.

Michelle doesn't just need a place to hide out. She needs a man who will bare her bottom and spank her until she is sore and sobbing whenever she puts herself at risk with reckless defiance, then shove her face into the sheets and make her scream his name with every savage climax.

She'll get all of that from me, and much, much more.

Austin

I offered this brute a ride. I ended up the one being ridden.

The first time I saw Austin, he was hitchhiking. I stopped to give him a lift, but I didn't end up taking this big, rough former Marine wherever he was heading. He was far too busy taking me.

She thought she was in charge. Then I took off my belt.

When Francesca Montgomery pulled up beside me, I didn't know who she was, but I knew what she needed and I gave it to her. Long, hard, and thoroughly, until she was screaming my name as she climaxed over and over with her quivering bare bottom still sporting the marks from my belt.

But someone wants to hurt her, and when someone tries to hurt what's mine, I take it personally.

BOOKS OF THE ALPHA BEASTS SERIES

King's Mate

Her scent drew me to her, but something deeper and more powerful told me she was mine. Something that would not be denied. Something that demanded I claim her then and there.

I took her the way a beast takes his mate. Roughly. Savagely. Without mercy or remorse.

She will run, and when she does she will be punished, but it is not me that she fears. Every quivering, desperate climax reminds her that her body knows its master, and that terrifies her.

She knows I am not a gentle king, and she will scream for me as she learns her place.

Beast's Claim

Raven is not one of my kind, but the moment I caught her scent I knew she belonged to me.

She is my mate, and when I claim her it will not be gentle. She can fight me, but her pleas for mercy as she is punished will soon give way to screams of climax as she is mounted and rutted.

By the time I am finished with her, the evidence of her body's surrender will be mingled with my seed as it drips down her bare thighs. But she will be more than just sore and utterly spent.

She will be mine.

Alpha's Mate

I didn't ask Nicolina to be my mate. It was not up to her. An alpha takes what belongs to him.

She will plead for mercy as she is bared and punished for daring to run from me, but her screams as she is claimed and rutted will be those of helpless climax as her body surrenders to its master.

She is mine, and I'm going to make sure she knows it.

MORE STORMY NIGHT BOOKS BY PIPER STONE

Claimed by the Beasts

Though she has done her best to run from it, Scarlet Dumane cannot escape what is in store for her. She has known for years that she is destined to belong not just to one savage beast, but to three, and now the time has come for her to be claimed. Soon her mates will own every inch of her beautiful body, and she will be shared and used as roughly and as often as they please.

Scarlet hid from the disturbing truth about herself, her family, and her town for as long as she could, but now her grandmother's death has finally brought her back home to the bayous of Louisiana and at last she must face her fate, no matter how shameful and terrifying.

She will be a queen, but her mates will be her masters, and defiance will be thoroughly punished. Yet even when she is stripped bare and spanked until she is sobbing, her need for them only grows, and every blush, moan, and quivering climax binds her to them more tightly. But with enemies lurking in the shadows, can she trust her mates to protect her from both man and beast?

Millionaire Daddy

Dominick Asbury is not just a handsome millionaire whose deep voice makes Jenna's tummy flutter whenever they are together, nor is he merely the first man bold enough to strip her bare and spank her hard and thoroughly whenever she has been naughty. He is much more than that.

He is her daddy.

He is the one who punishes her when she's been a bad girl, and he is the one who takes her in his arms afterwards and brings her to one climax after another until she is utterly spent and satisfied.

But something shady is going on behind the scenes at Dominick's company, and when Jenna draws the wrong conclusion from a poorly written article about him and creates an embarrassing public scene, will she end up not only costing them both their jobs but losing her daddy as well?

Conquering Their Mate

For years the Cenzans have cast a menacing eye on Earth, but it still came as a shock to be captured, stripped bare, and claimed as a mate by their leader and his most trusted warriors.

It infuriates me to be punished for the slightest defiance and forced to submit to these alien brutes, but as I'm led naked through the corridors of their ship, my well-punished bare bottom and my helpless arousal both fully on display, I cannot help wondering how long it will be until I'm kneeling at the feet of my mates and begging them take me as shamefully as they please.

Captured and Kept

Since her career was knocked off track in retaliation for her efforts to expose a sinister plot by high-ranking government officials, reporter Danielle Carver has been stuck writing puff pieces in a small town in Oregon. Desperate for a serious story, she sets out to investigate the rumors she's been hearing about mysterious men living in the mountains nearby. But when she secretly follows them back to their remote cabin, the ruggedly handsome beasts don't take kindly to her snooping around, and

Dani soon finds herself stripped bare for a painful, humiliating spanking.

Their rough dominance arouses her deeply, and before long she is blushing crimson as they take turns using her beautiful body as thoroughly and shamefully as they please. But when Dani uncovers the true reason for their presence in the area, will more than just her career be at risk?

Taming His Brat

It's been years since Cooper Dawson left her small Texas hometown, but after her stubborn defiance gets her fired from two jobs in a row, she knows something definitely needs to change. What she doesn't expect, however, is for her sharp tongue and arrogant attitude to land her over the knee of a stern, ruggedly sexy cowboy for a painful, embarrassing, and very public spanking.

Rex Sullivan cannot deny being smitten by Cooper, and the fact that she is in desperate need of his belt across her bare backside only makes the war-hardened ex-Marine more determined to tame the beautiful, fiery redhead. It isn't long before she's screaming his name as he shows her just how hard and roughly a cowboy can ride a headstrong filly. But Rex and Cooper both have secrets, and when the demons of their past rear their ugly heads, will their romance be torn apart?

Capturing Their Mate

I thought the Cenzan invaders could never find me here, but I was wrong. Three of the alien brutes came to take me, and before I ever set foot aboard their ship I had already been stripped bare, spanked thoroughly, and claimed more shamefully then I would have ever thought possible.

They have decided that a public example must be made of me, and I will be punished and used in the most humiliating ways imaginable as a warning to anyone who might dare to defy them. But I am no ordinary breeder, and the secrets hidden in my past could change their world… or end it.

Rogue

Tracking down cyborgs is my job, but this time I'm the one being hunted. This rogue machine has spent most of his life locked up, and now that he's on the loose he has plans for me…

He isn't just going to strip me, punish me, and use me. He will take me longer and harder than any human ever could, claiming me so thoroughly that I will be left in no doubt who owns me.

No matter how shamefully I beg and plead, my body will be ravaged again and again with pleasure so intense it terrifies me to even imagine, because that is what he was built to do.

Roughneck

When I took a job on an oil rig to escape my scheming stepfather's efforts to set me up with one of his business cronies, I knew I'd be working with rugged men. What I didn't expect is to find myself bent over a desk, my cheeks soaked with tears and my bare thighs wet for a very different reason, as my well-punished bottom is thoroughly used by a stern, infuriatingly sexy roughneck.

Even though I should have known better than to get sassy with a firm-handed cowboy, let alone a tough-as-nails former Marine, there's no denying that learning the hard way was every bit as hot as it was shameful. But a sore, welted backside is just the start of his plans for me, and no matter how much I blush to admit it, I know I'm going to take everything he gives me and beg for more.

Hunting Their Mate

As far as I'm concerned, the Cenzans will always be the enemy, and there can be no peace while they remain on our planet. I planned to make them pay for invading our world, but I was hunted down and captured by two of their warriors with the help of a battle-hardened former Marine. Now I'm the one who is going to pay, as the three of them punish me, shame me, and share me.

Though the thought of a fellow human taking the side of these alien brutes enrages me, that is far from the worst of it. With every searing stroke of the strap that lands across my bare bottom, with every savage thrust as I am claimed over and over, and with every screaming climax, it is made more clear that it is my own quivering, thoroughly used body which has truly betrayed me.

Primitive

I was sent to this world to help build a new Earth, but I was shocked by what I found here. The men of this planet are not just primitive savages. They are predators, and I am now their prey…

The government lied to all of us. Not all of the creatures who hunted and captured me are aliens. Some of them were human once, specimens transformed in labs into little more than feral beasts.

I fought, but I was thrown over a shoulder and carried off. I ran, but I was caught and punished. Now they are going to claim me, share me, and use me so roughly that when the last screaming climax has been wrung from my naked, helpless body, I wonder if I'll still know my own name.

Harvest

The Centurions conquered Earth long before I was born, but they did not come for our land or our resources. They came for mates, women deemed suitable for breeding. Women like me.

Three of the alien brutes decided to claim me, and when I defied them, they made a public example of me, punishing me so thoroughly and shamefully I might never stop blushing.

But now, as my virgin body is used in every way possible, I'm not sure I want them to stop…

Torched

I work alongside firefighters, so I know how to handle musclebound roughnecks, but Blaise Tompkins is in a league of his own. The night we met, I threw a glass of wine in his face, then ended up shoved against the wall with my panties on the floor and my arousal dripping down my thighs, screaming out climax after shameful climax with my well-punished bottom still burning.

I've got a series of arsons to get to the bottom of, and finding out that the infuriatingly sexy brute who spanked me like a naughty little girl will be helping me with the investigation seemed like the last thing I needed, until somebody hurled a rock through my window in an effort to scare me away from the case. Now having a big, strong man around doesn't seem like such a bad idea…

Fertile

The men who hunt me were always brutes, but now lust makes them barely more than beasts.

When they catch me, I know what comes next.

I will fight, but my need to be bred is just as strong as theirs is to breed. When they strip me, punish me, and use me the way I'm meant to be used, my screams will be the screams of climax.

Hostage

I knew going after one of the most powerful mafia bosses in the world would be dangerous, but I didn't anticipate being dragged from my apartment already sore, sorry, and shamefully used.

My captors don't just plan to teach me a lesson and then let me go. They plan to share me, punish me, and claim me so ruthlessly I'll be screaming my submission into the sheets long before they're through with me. They took me as a hostage, but they'll keep me as theirs.

Defiled

I was born to rule, but for her sake I am banished, forced to wander the Earth among mortals. Her virgin body will pay the price for my protection, and it will be a shameful price indeed.

Stripped, punished, and ravaged over and over, she will scream with every savage climax.

She will be defiled, but before I am done with her she will beg to be mine.

Kept

On the run from corrupt men determined to silence me, I sought refuge in his cabin. I ate his food, drank his whiskey, and slept in his bed. But then the big bad bear came home and I learned the hard way that sometimes Goldilocks ends up with her cute little bottom well-used and sore.

He stripped me, spanked me, and ravaged me in the most shameful way possible, but then this rugged brute did something no one else ever has before. He made it clear he plans to keep me…

Auctioned

Twenty years ago the Malzeons saved us when we were at the brink of self-annihilation, but there was a price for their intervention. They demanded humans as servants… and as pets.

Only criminals were supposed to be offered to the aliens for their use, but when I defied Earth's government, asking questions that no one else would dare to ask, I was sold to them at auction.

I was bought by two of their most powerful commanders, rivals who nonetheless plan to share me. I am their property now, and they intend to tame me, train me, and enjoy me thoroughly.

But I have information they need, a secret guarded so zealously that discovering it cost me my freedom, and if they do not act quickly enough both of our worlds will soon be in grave danger.

Hard Ride

When I snuck into Montana Cobalt's house, I was looking for help learning to ride like him, but what I got was his belt across my bare backside. Then with tears still running down my cheeks and arousal dripping onto my thighs, the big brute taught me a much more shameful lesson.

Montana has agreed to train me, but not just for the rodeo. He's going to break me in and put me through my paces, and then he's going to show me what it means to be ridden rough and dirty.

Carnal

For centuries my kind have hidden our feral nature, our brute strength, and our carnal instincts. But this human female is my mate, and nothing will keep me from claiming and ravaging her.

She is mine to tame and protect, and if my belt doesn't teach her to obey then she'll learn in a much more shameful fashion. Either way, her surrender will be as complete as it is inevitable.

Bounty

After I went undercover to take down a mob boss and ended up betrayed, framed, and on the run, Harper Rollins tried to bring me in. But instead of collecting a bounty, she earned herself a hard spanking and then an even rougher lesson that left her cute bottom sore in a very different way.

She's not one to give up without a fight, but that's fine by me. It just means I'll have plenty more chances to welt her beautiful backside and then make her scream her surrender into the sheets.

Beast

Primitive, irresistible need compelled him to claim me, but it was more than mere instinct that drove this alien beast to punish me for my defiance and then ravage me thoroughly and savagely. Every screaming climax was a brand marking me as his, ensuring I never forget who I belong to.

He's strong enough to take what he wants from me, but that's not why I surrendered so easily as he stripped me bare, pushed me up against the wall, and made me his so roughly and shamefully.

It wasn't fear that forced me to submit. It was need.

Gladiator

Xander didn't just win me in the arena. The alien brute claimed me there too, with my punished bottom still burning and my screams of climax almost drowned out by the roar of the crowd.

Almost…

Victory earned him freedom and the right to take me as his mate, but making me truly his will mean more than just spanking me into shameful surrender and then rutting me like a wild beast. Before he carries me off as his prize, the dark truth that brought me here must be exposed at last.

Big Rig

Alexis Harding is used to telling men exactly what she thinks, but she's never had a roughneck like me as a boss before. On my rig, I make the rules and sassy little girls get stripped bare, bent over my desk, and taught their place, first with my belt and then in a much more shameful way.

She'll be sore and sorry long before I'm done with her, but the arousal glistening on her thighs reveals the truth she would rather keep hidden. She needs it rough, and that's how she'll get it.

Warriors

I knew this was a primitive planet when I landed, but nothing could have prepared me for the rough beasts who inhabit it. The sting of their prince's firm hand on my bare bottom taught me my place in his world, but it was what came after that truly demonstrated his mastery over me.

This alien brute has granted me his protection and his help with my mission, but the price was my total submission to both his shameful demands and those of his second in command as well.

But it isn't the savage way they make use of my quivering body that terrifies me the most. What leaves me trembling is the thought that I may never leave this place… because I won't want to.

Owned

With a ruthless, corrupt billionaire after me, Crockett, Dylan, and Wade are just the men I need. Rough men who know how to keep a woman safe… and how to make her scream their names.

But the Hell's Fury MC doesn't do charity work, and their help will come at a price.

A shameful price…

They aren't just going to bare me, punish me, and then do whatever they want with me.

They're going to make me beg for it.

Seized

Delaney Archer got herself mixed up with someone who crossed us, and now she's going to find out just how roughly and shamefully three bad men like us can make use of her beautiful body.

She can plead for mercy, but it won't stop us from stripping her bare and spanking her until she's sore, sobbing, and soaking wet. Our feisty little captive is going to take everything we give her, and she'll be screaming our names with every savage climax long before we're done with her.

Cruel Masters

I thought I understood the risks of going undercover to report on billionaires flaunting their power, but these men didn't send lawyers after me. They're going to deal with me themselves.

Now I'm naked aboard their private plane, my backside already burning from one of their belts, and these three infuriatingly sexy bastards have only just gotten started teaching me my place.

I'm not just going to be punished, shamed, and shared. I'm going to be mastered.

Hard Men

My father's will left his company to me, but the three roughnecks who ran it for him have other ideas. They're owed a debt and they mean to collect on it, but it's not money these brutes want.

It's me.

In return for protection from my father's enemies, I will be theirs to share. But these are hard men, and they don't just intend to punish my defiance and use me as shamefully as they please.

They plan to master me completely.

Rough Ride

As I hear the leather slide through the loops of his pants, I know what comes next. Jake Travers is going to blister my backside. Then he's going to ride me the way only a rodeo champion can.

Plenty of men who thought they could put me in my place have learned the hard way that I was more than they could handle, and when Jake showed up I was sure he would be no different.

I was wrong.

When I pushed him, he bared and spanked me in front of a bar full of people.

I should have let it go at that, but I couldn't.

That's why he's taking off his belt…

Primal Instinct

Ruger Jameson can buy anything he wants, but that's not the reason I'm his to use as he pleases.

He's a former Army Ranger accustomed to having his orders followed, but that's not why I obey him.

He saved my life after our plane crashed, but I'm not on my knees just to thank him properly.

I'm his because my body knows its master.

I do as I'm told because he blisters my bare backside every time I dare to do otherwise.

I'm at his feet because I belong to him and I plan to show it in the most shameful way possible.

PIPER STONE LINKS

You can keep up with Piper Stone via her newsletter, her website, her Twitter account, her Facebook page, and her Goodreads profile, using the following links:

http://eepurl.com/c2QvLz

https://darkdangerousdelicious.wordpress.com/

https://twitter.com/piperstone01

https://www.facebook.com/Piper-Stone-573573166169730/

https://www.goodreads.com/author/show/15754494.Piper_Stone

Made in the USA
Middletown, DE
24 June 2024